Other Books by Robert Eisenhart

Occabot

The Spoken Word

Investigator

Maenads

MANLY

A Novel

by

Robert Eisenhart

For my brother, Gary

Chapter 1

That day in July 1972 in a normally quiet suburb outside of Cincinnati left an indelible impression on the minds of all those who were there. It was an unseasonably gloomy afternoon. There was no wind. The atmosphere hung oppressively over the house on Euclid Place, too thick to take a deep breath. If there is a God, He held His breath... and in the stifling vacuum, there could be felt the presence of a great cosmic clock ticking off the seconds.

The SWAT team moved into position.

A pair of field glasses focused on the porch of the house on Euclid Place.

What appeared to be a large black delivery truck was in fact the Mobile Command Post.

From inside: "I got a bad feeling about this one, L-T."

The lieutenant was standing behind the open doors at the rear of the CP. His response to the young officer's comment—he didn't say a word.

Lieutenant Gabriel Thompson was a 20-year veteran of the department. He had long ago seen too much. His craggy face was so deeply lined it was like a topographical map of some god-forsaken territory; most folks felt uncomfortable looking directly at him.

Then, "Scott, front and center."

Officer Scott stepped down from the CP and stood before the lieutenant: "Sir, yes sir."

The lieutenant eyeballed him. After a long three seconds: "Go join Mackay. He's gonna need some help keeping those TV fellas back."

Hesitation registered Officer Scott's disappointment: "Sir, yes sir." Then he hurriedly walked off.

The lieutenant returned to his binoculars, to the view of the front porch, and a truly frightening scene.

The man on the porch was a graduate student, a math major. A family man. He threw his head back and made ungodly noises like the pressure inside a pipe when you turn the faucet. His upper torso rocked back and forth like someone with autism— providing a most frustrating target for the marksmen. His left hand held unwaveringly onto the tangled tresses of his kneeling wife. On her face, a mask of unspeakable terror. In her arms, a newborn baby. In his right hand, a gleaming butcher knife.

There was little background to go on. The young couple had lived in the rented one bedroom bungalow for the past five years. Just a few blocks away was the university where he attended classes. She waitressed the night shift at an all night diner.

No one in the community seemed the least bit aware of them...

Until now.

It began early that morning with a visit from the Child Welfare Department. A reported case of child abuse. A case worker had been called out to investigate. During the course of her interview, the man of the house, one Michael Arthur Manly, became hostile and attacked the social worker.

The poor woman was severely injured. She had to be rushed to a nearby hospital.

The police were called in.

That was how it began. The question now... *How would it end?*

In the rear of the mobile command post, a policeman monitored radio transmissions. The officer's name was Mike Fransen. A former radio operator in Vietnam, he was an adrenaline junkie. If you stood close enough, you would swear you heard a constant buzz coming from inside his head. At the moment, you didn't have to stand all that close.

"Lieutenant, Meisner says he has a clear shot. Sir.... Sir?"

"Yeah, I heard you, Fransen."

He also heard the man on the porch. Michael Manly was screaming at his wife now. He was unintelligible. It wasn't language anymore; it wasn't even human.

The wife—maiden name, Polansky, Iris Evelyn Polansky— was trying so hard not to antagonize her husband. If she could've she would have put the infant back inside herself, away from this madman, away from the mad world. How could she have brought yet another life into such madness? She kept her eyes on the ground, glancing up every now and then—only to see the blade brandished just inches from her face.

And he would bellow like some kind of animal in pain.

Remarkably, the infant didn't cry. Or at least Thompson couldn't hear it. He listened for it. But he couldn't hear...

3

He glimpsed movement in the driveway of a neighboring house. He knew they weren't his... Civilians!

"Shit! The second house from the corner, south side of the street. Somebody, get those people inside. Now!"

"Adam 22, I'm on it."

Then another voice: "Sir, this is Bruckner, I'm in position."

Bruckner and Meisner, his two best sharpshooters. This was what Thompson was waiting for: in the cross hairs. He knew once he gave the order, they'd get one shot and one shot only. He needed a head shot, an instantaneous kill. Mother and child could afford nothing less. A single marksman might conceivably not hit it dead-on, but two...

"C'mon, get those civilians out of there," Thompson barked between gritted teeth. He feared they might not get another chance.

Nothing else had worked. They tried to talk the man down from his rage, but Manly tore the phone out of the wall. They tried several different approaches, but each time Manly backed them off by threatening to slash his wife. And Thompson believed he meant it! He could *feel* it, like you feel a chill up your spine. This wasn't some kind of childish cry for attention. This was deep-seated illness. This was—

"THIS IS HOW IT'S SUPPOSED TO BE!" Michael Arthur Manly bellowed into his young wife's face. He pulled back forcefully on her hair. "THIS IS HOW IT'S SUPPOSED TO BE!"

And having shouted those words, he began to cut.

4

"Fire!" Thompson gave the order.

The blade moved slowly across the young mother's throat, tracing a sickeningly widening line of red.

A scream surged up inside Thompson's brain threatening to explode through the top of his head if he didn't yell it out: *"Fire!"*

Shots rang out. Two shots in rapid succession.

Michael Arthur Manly's head jerked violently to one side, then the other—like a final, emphatic *NO!*

Through the 10 X 40 lenses of the binoculars, the front porch appeared as if it were less than ten feet away. As if Thompson could actually reach out and wipe the splattered blood. As if he could reach out and catch the infant as it slipped from its mother's arms, as it fell naked onto the spreading puddle that was forming at its father's feet. And once on the ground, the tiny baby lay still, face up, like a statuette of a cherub in a fountain—blood spurting down from the gaping wound in Mommy's neck. A shiny coat of red to cover the naked babe.

Then Mommy fell forward at the knees, landing on top. Then Daddy crumpled down, falling on top of Mommy. What was once a family lay in a messy heap on the porch of the house on Euclid Place.

Nobody moved.

For a split second, it was as if the same knife that had just rent a hole in the front of Iris Manly's delicate neck had poked a hole in the very fabric of life—a loose thread, a flaw that threatened to unravel.

Then suddenly everybody moved. A dozen pairs of feet ran

5

up the stairs, back and forth, this way and that, on the wooden floorboards of the porch. Spit-shined leather boots with heavy-treaded rubber soles. Then shiny oxfords.

And the dust kicked up.

And the blood dripped down.

Gabriel Thompson stood on the porch, his face pinched from the pervasive stench. It was more than just the slack intestines of the dead. It was as if he were standing over a cesspool, he had to breathe through his mouth. Talking to Mike Fransen on the radio: "It's all clear up here. The paramedics can come on up... but there're no customers for 'em. Just tag and bag.... The baby was dead all along—at least a couple of hours. Can you believe that? Mike, this poor woman was clinging to a *dead* baby. I wonder if she even knew..." The lieutenant coughed, almost gagged—for want of a strong breeze; the stench was overwhelming.

"What's that...?" the lieutenant asked Fransen. "No, there's no one in the house. No... I checked it myself. The whole place is only two rooms and a closet... How can that be? Are you sure?"

"Lieutenant, I just got through talking with one of her co-workers. She called from the hospital. The social worker's gonna be alright, but she keeps asking about a little boy... No, Lieutenant, this is a six year old. Of course she's sure... She was talking with Mrs. Manly about enrolling the boy in school when... Lieutenant...? Are you there?"

Thompson dropped the handset. He was startled by something he saw, something *under* the porch—a reflection, or a movement.

As he bent to pick it up he peered into a crack in the floorboards.

The reflection blinked.

"Dear God!"

"Come again... Lieutenant? That last message... I did not copy. Lieutenant...?"

Chapter 2

It was truly horrific to contemplate. They had kept that little boy locked up under that porch most of his entire life. His muscles were atrophied from nonuse. He'd never learned to speak. He wasn't even toilet trained.

"How sick can some people be?"

"Meisner, with all you've seen, I'm surprised that you—"

"I'm not talking about the parents, Fransen. I'm talking about the sleazebags who print shit like this..." He was reading one of those supermarket tabloids that tries to pass itself off as a newspaper. "Can you believe this? Bruckner, look at what these bastards wrote. That poor kid!"

Meisner was reading over Fransen's shoulder. Bruckner moved his chair closer so he too could get a look. Fransen spread the front page out on the table for the others to see.

The headline screamed: "Alien Baby Held Them Hostage." And printed underneath was a picture of Lance Manly. Frightened and malnourished, the six year old could truly have been from another world—with a body that belonged on a three year old and eyes that belonged to an eighty year old.

"That's deplorable!"

"Yeah, I guess..."

The area precinct's squad room was sometimes used by SWAT for debriefings. Most of the time they were training or in

8

the field. This morning, all anybody talked about was the kid, Lance Manly.

"What d'you mean, you guess...? Geez, Fransen, they make it sound like *he's* the monster and the parents are the victims, instead of the other way around. How twisted can you get?!"

Fransen shifted in his seat. "Bruckner, you're a good man, and you have a keen eye on the firing range, but your perception of human nature seems to be somewhat lacking. A lot of people, when confronted with an atrocity—too horrible to think about!—they go into 'fight or flight'. If it's flight, they run away, or they fall down and piss their pants. And if it's fight, they get a need to lash out at something. The poor victim is seen as the source of the discomfort and distress, and often gets turned upon. People can be vicious." Fransen made claws of his hands and bared his teeth.

"Is Fransen having one of his flashbacks?" said a voice from across the room.

"Okay, Lieutenant... joke all you want, but you know." Fransen tore the front page out of the paper. "*You* know..."

He stood up, went over to the bulletin board, and tacked up the picture of the "alien" boy.

"Go ahead, laugh. It's a defense mechanism. This kid makes us all feel uncomfortable. You look in those eyes and you get a glimpse of how primitive we really are. It's disturbing. And familiar. You don't like it.

"Imagine how *he* feels looking *out* through those slits. Just try to imagine..." Fransen exhaled with a shiver up his spine. "I don't

9

want this kid looking at me."

"That reminds me," the lieutenant interjected, "I need to make the following announcement: Department policy—any time there's an *OIS*, if any one needs to talk to someone, you're encouraged to see the department psychologist.

"Or you could talk to Fransen, who seems to be developing his own insights into the human psyche."

"I am!" Fransen heartily agreed.

"One other thing," the L-T added, "Chaplain Roeder wants you to know he's available, if that's more your style."

With that, the conversation shifted to baseball and the Big Red Machine: *The Cincinnati Reds, sure to clinch the division. Pure muscle and Charlie Hustle. It was rumored they were going to make a trade for Joe Morgan, one of the most intelligent ballplayers ever. Bobby Tolan had reportedly recovered from his injuries? So everyone said. Concepcion—the best shortstop in the league? All in all, the Reds could very well be the best defensive team of all time.*

Someone pointed out that it was lunchtime.

The conversation continued out the door.

Bruckner was the last to leave. He was about to close the door when he reached over and tore the picture of the "alien" boy off the bulletin board.

Right before he tossed it into the trash, he looked into the eyes of little Lance Manly. And he shuddered.

Chapter 3

Plainview Hospital was not in plain view. Such institutions are best kept tucked away from polite society. As for it being a *hospital*, that would depend. Is a *hospital* a place of healing? Plainview might be better described as a place for storing, where people are shelved and mental deterioration is documented—and, more often than not, accelerated. That's not to say that Plainview didn't have its share of well-intentioned staff. But these residents were perhaps the most delusional of all.

Be that as it may, Plainview was where Lance Manly was taken.

Gabriel Thompson and Mike Fransen got off the expressway at Deer Creek Pass. Under the exit sign, there was a smaller sign which read STATE HOSPITAL. They drove several miles east before spotting a second sign; this one at the mouth of a nameless blacktop tributary. Gabe turned onto the road and proceeded several hundred feet. He was beginning to think he'd made a wrong turn when the approach opened onto a gravel lot. The end of the line for the confused of mind: Plainview State Hospital.

Mike turned to look at their backseat passenger. He'd been riding along with them ever since they left the toy store. Not a peep out of him. The big stuffed bear sat up straight, looking

11

right back at him.

"Mr. Bear don't let on much, but I think he's glad to be out of that toy store. Aren't you, Mr. Bear?" Fransen reached back and grabbed up the teddy. "If this goes right, Mr. Bear, you're going to get a real live boy all your own to play with."

"I don't know, Fransen. Maybe the kid is too old to be playing with a teddy bear?"

"Are you kidding, Lieu?" Even when they were off-duty, Fransen called Gabriel *Lieu*. "The kid's the perfect age. Besides, what he's been through... you know he's never had a teddy bear. You'll see, they're gonna hit it off."

Stepping from the car, the two men stood in the parking lot of the state asylum. These were men accustomed to braving the flashpoint. Now they wavered in the pale light of the late afternoon.

"Lieu," Fransen said, "listen.... What do you hear?"

He keyed in on the pervasive silence all around.

"Nothing. Not a thing."

"Me neither.... So how come it don't feel peaceful?"

Gabriel didn't answer. It wasn't so much a question as it was a *feeling*.

A series of buildings faced the parking lot. There were four buildings in all, all three stories. A narrow tree-lined walk linked the structures. There was little doubt it was an institution. Neither the gentle gardens, nor the neat brown brick of the colonial architecture could betray the nature of the place. Behind those walls, behind a glaze of medication and a pile of psychiatric jargon, languished a hundred agitated minds.

"Let's get this over with."

Fransen switched hands, holding Mr. Bear under his left arm while he fished in his pocket for a stick of gum.

"You sure visiting hours aren't over by now?" The lieutenant raised his eyes to the dwindling daylight, then down to his watch.

"That's not what the lady told me."

The two men strode quickly across the lawn and into the administration building.

Just inside the front doors, a nurse was seated at a desk.

They told her who they were and who they were there to visit.

A doctor, name tag of Farnsworthy, came out to meet them. He was equal parts courteous and contrived: "I am so sorry, Lieutenant. Had I been made aware of your visit earlier I could have saved you a trip. Lance is presently undergoing a battery of tests... specially designed tests. They require a carefully controlled environment. I'm not sure you can fully appreciate this, but a singular group of distinguished psychologists and linguistic scientists from Harvard are personally monitoring this case. So you see, we can't allow any outside visitors at this time. I'm sure you understand."

The two police officers didn't look like they understood.

"The boy presents a unique opportunity to study the development of conceptual ideation apart from language."

"Hey, Doc," Fransen wasn't impressed, "all we want to do is

give the kid the bear."

"Well, if that's *all*, I'll be glad to see that he gets it."

The lieutenant spoke: "That's very nice of you, Doctor, but I'm sure you can understand, Officer Fransen and I, we would like to be the ones glad to see that he gets it."

"I'm afraid that won't be possible. Perhaps another day—"

"Doctor, I'm afraid *you* don't understand. The boy is the victim of a crime, which makes him a witness. You are preventing a victim from reporting a crime? That's interfering with a police investigation. I could arrest you for that." The lieutenant was smiling the whole time, making it impossible to tell if he was being serious.

"We needn't go to that extreme." A freakishly tall man with white hair had spoken. He ducked as he stepped through the doorway. He remained stooped and round-shouldered as he approached. Like Farnsworthy, he wore a white coat. The name tag on his pocket said H. KRONSBERG, M.D. He introduced himself as Dr. Herbert Kronsberg, Director of the Children's Ward.

To his colleague he said, "Thank you, Dr. Farnsworthy. I appreciate your vigilance, but I think we can make an exception for the officers."

And with that, Farnsworthy was dismissed. He shook hands with both Thompson and Fransen, and left.

"Excuse the hindrance," Dr. Kronsberg explained as he led them down a long corridor. "As you might expect, we've had to contend with an unusual number of visitors, journalists and photographers mostly. They find young Lance to be newsworthy, a curiosity. And to tell the truth, the same might be said of the scientific community."

"How do you mean?" the lieutenant inquired.

They exited the building, proceeding down a short flight of steps to a leaf-strewn walkway. Starting up the path, the doctor pointed to a building at the far end of the grounds. "The children's facility is kept segregated from the rest. I hope you don't mind a walk?"

"No," Fransen swiped the air, "it feels good to stretch the legs."

Kronsberg bestowed a short, shallow smile. "It also gives us an opportunity to talk. Lieutenant, you ask why we in the scientific community find young Lance Manly so fascinating. It is because he presents a unique opportunity... to observe a human being who, for all practical purposes, was denied the most basic interaction with others. He is completely devoid of the most rudimentary precepts. Do you realize that this poor youngster has never been out in the daylight? His eyes have probably sustained permanent damage. He may never be able to see normally in the light of day. We have a team of neuro-opthamologists coming to see him tomorrow. One hypothesis is that, as with some nocturnal animals, they may find specialized nerve cells that have adapted to lower levels of light. They're going to run tests on the boy's retinas. Actual developmental changes in the structure of the eye!—it's really quite mind-boggling."

As Fransen listened to the doctor's discourse, the distance between them and the little boy in the building just ahead seemed to grow wider.

"This is a state facility," Kronsberg went on to say, "unaccustomed to this kind of attention. There was some talk of transferring Lance to a teaching hospital at one of the big universities. But in the meantime, the researchers are coming here. They're vying for grants from government agencies and private foundations. There's a lot to be gained—for the researchers, for this facility, maybe even for young Lance."

Gabriel Thompson stopped walking; the others automatically stopped as well. "I thought research was supposed to benefit mankind."

"It is!" Kronsberg seemed bemused. "That goes without saying. Mankind. Yes, indeed!"—like he was reminding himself. "Ultimately the purpose *is* to benefit mankind!"

Fransen had a question. "You mentioned that this research might benefit Lance. That's what I'd like to hear."

"Yeah, how 'bout that?" the lieutenant seconded. "How is all this going to help the boy?"

Kronsberg sighed. "Well, it's like this..." He directed them along the path as he explained. "The Department of Social Services hasn't been able to find any living relatives, at least none that are willing to take the boy. Which means, if he's lucky, he'll be adopted. Given his history and special circumstances, that is unlikely. The greater probability is that he will be placed in a foster home, waiting for an adoption that will never come.

16

However, it's not all bleak. Whatever happens, he will likely remain a patient in an institution such as this as part of a long-term research program. As such, he receives better care—just one of those things. And research grants provide funds, making him more 'placeable'." Kronsberg paused outside the building. "Let's not forget," he held the door for the two visitors, "Lance will continue to need special care for many years to come."

Fransen reached across to hold the door. "After you, Doc."

Kronsberg kept talking as they entered, looking back over his stooped shoulders as he proceeded up a flight of stairs. "The extent to which further studies prove practical... that remains to be seen. The boy does not appear to possess normal intelligence, which is not at all surprising considering that his nutritional needs have been totally neglected. Nevertheless, it is my understanding that there is already a trust fund being set aside to cover basic educational expenses—a special tutor, and so forth.... So you see, there is something in it for Lance."

The interior lights flickered sallow. The director of the children's asylum looked straight ahead as he led them down the corridors. Sounds and smells from adjoining quarters drifted into the hall, and Fransen thought of the primate house at the zoo.

The director explained, "For the time being we've isolated Lance from the other children. If you think about it, I'm sure you can understand why. We must try to acclimate him gradually. We don't want to overwhelm him with external stimuli. That could result in unforeseen and possibly injurious consequences."

Joined by a nurse, the three men stood in front of a two-way mirror, peering into the cramped darkness on the other side. As Gabe's and Mike's eyes began to adjust, they could make out several pieces of playroom furniture—plastic and brightly colored undersized chairs and table; there were building blocks strewn about, and other toys including two other Mr. Bears seated on a cot in the far corner.

Gabe was about to ask *Where's the boy?* when he caught sight of him.

Two red flecks of light reflected off the eyes cowering beneath the cot.

Chapter 4

Friday nights Margie Danser played darts. She took up the pastime just a little over a year ago. And she was turning out to be one of the better players on the team. They were glad to have her. The team was comprised of employees from the Greater Cincinnati Airport: more specifically, the ground crew. Most of her co-workers knew about her private life, or had heard rumors. But she did her job and minded her own business. Most figured they should do the same.

It was the last Friday in March and as scheduled, the Flight Crew, as they were called, was facing off against the guys from Tally's Tavern, a.k.a. Tuff Darts. It was an important game. Last year, the Flight Crew was unbeatable. They were intent on maintaining their bragging rights as the league champs. The only real obstacle in their way was Tally's team. The last time the Flight Crew met Tuff Darts they were on home turf, at the Flight Deck Bar and Grille, a quarter mile down the boulevard from the airport. On this night, the Flight Crew found themselves in enemy territory.

Tally's Tavern was located in the warehouse district, by the train yard, far from the 24-hour bustle of the airport. At day's end, after the last of the loading docks rolled down its iron gate and the last worker dragged his weary ass on home, a spooky desolation settled in. You could hear the traffic lights click and the electricity crackle in the high-power lines overhead. And on a corner of this now nearly deserted neighborhood, a hazy glow surrounded the dingy neon that buzzed in the damp and the gloom. Tally's Tavern.

Through the portal of Tally's double-doors marched the Flight Crew, ready to do battle. Margie led the way: "C'mon out, Tuff Darts." The entire eight-man team from Tally's was standing right there in front of her, along the bar. "Where are you hiding?" She brushed back her strawberry-blonde hair from her face and made like she was searching the bar. "C'mon out. Fight like men."

Typical Margie. A real kidder—a spunky monkey. Everybody liked Margie. She was the only woman on the team. And there were no women on the Tuff Darts team. Some of the other teams in the league had women, but Margie was one-of-a-kind: an open-faced farm girl, everybody's kid sister. A sturdy little frame and a sharp mind. She brought a vitality to whatever she did. She brought a measure of shine to the dismal old bar.

A lot of women wouldn't feel comfortable in Tally's. Chipped ceiling tiles, wallpaper curling down at the edges, and if that wasn't grim enough, somebody painted silhouettes of rats along the baseboards—probably to camouflage the real thing.

Margie reached into the pocket of her green woolen cardigan. She always wore that sweater for the tournament. Her friend J.J. knitted it; it was supposed to bring her good luck. She took out the little carrying case that contained her darts. Without looking she screwed on the tungsten steel-tips, unfolded the flights, and fitted them into the notches at the ends of the shafts. Ready to go.

She took a few warm-up throws. The team followed suit.

Tom "Smitty" Smith, Captain of Tally's Tuff Darts, surveyed the playing field: "Okay, everyone's here. Let's get started." He read off the names he'd written on a piece of scrap paper. It was the opening pairings in the doubles matches; the game, 301.

Paul Duberry was partnered with Margie. Paul was as a tractor operator towing the airliners to the boarding gates and in and out of the hangers. Margie liked him, and more importantly, he threw a tight cluster. He was especially effective on the outside doubles ring. A thin man with a distinctive toss, he'd crouch at the line holding the dart high alongside his cheekbone. Then he'd uncoil upward, his head would go back slightly as his wrist flicked out the dart. Like he was spitting darts. Not much follow-through, but it worked for him.

Margie used a longer toss, more of a push.

There's a lot to be learned about a person by the way he, or she, throws a dart.

On regular nights Tally's has only one dart board. But on league nights they clear away the pool table and make room for a second and a third. Still, it was a lengthy process. There were four matches of 301 doubles, four of cricket doubles, and four of cricket singles. There were eight pitchers of Guinness, one pitcher of Michelob Light, two jumbo bags of salted peanuts, four bags of pretzels. And finally, there was a clear victory. The

Flight Crew won, taking three of the four cricket singles matches, a clean sweep in the doubles, and tying at 301. If you had to pick a most-valuable player award, it would've been Margie. Not only was she the "Bull's-Eye Queen," she was the Flight Crew's steadfast cheerleader, their team spirit, their reason to show off.

As was the custom, the losing team paid the tab. Dart players are very sportsmen-like; the two teams shook hands, offered up the accolade of "good darts," and promised to kick butt the next time they meet. Talking a little too loud and strutting a little too proud, the Flight Crew tumbled out into the night. Everyone was pleased to find their vehicles unmolested; in that neighborhood, that was an accomplishment in and of itself.

"Hey, what d'you say we meet over at Dolly's Diner?" Paul suggested, which was purely formality. The post game gathering was by now routine. After a victory, they always went to Dolly's. It was tradition. Nevertheless, they went through the usual rigmarole—giving it careful consideration. That was part of the tradition. It took about a minute, standing around, their breath vaporizing in the cold night air, arms pressed close to their sides to keep away the chill.

"I could go for a Dolly burger."

"What else is open this late?!"

And so it was that the victors found themselves seated around a booth inside Dolly's Diner. Only Lester didn't join them. His wife was expecting and he was anxious to get home. Richard pulled some chairs over from the next table to make room for Danny and Ned. Dan was a little bummed, he'd lost his singles and his 301 match. But soon it was all forgotten. Inside Dolly's Diner was steamed with warmth and home cooking. Together with the comradery of co-workers, it was an unbeatable combination. They all felt fortunate indeed.

Over plates of burgers and fries, tuna melts and onion rings, they talked shop, they talked sports, they talked about movies—old movies, new movies, ones they liked, and ones they didn't.

Eventually Danny got around to retelling the story of Ned's meeting with Bongo the gorilla. They were laughing so hard they nearly got asked to leave. George had soda come out of his nose. Jack thought that was hilarious. He was holding his sides trying not to laugh. Margie had to wipe the tears from the corners of her eyes. It really wasn't *that* funny! But once they got started...

The legendary meeting between Bongo and Ned took place on a stopover from San Diego. Unknown to Ned, the cargo hold of the 747 contained Bongo. The gorilla was being transported from one zoo to another. Ned walked into the cargo hold without noticing the cage. When he looked up he was face to face with Bongo. To hear Danny tell it, Ned's mouth dropped open, his eyes popped out of his head—*whammo!*—Bongo hit him square in the face with a fresh gorilla turd.

Every time Margie looked over at poor Ned, she couldn't help but start laughing all over again.

It took a while, but they finally got it back under control.

Jack asked the waitress if she knew who won the game. An exhibition game between the Reds and the Angels. She didn't know but some guy two booths down said it was the Angels, 6-2.

A sorry bit of news but not so sorry as to put a damper on the celebration.

By the time they were down to refills on coffee the conversation had shifted to current events. Ned and Danny left after they finished eating; they had to be at work early. Then Jack and George bowed out, each saying he had to get up early for something or other. Margie had a feeling they were going to go over to the Music Machine. It was early enough, maybe they could still meet some girls. So that left Paul, Margie, and Richard.

Richard mentioned, "Did you hear about this fertility doctor on the news? He supposedly used his *own* sperm to impregnate a bunch of his patients."

Paul offered, "I personally don't believe in artificial insemination." Then he added, "Unless they use the husband's sperm, I don't think it's right."

"Why would they use the husband's sperm?" Richard wanted to know. "I mean, if they're going to use his sperm anyway, why not do it the old-fashioned way? It's a lot more fun."

"It's not a question of *fun*, Richard. There are some couples that can't conceive the old-fashioned way. I don't see anything wrong with helping nature out a little." Margie seemed adamant on the subject.

"Margie, did you see the picture of this doctor?" Paul made a face of disgust. "Who would want to have this guy's genes?"

Richard laughed.

Margie didn't.

"Think about it, Margie. What kind of man donates his sperm to a stranger—someone he doesn't even know? What kind of man doesn't want to know his own child? There's got to be something wrong with him."

Margie didn't say anything. She seemed to be considering what Paul had said. Paul was the father of two little girls, 6 and 8, which gave him a different perspective on the issue.

Margie turned to Richard: "Richard, you're divorced, right?" She didn't wait for the answer she already knew. "Your wife remarried. She lives in another city. So, for all practical purposes, the stepdad is raising *your* child."

"Uh... not exactly, Margie. I do visit from time to time and—"

"I'm sorry, I'm not picking on you, Richard. I'm just trying to make a point. Not everybody is as lucky as Paul here, with 2.2 kids and a house in the suburbs. Plenty of children are raised by someone *other* than their biological father. How is that any different from what we're talking about?"

"It's plenty different!" Paul chimed in. "In one case you're talking about people doing their best to deal with mistakes that have already happened—I'm sorry, Richard—"

"No, that's okay. I know what you're saying."

"...and in the other case, you're talking about people actually *planning* mistakes."

"I can't believe you're saying that!" Margie pushed the hair from in front of her face and held it aside as she glared at Paul. "If you have a couple who wants a child so badly that they're

25

willing to go to such lengths, how can you call that *a mistake?*"

"You're not listening to what I'm saying, Margie. I understand that these couples are acting out of desperation. That's all the more reason to examine the wisdom of this kind of decision. There are a lot of issues at stake here. There's the ethical issue, as well as a social issue, a psychological issue—"

Richard added, "...a legal issue." This was clearly becoming a debate between Paul and Margie, with Richard providing running commentary.

"I think you're forgetting the human issue."

"Not at all. Let's think about the child for a minute. He's being deprived of the opportunity to know his real father. That's not right! It's taking away a part of him."

"...Or her."

"Yeah... or her."

"Is it better not to exist at all? Is that what you're saying?"

Paul didn't say anything; he didn't have a response for that. He'd have to think about it.

"You know," Richard seized on the sudden lull in the discussion, his chance to complicate matters, "I can see both your positions. Now, given that technology has created this dilemma, or rather this medical breakthrough—depending on your point of view—let's take it a step further. Let's say science finds a way for a woman to donate an egg to a man. He buys the egg, adds a little sperm, and then, with the help of that same science, he is able to... What's the word I'm looking for?"

"Gestate."

"Thanks. *Gestate*—he's able to gestate the embryo in an incubator.... What do you feel about that scenario?"

Now it was Margie's turn to fall silent. She definitely had a gut reaction—that didn't seem right. She was going to have to think about that one.

Just then J.J. Twomey walked into the diner.

She was with another woman several years older than herself. Paul guessed J.J. to be somewhere around 35, about his age; Margie, he knew, had just turned 25. The two woman entering the diner were wearing pantsuits with vests; fairly dressy except that neither wore any makeup, though the older woman did have earrings. J.J. wore no jewelry, nothing to soften the short cropped hair. Her face was actually very pretty: a bow-tie mouth, high round cheeks, a button nose. In from the cold, her nostrils flared slightly as she stepped into the harsh light inside the diner. At first glance she looked to be a little on the chunky side. But it was the outfit; it did all it could to conceal. Paul, however—a remarkably perceptive man—could see that beneath the suit jacket and the starched white collar was milky smooth and voluptuous.

Margie's back was to the door, so Paul got her attention: "Hey, isn't that J.J?"

Margie turned, smiled. The two woman waved.

"I'll be right back." Margie got up and went quickly to J.J.

As the ladies stood there talking, Paul glanced at his watch. "You know, Richard, I think I'm going to call it a night."

"Yeah, I guess I will too. You played good darts tonight,

Paul."

"Yeah, we all did good. We got a good team this season."

The two men counted out some dollars, putting their money into the center of the table, adding to the jumble of bills and change already left by the others—tab and tip.

"Hey, where's everybody going?" Margie asked as Paul and Richard shuffled past her on their way out the door.

"We're gonna get going. It's getting late—"

Remembering her manners, Margie interrupted, "Richard, this is J.J... Paul, you already know J.J. And this is Terry."

The other woman, who was standing slightly apart from and behind J.J. and Margie, leaned forward to say a brief hello to the two men. They said hello back.

"Why don't you come over and sit with us? Have some more coffee?" Margie offered.

She didn't quite sound like she meant it. Somehow it had suddenly become Paul and Richard who were being invited to "sit with *us.*" Weren't *they* the ones who were there first?

Oh well, thought Paul, no matter. "Thanks anyway, but I'm all coffee'd out. I really should be getting home."

"Yeah, me too," Richard said.

"Okay..." Margie hesitated, then gave Paul a little hug. Then Richard. "See you at work Monday."

"Good night."

"Good night."

"It was nice meeting you." Richard shook hands with both Margie's friends.

"You, too," Terry said.

"Good night."

Once outside, Richard commented, "They seem nice."

"You know, they're gay."

Richard stopped in his tracks. "No, I didn't know that."

"Well, they are! J.J. is Margie's lover."

"No, you're kidding!"

"I'm not kidding. They've been living together for the past year."

"Jesus, I didn't know that... Gay! Really...? And Margie's so..." Richard didn't know what to say. "Seems like an awful waste."

"Maybe so... Don't tell that to J.J."

Chapter 5

The world seemed to be divided into blue and green—smooth crisp cerulean and sweet soggy verdure. Each dawn unrolled an endless expanse of sky above and a glorious carpet of grass under hoof. She wiggled her ears to chase off the flies. Something was attached to her ear, something that wasn't a part of her. An ear tag, #60N, was used to identify the 14 month old heifer.

The man walked behind her and she moved off, out of his way. He kept walking behind her and she kept moving before him, going away from the open field of green, leaving it now for the fenced in patch of brown.

There were several men nearby.

The young heifer's udders shook slightly from side to side as she quickened her step in response to a hand landing firmly though not altogether unpleasantly against her rump. Playful and spry, kicking up an orange dust cloud with her hindquarter, she let out a little *moo*—to register surprise, or perhaps only to feign indignation.

The farmer dropped the ampul of frozen sperm into the thermos of warm water to let it thaw. The farm hand closed the gate behind the heifer, closing her in.

Her downy beige hide gave off a healthy, fertile shimmer in the early morning sunshine. The farmer stopped what he was doing to look out at her. In the barn, he loaded the sperm into the gun. He placed a rod over the gun, tightened it and, pulling a transparent plastic glove over his left hand up to the elbow, he walked into the corral.

Swiftly the heifer was subdued. Her head was placed in stocks, wooden slats snapped into place. She mooed, pleading, frightened, eyes wide, trying to pull away. The man buried his arm high up into her rectum, his other arm positioning the sperm gun to release its load of bull semen—more precious than gold—into her defenseless vagina, her fertile young vagina.

And then, just as suddenly as it had begun, it was all over. She was released, allowed to get up. As the fear lifted, the oddness of the sensation swept through her. Her front legs trembled slightly as she raised up her head, regaining her footing. One of the farm hands slapped her hard on the rump. She hesitated, then trotted off, back through the open gate of the corral, back to the pasture to resume grazing amidst the serenity of the blue and the green.

"I can't explain it, J.J." Margie had failed to come to bed. She just sat in front of the window in the living room and looked out, seemingly lost in thought.

"It's only natural that you should have second thoughts. This is a *very* major decision. But we both know... it's what you want." Coming alongside Margie, J.J. dropped down to her knees. At eye level with Margie now, she carefully and caringly touched her, taking hold of her hand. Margie turned slowly from

31

the window. As their eyes met, their hearts went out. J.J. smiled warily; her eyebrows raised up, making it a kind of questioning smile, yet filled with warmth and concern, and more than a bit of love and admiration. "You're going to be *a mom*.... *We're* going to be parents. What could possibly be wrong with that...?"

Margie's eyes held steadfastly to those of her lover, she lifted up J.J.'s hand and pressed it to her lips. She kissed at a finger. Then, turning the hand over, she bit ever so softly at the fleshy side of the palm, scraping her teeth along the skin absentmindedly, in the same fretting manner in which one might chew on one's own finger.

"It's more than just second thoughts, J.J. There's something about the whole *procedure* that I'm beginning to find... *disquieting.*"

Beyond the window panes, background noise intruded from the street below. Their apartment was on the third floor, facing away from the main road, but sometimes, especially late at night, the lonely sound of a motorist taking the route less traveled drifted up. A sympathetic vibration on the edge of yearning. It seemed to reverberate in a nascent corner of her brain. Margie felt the unseen pull of divergent forces. She didn't dare look away from J.J. while their most private desires and fears swam back and forth between their eyes. And if truth be known, they were not altogether the same desires—or even the same fears.

"This has to do with Paul, doesn't it? Something he said set you off."

Margie started to say something, but J.J. wouldn't let her.

"No, no, you can't tell me it's not so. I know you, Margaret, better than you know yourself." J.J. was one of the few people, outside of her family, that ever called her *Margaret*. "You had no problem with 'the procedure'—as you call it—before you got into this little discussion with *Mister* Duberry."

J.J. was beginning to shake, just a little, from the frustration she was feeling—which caused Margie's face to become awash in worry and concern. ""You're not...?"

"No, I'm not having one of my seizures." There were times J.J. regretted ever telling Margie... but you can't hide something like that, not from the person you live with. "Can't I even have a normal show of outrage without your assuming..."

"I'm sorry... I just..."

J.J. could see that Margie was feeling bad enough already, she didn't need any of J.J.'s indignation to make her feel worse. So, acting to smooth things over: "Oh... don't start crying! It's no big deal.... Really, I'm used to it."

It was true. J.J. had had to learn to get used to a lot of things, things you cannot change. People have a tendency to treat you differently when you're an obvious lesbian. That never bothered J.J. She was upfront and out of the closet. But when you're an epileptic, people treat you differently still. J.J. had learned she prefer hatred and contempt to pity and fear. So she made an effort to hide her epilepsy, to not let others know.

Hers was not a very severe case, she was able to keep it under control provided she adhered to the regime—an anticonvulsant medication called Dilantin. It had been over two years since she'd suffered a seizure, and so she'd been able to reduce her dosage—with still no return of symptoms. If she was going to have a seizure, she would know it. She would be the first to know. It was called an "aura." In her case she would get an odd sensation followed by this particular unpleasant taste in her mouth. And then she remembers—no, more than remembers, she actually *sees*—a scene from her past. She's very young and her father is sitting next to her.... Consciousness is lost soon after the appearance of the aura. She usually falls to the floor, skeletal muscles undergo strong tonic contractions, generalized clonic convulsions begin a few seconds later. It's during this stage that tongue biting, frothing at the mouth, loss of bladder and bowel control, and bruising are all apt to occur. A period of flaccid coma follows. Then a period of deep sleep.

Resuming the conversation: "J.J., I do love you, you know that... but I can't help wonder if we're doing the right thing. A child needs a father and..."

"No, I don't want to hear it. Not after all the bullshit we had to go through. Not because of some offhanded comment made by some dickhead who belongs on a farm."

"That's not nice, J.J. Paul's been a good friend. He's never said a bad word about you.... And as far as him being from a farm... I was raised on a farm. Does that make *me* a dickhead too?"

"Now you know I don't mean that! Don't twist my words. I just don't want you to do anything to louse things up. We've come so far. Remember the first time we went to the Women's Health Center and they had us sit through that three-hour orientation. I thought I was going to puke.... And that lady lawyer—what was her name?"

"Melissa Rawlin."

"That's right. Melissa. She started going over the legal and emotional implications, How do you think I felt? She starts saying how lesbian co-parents have no legal rights, that the state doesn't allow a second parent of the same sex to adopt. If something should happen to you—God forbid!—the courts could take away *my* relationship to *our* child. That's scary shit. I had to ask myself, Am I being stupid? I was looking at a lot of emotional liability. But you, you didn't have any doubt. You were so determined. I watched you plan out everything, from the finances to the charts of your fertility cycle. And little by little I started to let go of my fears. I started to feel like I was a part of it. Then suddenly, all the questions, they didn't mean anything anymore. *We* were going to have a baby. That was all that was important."

The tears were beginning to flow. The two women jumped into the safe harbor of each other's arms. Caught off balance, J.J. let out a little screech and went tumbling backward onto the pile of pillows that lay strewn about at the foot of the fireplace. Margie quickly cupped J.J.'s head in her hands.

"I'm fine," J.J. assured. And she was.

And she proceeded to rock Margie in her arms, to soothe her worries, to affirm their love, to initiate their lovemaking.

It was so very late, and the tears they'd spent had left them both drained. Yet the warm creases knew no such bounds. A readiness drew each to the other, to the sweet familiarity, to the moist secret. Both hearts raced, their blouses hastily flung open and tossed aside. Breasts to breasts, lips to lips. Tear-streaked cheeks were lavished with kisses. Kisses that traveled down warm soft curves.

A mini-shudder rippled up Margie's body—the first of what she knew would be many.

A thought occurred to her. It was a thought she knew better than to articulate: *I wish I didn't have to go back to that clinic tomorrow. I wish J.J. had a big fat syringe full of semen. I wish she had it with her right now.*

Chapter 6

The young man arrived as prearranged, at 7:30. The Women's Health Center was not scheduled to open for another hour yet. He went around to the back where a young woman in a crisp white uniform let him in.

This was a different young woman from the one he'd seen the last time. She smiled briefly. She had a pretty mouth but it almost immediately began issuing instructions: "You are to have a seat in this room and wait for the doctor. The doctor will be along in a few minutes. In the meantime you are to change into this gown. There's a hanger behind the door for your clothes. There's a medical release form here." She indicated a clipboard atop a small desk, like a shelf that folded down from the wall next to the sink. "It's a triplicate form," she went on to say. "Sign here. The pink copy is for you to keep. This envelope is for your copy." She lifted an envelope, then laid it back down on top of the clipboard. "This envelope..." she lifted a second envelope and laid it down alongside the clipboard, "...contains the agreed upon remuneration. When the procedure is completed, you are to leave the premises immediately—that includes the parking lot and the immediate vicinity. You are to exit the same entrance you just came in.

"On behalf of the clinic and our patients, I extend our appreciation for your participation in the program."

The young man started to say something but she cut him short.

"If you have any questions, the doctor will be along shortly." And she was gone.

At first the young man sat without moving. He was concentrating, thinking about his anatomy like a yogi contemplating his navel, though not quite. His focus was a little lower; his demeanor, more like that of a scientist seeking to provoke a response. A chemist mixing one part intellect, two parts testosterone, three parts determination. And the stirring was occurring. In vivo, inside his personal test tube—the crotch of his loose fitting khakis began to rise. Bigger and bigger. He looked down at himself with satisfaction. It occurred to him that it was like a scene from one of those sci-fi thrillers where the main character undergoes a supernatural transformation, except there wasn't anything so supernatural about an erection.

He hopped down off the exam table and lifted his shirt off over his head.

He was exceptionally thin, making his body look more boyish than one might expect of a man in his mid-twenties. He was almost entirely devoid of body hair. He went to the desk and signed the release form without reading it. He tore his copy off, folded it, and put it in his shirt pocket. Then he folded his shirt—he didn't use the hanger—and placed it on a chair in the corner of the room behind the door. Next he removed his pants.

His tumescent manhood stood straight out in front of him.

Just then the door opened and the doctor walked in.

A lady doctor.

The doctor stepped hurriedly into the room, partially closing the door behind her. The young man had just finished folding his pants. He was holding them out in front of him. The doctor turned and as she did, the young man fumbled nervously and dropped the pants onto the chair.

"Good morning, Doctor," he stammered. "How are you this morning?"

Part of any physician's profession demeanor is the ability to not act surprised or astonished by the wide variety of symptoms one is apt to come across in the course of his, or her, career. Such reaction would only cause the patient to become self-conscious and concerned.

Dr. Shirley, as she was affectionately known by her patients, was an older woman; she had been in family practice for more than a quarter of a century. She, herself, had raised three boys, so she was not one to balk at the sight of a naked man.

Yet this naked man startled her.

The feeling must have been mutual. The young man backed away from her, and he seemed to be having trouble swallowing.

It was very unusual for a patient to get an erection in the decidedly clinical environment of the doctor's office. And the erection itself was nothing short of colossal. Dr. Shirley dropped the glass container in her hand. It fell to the linoleum but did not break. Because of its conical shape it rolled around in a little circle and stopped halfway between the doctor and the young man. Instinctively she knelt to retrieve the beaker. Looking up, she found herself at eye-level with an engorged red member—the owner of which grinned sheepishly down at her. She almost dropped the beaker a second time, but managed to get a firm hold on it. Standing up quickly, she attempted to get a hold of her composure as well. She couldn't remember the last time she felt so flustered.

"I usually suggest that there are some erotic magazines in the bottom drawer..." she pointed to an antiseptic-looking steel cabinet. "Some donors find that they help to achieve arousal; however, I see that you won't be needing them."

"Doctor, I have a few questions I'd like to ask you, if I may?"

His timid manner was starkly contrary to his presentation, so to speak. And for the first time since she entered the room, Dr. Shirley made eye contact.

"I'd be happy to answer any questions you might have, Mister..." She needed to refresh her memory. She reached for the donor's chart. "Mister Manly... Lance Manly. Is it alright if I call you Lance?"

He nodded; it was alright.

He had the strangest eyes.

"Why don't you put on the gown, Lance—that's why it's there—then have a seat over here," she indicated the exam table, "and we can discuss your questions."

Those squinting eyes—the doctor found herself unable to look away.

Thankfully he kept his eyes fixed on the floor. She really did not want him looking back at her. There was something too uncomfortable in those eyes. Dark scary slits.

Chapter 7

It was an hour later that Margie Danser arrived at the Women's Health Center. As usual, J.J. Twomey was with her. Dr. Shirley greeted the two women in the reception area, chatting casually as she lead them back to the exam room.

The donor had left the building minutes before. Though he didn't come right out and say it, Dr. Shirley got the impression that he wasn't completely comfortable in his role as donor. What was worse, he managed to make Dr. Shirley feel uncomfortable in her role as doctor. She was beginning to suspect that Mr. Manly had lied on his application. Maybe he wasn't even a medical student, just someone looking to make a quick fifty bucks. It wouldn't be the first time someone pulled a fast one, she thought, giving new meaning to an old expression.

She made a mental note not to use Mr. Manly again.

Artificial Insemination guidelines dictated that donors and recipients were not to meet. The clinic went to great lengths to enforce this policy. It wasn't always easy. In vivo fertilization required the specimen be used 1 to 2 hours after collection. There was always a chance the A.I. recipient might catch a glimpse of the donor in the parking lot, or as he exited the building. For that reason, careful scheduling and separate entrances were set up. It didn't always work, but they did the best they could.

"Margie... J.J., it's good to see you both." Dr. Shirley noticed that Margie looked slightly piqued, as though she wasn't getting enough sleep. "You're early today. Is everything alright?"

J.J. assured the doctor that things couldn't be better.

Dr. Shirley smiled knowingly. Over the years, with each A.I. attempt she had learned to except a certain degree of emotional wear and tear. The process itself engendered stress, there was no way around it. The good news was, if the statistics were right, Margie Danser would not be undergoing the procedures much longer. Dr. Shirley performed A.I. two or three times during each cycle. Since sperm could survive up to 72 hours in the hospitable environment of the cervical mucosa, she usually scheduled the procedure on days -3, -1, and +1; day 0 being the day of ovulation. An 80% success rate was average, with pregnancy being achieved within six attempts. This was Margie's fifth attempt.

And in light of what the lab findings indicated about Mr. Manly's specimen...

That was something else that bothered Dr. Shirley. Perhaps it shouldn't have, but it did. She glanced again at the report in the file: a normal ejaculation contains about 2 to 4 c.c. with a 20×10^{10} sperm count and a 60% motility; this specimen contained 6 c.c., a 35×10^{10} count, with an 80% motility—a very dangerous man indeed. In and of itself, that should not be a cause for concern.

Lance Manly had been pre-screened. On paper at least, he seemed to have all the right qualities. He was of average height, of European extraction; he was certainly slender. He had no apparent diseases, and claimed to have no history of familial disorders. Unfortunately there was no way to check. Most of the donors were graduate students from the nearby medical school. The advantage in using graduate students was twofold: Not only did it assure a certain level of intelligence, but most were from outside the area. After they completed their studies, they would move away. That was important since it decreased the risk of future contact between donor and offspring. Mr. Manly's profile seemed particularly attractive on several other accounts. He stated that he'd never been a donor at any other clinic. With some donors fathering as many as twenty-five children, the spectre of "innocent incest" had to be considered. And Mr. Manly was married with a healthy child from that union. In choosing donors for the program, those who are married with healthy offspring are definitely preferred.

So why was Dr. Shirley so uneasy about proceeding with the procedure?

Margie quickly disrobed and got into a blue hospital gown. She was anxious to get it over with. She hated the examination tables—another indignity of being a woman. She got onto her back with her butt elevated by a pillow. The exam table paper felt cold and crinkly. Her feet were placed into the stirrups with her knees open.

The doctor drew the semen into a glass syringe. In place of a needle there was a soft flexible tube placed. Using only water as a lubricant, a speculum was placed inside and opened, permitting direct visualization of the cervix.

J.J. stayed in the room—for moral support. It was her wish to go along with Margaret through each step of the way, to share in the experience. It was supposed to make it easier for her. It was supposed to create an even stronger bond between them. At moments like this, Margie would've just as soon it was only her and the doctor. But looking over at J.J. and seeing the expression on her face, she understood it was probably more for J.J.'s benefit. And she did love J.J.

She would go along with the program.

With the speculum in place, the donor semen was placed on the anterior lip of the cervix. A small amount was also placed in back of the vagina. The speculum was removed, careful not to remove any semen on the lower blade of the instrument.

And that was it.

It was over.

Margie couldn't understand why she always felt such anxiety over what was essentially a very simple procedure. But she did.

Now all Margie had to do was to remain lying down with her hips elevated for the next fifteen minutes to an hour. J.J. had already gathered up a stack of magazines for her to read.

"Thanks, but no thanks." Margie said, "I think I'll stick with the book I'm reading. You know, I left it in the car. Would you—"

"You just stay put, I'll go get it. Be back in a flash."

The instant J.J. was out of the room, Margie asked the doctor, "Did you use the same donor this time as last time?"

45

"Now Margie, what difference does that make?"

"I don't know, I have a different feeling this time. I think this time may be the one."

"Well, I certainly hope so, Margie."

"Is he a medical student?"

"Yes, he's a medical student." Dr. Shirley began to feel uneasy. "But that's all I can tell you." Then she added, "He seemed like a very nice young man."

But that wasn't saying anything. It was worse than nothing; it sounded like what you might say about a supermarket clerk who helped you to your car with your groceries. Margie stared at the doctor, probingly. Dr. Shirley turned her back, moving things around on the desktop.

"He seemed like an intelligent, healthy young man." She could still feel the drill of the younger woman's gaze, prying into her. So she added, "...With beautiful eyes."

Which made Margie smile.

And the drilling stopped.

J.J., as always, was good to her word; she was "back in a flash," bounding into the room holding Margie's paperback extended out in front of her—a Stephen King novel. Margie was a big fan of horror stories.

"And now, ladies," Dr. Shirley straightened the file, tapping it on the counter before tucking it under her arm, "I bid you both adieu. Nancy'll be in in a while—to let you know when time's up."

Stepping from the room, closing the door behind her, Dr.

Shirley experienced a peculiar sensation. All of a sudden she felt sad.

She thought about something a male colleague had once said: "Every time, after I perform an A.I.," he'd joked, "I want to share a cigarette with the patient and buy cigars for my friends."

But this was different. Dr. Shirley couldn't explain it but she didn't feel like celebrating or congratulating. She felt like seeing a priest, to ask forgiveness—and she wasn't even Catholic. She hadn't done anything any different than usual, she hadn't said anything untrue—yet she couldn't shake the feeling... *Who were they fooling? Were they being untrue to Love? Were they lying to God?*

Chapter 8

Lance Manly was not a first year medical student, as he'd led them to believe. He couldn't help thinking out loud: "Those women at the Health Center, they're not as smart as they think."

The fact that he was capable of functioning outside of an institution was, in and of itself, nothing short of a miracle. Credit where credit's due, despite his horrendous beginnings he had persevered. His early interaction with doctors and hospitals had proven to be quite influential. When it came time to select a career, it seemed only natural that he should choose something in the health field. He managed to get accepted to a small vocational school where they promised to train him as an x-ray technician. And so, using the money set aside for his education, young Manly embarked on a promising future.

Radiological technician school was turning out to be very difficult for Lance. He'd already had to repeat one semester. But he would not let himself become discouraged. He was able to derive a very special strength from the fact that he was not alone. With him was a young girl whom he had met at a foster home. Her name was Eunice. And although as children they were raised as brother and sister, she eventually became his wife.

Theirs was not a typical love.

Nothing about Lance and Eunice was typical.

They lived with their one year old daughter in a trailer park, on the northeast edge of town.

The sky over the trailer park seemed to be a constant sheet of gray, stained and faded in places, tucked in low on the horizon. Eunice Manly suspected that a different sky hung over other homes. She further suspected that the daily barrage of gloom was somehow there because of Lance. He never had any love for the sky. It was days like this, overcast and shadowy, that caused him to hum to himself. It's odd but that was the very quality which drew Eunice to Lance: he was cheerful when all around him was dreary, and sorry, and sad.

And in that, they complimented each other. For Lance's wife was a chronically depressed person. She carried around a kind of raging hopelessness which could spread like a rash. Her voice was grating, like a cough fouling her surroundings with glum.

And for that, Lance loved her.

He not only seemed immune to her malady, he actually seemed to thrive on it.

It was there from the start; they were made for each other.

When Lance arrived home that day after class, he brought with him two large bags of groceries purchased with the money he'd earned for donating his sperm at the Women's Health Center. He didn't like having to lie, but they needed the money. Carrying the heavy bags, one in each arm, he proceeded on the path between the narrow lots of land each housing a dilapidated box of tin propped up on cinder blocks. One practically on top of each other.

It was a little past eight. Smells left over from dinner hung to the air along with the noise of a half dozen TV's. An occasional holler got thrown in and passed for conversation.

The Manly residence was an old Airstream. A classic. Pushed off into a dark corner of the park, its curved silver skin was barely able to glean enough light for reflection. The neighbor in the next trailer over tried to beautify the grounds with flowers, but there never seemed to be enough sunshine to raise a decent patch of color. On the ground outside of Lance's trailer—Eunice had a tendency to throw garbage out the front door.

She seldom bathed and was constantly eating.

But Lance never criticized.

On the contrary, it was Eunice who took every opportunity she could to berate "Lance in the Pants," as she called him.

"Honey..." he poked his head forward to peer through the screen door. Only his meek voice ventured inside. "Honey, wait till you see what I got." He waited. "Eunice, dear...?"

The grocery bags were getting heavy. Holding one bag between his skinny forearm and bony body, he managed to free his fingers to get a hold on the handle. Nudging the door aside with his head, he got a foothold on the first step and angled in sideways. As the screen door swung closed behind him, he stuck his foot out to try to prevent it from banging. Instead he ended up kicking it closed. The screen rattled noisily, and Lance almost lost his balance. He pulled his foot back onto the stairs. The door banged closed.

"You inconsiderate little shit!"

Now he had done it. He woke Eunice.

She cleared her throat. It was a long disgusting sound. Coming out of that corpulence, it resounded like a tuba.

"Yaaah!" she screamed.

The whole trailer quaked under her charge. Completely naked, she barreled down the midway. Her huge pink body was covered with freckles and orange-red hairs—on her arms, and under her arms, on her loose hanging belly, and a great mat of pumpkin hair under her belly. It was too late, there was no getting out of her way. With a backhand, she clobbered him. With plenty of power behind the blow. Eunice Manly was about 5 foot 7 inches tall, and weighed at least 200 pounds. She made solid contact with the right side of his head. With his arms full he was unable to fend off the blow. And having absorbed the full impact, there was no place to fall. The trailer was too narrow. He leaned against the door of the wardrobe, letting the packages slide from his hands. Eunice was just about to deliver a balled up pudgy right hand to his mid-section when she noticed the box of cookies sitting atop the bag.

Lance made no sound. He was careful to avoid eye contact.

"Oh, you brought me my favorite, peanut butter chocolate cooookies."

She knelt down. Rolls of fat bunched up and overlapped her sides.

She went right for the box of cookies.

Standing back up, she brought her warm breasts and belly smack against him, her breath within an inch of his face. There

51

were some cookie crumbs on her cheeks.

"You're such a sweetheart, Lance in the Pants. That was so nice of you to bring me my favorite cooookies." She put one hand on his buns, the other on his crotch; his head was turned to the side—still not looking at her—and she kissed him hard on the mouth, the weight of her head squishing his ear painfully against the wall paneling.

And just then—*Wouldn't you know it!*—the baby started crying and interrupted their romantic moment. Coming from the back of the trailer, it started up like a small siren and rapidly lifted up into full, ear-splitting cacophony.

"Oh, she must've crapped herself...." Eunice announced.

And immediately Lance jumped—on his way to see to the little Princess's needs. That's what he called her, *Princess*.

"Hold on, Lulu. Mommy's coming." Eunice also started in the direction of their daughter's cry. The result was a collision.

Lance got the worst of it. He was knocked partly down, his legs sticking out into the aisle, almost tripping Eunice as she hurried to her little baby, Lulu.

"You're always getting under foot." Her face grew flush with anger.

Two slaps landed in rapid succession. A right across his face, then a left hammering down on top of his head. She batted him with open-hands, heavy hands.

"Fuck! This trailer is too small to have you getting in my way."

And as he cowered, expecting another blow, she lifted him

up by his hair. He didn't let out a sound, not even a peep. She tossed him like trash, out the door and onto the soggy ground.

With his head still ringing from the force of the slaps, he could hear her say: "There now, Lulu. Stop your crying. Mommy's here." And Lance thought, *Princess and I are really lucky to have her. She really is a good mother.*

He got to his feet and brushed himself off.

There was only one thing to do now.

He walked slowly back to his car, an old brown four-door Plymouth. He retrieved his *X-ray Positioning* textbook and his *Anatomy Coloring Book.* Then, returning to the Airstream, he glanced around to see if anyone was watching. And very quickly and very quietly he got down on all fours and crawled under the trailer.

A small hole in the floor allowed the flickering light from the television to thread its way down to where Lance pored over his books. Eunice was always baffled how he could read without hardly any light.

"How you doing there, Lance in the Pants?" she absently called down to him, not taking her eyes off the TV.

"Fine, dear.... Thank you."

He glanced up through the hole to where his wife was sitting. He could see between her legs to where the fleshy pink labia protruded down out of the tangled orange bush.

He found her terribly beautiful.

And he loved her very much.

Chapter 9

The sun washed in through the curtains of Margaret Danser's room, lending a feminine touch to the morning light. The furnishings within the bedroom weren't particularly female: no flowery linens, no frilly doilies on dressing tables strewn with cosmetics. The most feminine article of furniture in her bedroom was a freestanding mirror. It was a full-length oblong mirror that swayed between lathe-turned posts, on a rosewood base. She only recently purchased it, and now, standing completely naked in front of it, she felt that maybe, subliminally, she had purchased it with this very moment in mind. It had been over a month since the results of her pregnancy test came back.

She was in her eighth week.

She'd been doing a lot of reading lately, reading up on the various signs and symptoms associated with her new condition.

Signs! Symptoms! Condition!—they made it sound like it was a disease.

Whatever... For these nine months it was going to be the condition of Margie's body, so she might as well learn all she could.

That went double for J.J. She was going to let Margaret know that she was not alone in this. The Women's Health Center provided a variety of educational pamphlets and brochures, but J.J. took it a step further. She went to the library intent on taking out every book they had on the subject. That was where she was that morning. She'd received a postcard letting her know that the book she'd ordered had come in. They were holding it for her.

So this moment belonged solely to Margie.

She stepped back from the mirror and sighed heavily. Her reflection sighed heavily. She took a step in closer, focusing long and hard at the naked woman in front of her. The wonder of it all began to dawn on her. She wasn't showing—it was too early for that—but she was undergoing changes. There was the vomiting. The doctor assured her that the bouts of morning sickness would subside by month three. And there were other signs. She was feeling overly-sensitive. And now, as she stood in front of the mirror, she studied the skin of her nipples which looked darker, more pigmented. Maybe it was her imagination but she thought her breasts felt heavier. And she was going to the bathroom all the time. The doctor told her that was to be expected.

Margie turned to her side, purposely sticking out her abdomen, trying to envision what she might look like in the months to come. Suddenly a wave of emotion swept over her. The image in the mirror twinkled like crystal as she blinked back the tears. She couldn't help herself, she sat down on the floor in front of the mirror and wept. She didn't even know why. She supposed it was just another symptom. Her hormones playing havoc. It was all so strange. So perfectly natural... and yet so strange.

She thought of all she'd been through to get to this point.

The frustration, the indecision—not to mention the expense!—it was no wonder she was crying. Right from the start, the A.I. option was met with concern and criticism. Margaret recalled when she first broached the subject of artificial insemination with her parents. Poor Mom and Dad, it had taken them so long to get used to the idea that their only daughter was a lesbian. Now this! There was no going back from this!

Then there was the insurance company to deal with. Margie's job provided good health coverage, or so she thought— until she, as a "single" woman, started the A.I. procedure. Right away, medical coverage was denied. Not a medical necessity. It became a long-drawn-out paperwork battle. The insurance company called the procedure "experimental." This despite the fact that the first recorded artificial insemination involving humans was done two hundred years ago.

In 1790, a British M.D. named John Hunter performed a homologous A.I. for a husband who had a hypospadius deformity of the penis. Margie decided that that was what the *men* at the insurance company meant by "medical necessity."

The first recorded donor A.I. was performed in the 1890's, a hundred years ago, and yet it appeared it was still nearly as controversial now as it was then.

History notwithstanding, the insurance company finally agreed to cover the cost. At three hundred dollars each attempt, plus physical exams and lab work, Margie would've been hard-pressed to pay that out of her own pocket. But all that was in the past. Now that she was pregnant, they would cover the cost of prenatal care and hospital delivery, no questions asked.

J.J. said the insurance company's initial reluctance was part of a conspiracy to undermine women's rights to reproductive freedom.

Margie wasn't quite so cynical.

Besides, she had more pressing concerns.

Though she was, on some level, enjoying her little cry, she had no choice but to rush off to the bathroom. Self-discovery in front of the mirror was going to have to wait; dry heaves took precedence.

When J.J. returned she found Margie vigilantly guarding the toilet.

Quick to embrace the role of doting spouse, and adhering to the instructions in the prenatal literature, J.J. prepared a light carbohydrate breakfast of biscuits and milk. It was supposed to ease the nausea.

"There... That help...? Feel any better?

Margie took another nibble on the biscuit. Some of the color was returning to her face. Her stomach was settling back down.

"Well, it's not as bad as the night we drank tequila at the Baja Cafe. " J.J.'s smiled across the table to her friend. They were lovers, of course, but Margie had been a friend first and would always be.

It seemed like so long ago, but it was really only three years. They met in a class for women's studies at a community college. Margie wasn't sure why she'd enrolled. It was something to do.

She'd recently gone through a painful breakup with her boyfriend and she needed to give her heart a breather, to take inventory, and to learn how to feel good about herself again.

J.J. had also just ended a long-term relationship. The two women commiserated over frustrations and disappointments. They found a common bond.

And all along Margie never thought to ask J..J. if her lost love was male or female. And J.J. never mentioned it.

Until one day, they went to the movies together. It was a foreign film. At the onset of the class, their professor had provided a list of suggested books, plays, and movies. This particular movie was on the list.

Margie was not a lesbian. Not in the same way that J.J. was. Margie had always enjoyed the company of men. So it was curious when she felt herself becoming aroused at the sight of two women making love on the screen. It was even more bewildering when J.J. kissed her, and she found herself responding. More than responding. Thirsting.

~~~

J.J. glanced at her wristwatch. "You'd better hurry up and get ready. We've got to be there by eleven-thirty."

"I still don't understand...What's the purpose of these meetings?"

"Margaret, don't be difficult. It's like Dr. Shirley says: A.I couples, especially lesbians, we don't have the same social support as traditional expectant mothers—baby showers and that sort of thing. This will provide a sense of extended family. It's important."

"I think I'd rather stay home and throw up."

J.J. screwed in a stern face meant to look as if she was losing patience. Truth was, where Margie was concerned, J.J. had an endless reservoir of patience. "Maybe *you* don't need this, but there are other people who might benefit from getting together with other people who are going through the same thing."

It came out a little awkward, but the idea got across.

"Okay," Margie gave in, "you win. So maybe I'll be of help to someone else."

"There you go. That's one way to look at it." J.J. was boosted.

To herself she mumbled, "It certainly might do me some good."

Chapter 10

The support group met at the Women's Health Center, in a
comfortable back room. Chairs with cushions on them were
arranged in a circle. Everyone helped themselves to herbal teas;
the red-capped spigot on the water cooler provided hot water. A
tray of butter cookies had been put out on a table. J.J. went over
and helped herself. After sampling a few, she piled a handful into
a napkin, to share with Margie. The meeting was getting
underway as she returned to her seat. She laid the napkin out on
the coffee table between her and Margie's.

Margie waved off the offer; she whispered, "No thanks, you
eat 'em."

J.J. simultaneously shrugged and nodded, as she put another
cookie in her mouth.

There were five other people in attendance, three women—
not counting Dr. Shirley—and two men. Margie had already met
one of the women. When she was first considering A.I., the
woman had been nice enough to talk to her about it. She was an
older woman, without a partner, male or female. Margie gave her
a lot of credit; it took a lot of guts. When Dr. Shirley first
introduced Sigreid Calhoun, Margie was taken aback. Sigreid
seemed too old to be having a baby. But apparently she didn't
think so, because here she was, three months pregnant and
glowing like a girl, a girl with a wondrous secret.

Sigreid was a German national. She'd married a G.I. who was stationed there. He was much younger than she. They divorced shortly after she returned with him to the States. She'd been on her own ever since. A strong-minded, no-nonsense woman—you have to be if you're going to raise a child by yourself—she decided to take matters into her own hands. It was a race against her biological clock. Her methods were a bit unorthodox, but it appeared she won. Not that she couldn't have gotten a man. One look at her was enough to dispel that notion. Sigreid was a good-looking woman, regal in bearing. She had a trim, hard body, though not lacking in soft curves. It was obvious she kept in shape. She had a somewhat hard-looking face, but the eyes told a different story. A lively intellect danced behind those eyes. She looked at the world with constant amusement. Margie liked her right off.

The other participants in the group included a very sweet-looking girl sitting very close to her handsome young husband. Mandy and Howard Greenleaf were seated on the couch. Neither one leaned back; they both perched on the edge of the seat cushions. Neither one looked comfortable, but he looked the more uncomfortable by far. When it came their turn to speak, she did the speaking. Childhood mumps had left him sterile. Shame and resentment left him brooding in silence. Meanwhile, his wife, cradling her little pregnant belly, was telling these strangers his most personal problems. The couple was undecided whether to tell the in-laws that their grandchild was not of their bloodline. Every once in a while Howard smiled ungracefully.

The group listened to Mandy go on about her "happy little problem," as she called it, and Margie thought, *This support group may turn out to be interesting after all.*

And there was more to come.

The next couple introduced themselves as Monty and Rebecca "Becky" Mandell. Becky was a former Las Vegas showgirl, and Monty, a retired businessman. Unlike Howard, Monty wasn't the least bit bothered. He was more than happy to do anything he could to indulge the wishes of his young bride. If that meant having a baby, he was onboard. He didn't come right out and say it, but the man had to be at least sixty. What he did say was that he had a vasectomy years ago and it probably wasn't reversible. He already had several children of his own, all grown and on their own. Judging from his clothes—Farrentino shoes, Ike Behar sport shirt—money was no problem. He was a man with no problems. And like he told the group, he enjoyed raising his family the first time around; this time was going to be even better.

Margie found herself smiling.

And then, to her amazement, Monty winked at her.

What a character! How extraordinarily outrageous! This old bandit, lucky as aces, married to an incredibly beautiful showgirl, and he's flirting with a pregnant lesbian. *Unbelievable!* Margie couldn't get over it. She couldn't stop grinning.

She looked over at J.J.

J.J. wasn't grinning, not in the least.

"So, what did you think of our first support group meeting?" Margie wanted to know. "What do you think of our fellow *conspirators?*"

They were on their way home. J.J. was driving, proceeding down Brand Avenue, past a stretch of markets and shops.

"I'll tell you what I think," J.J. said, steering the car into a diagonal parking spot, "I think I should pick up some fish for tonight. Maybe orange roughy, with a little rice on the side, some steamed veggies. How about chocolate mousse for dessert, huh...? What do you think?"

"I think you got your nose out of joint because some old Romeo came on to me. That's what I think...." Margie's tone was plainly teasing, playful. Her spirits had been lifted by the meeting.

J.J., on the other hand, was being unusually quiet, pouty even.

"C'mon, J.J., the old boy's funny! He reminds me of my dad, for Christ sakes. You can't really think... I mean... get serious!"

"I know, I know... I'm sorry, Margaret. Sometimes I don't know what gets into me."

"Eh, forget it."

"No, I don't want to forget it. Not yet. I want to say something first. You know, sometimes it scares me how much I love you.... No, listen! I know that you're not like me, you weren't always attracted to women. And I get frightened sometimes that maybe you miss... men. There, I said it."

"Okay.... So now can we forget it?"

J.J. stared lovingly at her partner, like she might cry at any minute. Then suddenly she reached across the front seat and hugged Margie so violently that Margie thought she might pop her back. But it was not a hug to be denied. She felt the kiss on her cheek, mingled with the wetness of tears—and she held J.J. even tighter.

Before breaking off the embrace, J.J. dabbed her eyes dry. "Okay, we can forget it now." She smiled. "I'm going to fix you the best chocolate mousse you ever tasted."

"I don't know if that's on my prenatal diet."

"What! Are you kidding? Fetuses love chocolate mousse. It's their favorite food."

The two women laughed. Not that it was that funny—they just needed to laugh.

"Okay, enough *putzing* around. Let's get cracking." J.J. liked to say that: *Let's get cracking*—lesbian humor.

She handed Margie a dry cleaning receipt. "I'll go to the market and pick out a nice piece of fish, you go to the cleaners and pick up the dry cleaning. See you back here in ten minutes."

The cleaners was up the block from where they parked, on the same side of the street.

The day had become cloudy again, a pattern that had been repeated as of late—a smattering of sunshine in the afternoon, fooling you into leaving your sweater home.

With her arms filled—one hand looped through hangers from which several plastic-draped garments hung, slung over her shoulder; the other hand clutching a large cumbersome shirt box—Margie was making her way back to the car. She was crossing in front of an alleyway that ran between two buildings when she stopped and turned. She wasn't sure if she was seeing correctly. Perhaps it was the low, grunting sound that got her attention. But once she was facing him, it should have registered. It shouldn't have taken her so long to see what was going on. To turn away and keep walking.

But she didn't. She just stood there.

Why was she just standing there?

At first she thought he was a panhandler. Then it occurred to her that perhaps the man was injured. He seemed to be in some distress. His eyes seemed to be pleading and his tongue rolled out across his dry, cracked lips—as if he were going to say something. Then he looked down at his hand. His pants were open. He was masturbating in front of her. *Masturbating* in front of her.

As the realization of what was happening finally sunk in, Margie's mind played a cruel trick. She thought about the father of her child. She superimposed the image of this flasher onto her image of *the donor.* Against the backdrop of the alley, she envisioned the exam room at the Women's Health Center. And when she glance down again at the man's hand feverishly jerking off his dick, there *he* was, leaning against the wall: the flasher, the donor—one and the same—performing the same crude act, into a jar, the contents to be injected up into her womb.

The next thing she knew she was being roused from her dreadful daydream by a ruckus:

"Show me, you pervert." It was J.J. She'd run up to the flasher and before he knew what was happening, she'd smacked him savagely in the head. "Show it to me," she screamed at him. "I want to see your stinking little pee pee. I'll kick it up into your lungs, you filthy..." She started kicking him mercilessly. He stumbled back, trying to get away and, at the same time, trying to get his penis back into his pants. J.J. had become a fury of fists and feet wailing away at the sorry sack of human debris.

He took a few more vicious shots that knocked him down onto his hands and knees before he finally managed to scamper off down the alley.

J.J. started to go after him when she heard Margie say, "Let him go, J.J. He's just a sick individual. Don't dirty your hands on him."

It was like a bad dream. The plastic garment bags and the shirt box lay on the sidewalk. She didn't even recall dropping them.

"That pervert bastard," J.J. was fuming as she helped Margie gather up the packages. "He's lucky I didn't have my knife on me, I'd've cut off his balls.... You know, I always have my knife—" Looking up, J.J. saw how shaken Margie was. "Are you alright?"

"Yeah, I'm okay...."

J.J.'s eyes didn't let go; she looked deeply, she looked concerned.

"Really, I'm okay. I just never had anything like that ever happen to me before, is all."

"You sure you're alright?"

"Don't be silly, I'm fine," Margie said, and she put on a brave face for her lover and protector.

And for herself.

Chapter 11

The months that followed were indescribable: they flew by, they dragged on; they were joyous, they were abysmal; and whatever else... they were truly transforming. And throughout the entire time, Margie was often put in mind of something her mother used to say: "Wait until you have a child of your own, then you'll understand."

And that was precisely what was happening. Margie was beginning to *understand*.

Not the same way one understands a math problem, or understands that the world turns on its axis. The only analogy that bears any correlation might be in the way one eventually learns to understand death—not with the mind, but with every mortal fiber of one's being. It takes the loss of a someone so close that it's like your own death. It took the birth of someone so close that it was like her own birth. And so it was that with every nurturing cell of her body, Margie was learning to understand life. To fathom the incomprehensible. That was what having a child was about.

Wait until you have a child of your own, then you'll understand.

~ ~ ~

On November 3rd, 1992, Margaret Danser gave birth to a healthy baby boy. The child was delivered at four forty-five in the afternoon, weighing seven pounds seven ounces, measuring 20 inches in length. Both mother and child were resting comfortably.

J.J. Twomey strode into the room like a proud papa. The only thing she was lacking was a cigar in her pocket. She was all puffed up and leading a contingent of well-wishers: Dr. Shirley; Sigreid Calhoun; the Mandells; and her friend, Terry. They all came to see the new baby.

In Sigreid's case, her coming to the hospital showed exceptional strength; Sigreid had lost her child in the sixth month. It could not have been easy for her. When Margie saw her standing there, for an instant she felt an irrational pang of guilt. Her heart went out to Sigreid, and her smile—bittersweet. Sigreid smiled back. No sign of sadness, no trace of envy. A truly remarkable woman.

Someone was saying, "Mandy and Howard Greenleaf were unable to come, but they send their *congratulations.*"

Mandy Greenleaf had given birth three weeks early. Her baby, a little boy, Brad Vincent, had some respiratory difficulties, and so he had to remain in the hospital for a few days. Just last week they finally got to take him home.

Margie heard Dr. Shirley speaking, but she wasn't really listening; she was too excited, too busy taking it all in. What a moment! The nurse came into the room carrying a little bundle, straight to the arms of mama. What bliss!

The newborn yawned; his perfect little arms and shoulders trembled with the breath as his new lungs drew new life. Margie was speechless. She wanted to say something, to talk to these dear people who'd come to be with her, to share her joy. But she was unable to utter even a syllable. She just looked at the perfect little angel. Her eyes grew enormous as she beheld her child. Those at her bedside crowded in to witness the wonder. And Margie reveled in the chorus of *oohs* and *aahs*.

His birth certificate read: Kenneth J. Danser.

The *J* was J.J.'s idea. When Margie asked her, "What will he say when people ask him what the *J* stands for?" J.J. simply replied, "It doesn't stand for anything. It's not an initial, just the letter *J*. It stands for there being part of me, J.J., in him.

On the birth certificate, the space for the father's name was left blank.

The subject of the donor was not mentioned in the Danser household. More than not mentioned, a deliberate effort was made to forget. To deny. Both women knew that the "straight" world was not to be trusted. There were cases in which divorced mothers lost custody of their children when it became known that they were lesbians. What hope could there be for a lesbian mother without a husband. J.J. read somewhere that "Legitimacy is a concept invented by men for men." Despite written agreements, donors could make claims for paternity. The legal system couldn't be trusted. In the past, visitation rights have been awarded to donors. Courts have even awarded visitation to donor's parents. And the most scary of all, donors could challenge for custody based on the lifestyle of the mother, meaning sexual preference.

The donor became a skeleton in the closet, a skeleton that threatened to waltz out into the light of day and snatch up every ray of sunshine.

So it was understandable that little by little, Margie and J.J. became increasingly private, choosing to live their lives in a closed circle among women whom they could depend on not to hurt them. You could almost call it a siege mentality. Such was their vulnerability.

Chapter 12

Cave City's Urgent Care was having difficulty filling the position. There simply weren't many applicants who wanted to live in South Central Kentucky, miles from anywhere. The patients were, for the most part, locals, with a smattering of tourists. The staff was comprised of a doctor, a nurse, and the currently vacant position of x-ray tech. In an office this size, job title doesn't mean much; you have to be ready to step in and do whatever needs to be done. And that was exactly how Nurse Francine Johnson explained the position to Lance Manly. She wasn't particularly impressed by the young man's deportment. He seemed to blink a lot. But then Francine didn't exactly have a field of applicants to choose from. The fact was she only had the one. So that was that! He would have to do. She would call Dr. Carter and let him know that the position had been filled. That ought to make the doctor happy; he hated having to take his own x-rays. They always came out over-exposed. He would squint at them and grumble, polish his glasses, and grumble some more.

Dr. Carter was a kind and caring man. But he wasn't actually in the office very often. He would spend a couple of hours a day, three or four times a week. Nurse Johnson saw most of the patients. The doctor had moved down to Cave City from Lexington about ten years ago, and at that time he considered himself to be semi-retired. In truth, he should've retired years ago except, like many men, his identity was wrapped up in his work. And though he had trouble reading the labels on the medicines, he would continue to practice until the day he died.

Lance Manly's first day on the job: After a quick hello to Nurse Johnson, he went directly to the darkroom and closed the door.

Several hours past.

It was an unusually quiet morning, even by Cave City standards. There were only three patients scheduled and none of them required x-rays. The new x-ray tech stayed holed up in the darkroom all morning. He came out once to use the bathroom, then went right back in.

Then, about eleven-thirty, Nurse Johnson stood and listened outside the door for a moment before knocking: "Mr. Manly... we may have a patient for you."

The door opened slowly.

"A patient... for x-rays." He sounded surprised.

What did he expect? He is the x-ray tech. Sometimes patients need x-rays. It was bound to happen.

Nurse Johnson didn't say anything. She figured she'd cut him some slack—his being new and all.

She couldn't help thinking that he looked like a rodent, a frightened shiny-eyed rodent.

"B...b...by all means," he stammered, "have...have the patient come in."

"Hey, relax. I said we *may* have a patient for x-rays.... I'm not sure yet. I just wanted to let you know, in case you have to warm up the processor, or anything like that." She turned her back and mouthed the words: *This guy is weird!* As she walked away she muttered under her breath, loud enough for Lance to hear, "What the hell you been doing in there all morning?"

He made like he didn't hear anything.

How Lance Manly made it through each day was a minor miracle. Throughout high school and vocational school, he was always the non-person, a pale presence. In later years, should classmates ever be asked to recall the frail face in the back row of the graduation picture, he would be the person that no one could quite recall.

The patient didn't wait for Nurse Johnson to show him back; a bearded muddy man came rushing into the x-ray room.

"Otto Gothard. President of Otto's Speleological Tours." The man took hold of Lance's hand and pumped it like a well handle. "So you're the new x-ray guy. Glad to make your acquaintance..." he leaned in to read the name tag, "Lance. Lance Manly."

People were always a problem for Lance. When he decided to become an x-ray technician that was the one thing he'd overlooked. He knew he'd have to study hard, he knew he'd have to make sacrifices, but he never stopped to consider that when all was said and done and he finally had his certification, he would have to deal with... *people!*

Faced with Otto, Lance found himself tensing up, wanting

to run.

"You know what *Speleology* is?" Otto asked.

Lance managed to speak: "Yes, I do."

Though he must've heard, Otto was determined to tell him anyway: "*Spelaion* comes from the Greek, meaning cave, and – *ology* means the study or exploration of... Speleology is the study or exploration of caves."

It was a good thing that Otto was a take-charge kind of guy. For Lance's fear of his fellow man had been steadily worsening, at times rendering him practically incapacitated. It had cost him three jobs in as many months, and as far as Eunice Manly was concerned, this was the end of the line. She had warned him in no uncertain terms: If he couldn't hold onto this job, he was going to lose her.

"See, Lance, I'm a cave guide." Otto pushed a business card into the pocket of Lance's lab coat. "Not like those exhibition guides that take twenty people for a walking tour in a lighted cavern with staircases and elevators—every hour on the hour. No, not me. That's strictly 'Mickey Mouse.' I put together *expeditions*. Up to four or five people. Out all day. At least usually we're out all day. Today, we ran into a little problem."

Lance didn't need to say a word; Otto was handling both ends of the conversation without any help. He was very well-spoken for a caveman. And what was even more remarkable, he smelled... *fantastic!* It was the strangest thing. Lance was enthralled by the smell coming off of this man's clothes. A dank primordial scent. It almost caused Lance to forget where he was.

"...Lance? Did you hear what I said...? She may have broken an ankle."

The patient was not Otto Gothard after all, but rather some young woman from San Diego. She and a couple of friends had hired Otto to take them spelunking. It turned out to be more than they bargained for.

Dr. Carter had been notified. He was on his way. In the meantime, they all stood around looking at the patient while Nurse Johnson proceeded to examine the offending extremity. The range of motion was good, and there was little swelling. Nurse Johnson and Otto agreed it was probably just a sprain.

However, the patient was in pain. Dirt tears streaked her cheeks. "Are you going to take x-rays?" she wanted to know.

Otto took Nurse Johnson aside. "Francie, why don't you have Lance here take a few x-rays. It won't hurt any, and Doc Carter will probably want to see x-rays when he gets here." They looked over at the woman sobbing on the exam table. "And it'll make her feel better."

Otto lowered his voice even further and added, "Caving is not for everyone. Some people don't realize it until it's too late. Claustrophobia, acrophobia, maybe they can't stand being in the dark too long—it's not for everyone." Nurse Johnson understood what Otto Gothard was getting at. But it didn't matter; she'd handle the situation the same either way.

Otto rested a hand on Lance's shoulder and said, "No one wants to be the one to back out. It's a question of saving face. It happens more often than you think."

Again that dark smell swam in through the limbic centers and the olfactory cortex of Lance Manly's brain.

And he understood.

Not about the patient. She was just a silly woman, of no consequence. He would x-ray her ankle if it would make her feel better. Whether there was something wrong with her leg or not, that didn't matter. *He understood.* The sense of smell is the most primitive of all the senses. He didn't bother to question; it wasn't a cognitive understanding. It was *instinctual.*

Otto gave Lance a hand assisting the young woman as she hobbled from the exam room to the x-ray machine.

It was some time later when the doctor finished administering to his patient. The x-rays turned out to be negative—no fractures or dislocations. After applying an ice pack for fifteen minutes, Dr. Carter wrapped the ankle in gauze and an Ace bandage. Nurse Johnson assisted, preventing the doctor from applying *estrogen cream* instead of *analgesic cream.*

Otto Gothard made sure to ask all the right questions: "Should she try to keep the ankle elevated whenever possible? ...Yeah that's what I thought. Guess she should try to stay off of it for a while? ...How about a crutch, Doc? ...Yeah, that ought to do it. Just for a day or so. Thanks, Doc. Thanks, Francie."

And finally, with the young woman leaning heavily against his arm, they headed slowly to the door. Otto's easy-going manner was really very reassuring. "Okay, ma'am, I'm going to take you back to the lodge now."

As he reached the door he turned and looked at Lance:

"Hey, Lance, any time you want to go caving, you just let me know. You'll be my guest. I provide all the gear you'll need. Who knows? Maybe I'll make a spelunker out of you."

Suddenly Lance Manly felt joyous. He practically jumped. "Really! You would take me with you... caving?"

Otto Gothard laughed. "Why sure, Lance, I'd be happy to have you along."

Chapter 13

From stroller to walker, to runner. First steps soon gained momentum and little feet in high-tops became the terror of the playground, chasing pigeons through the autumn leaves. Only a child can shout so gleefully at the changing of the seasons.

Only through a child does an adult get to shout along.

It didn't matter what season it was—on steely winter mornings, or chameleon autumn afternoons, with clouds overhead and leaves shimmying in the breeze—there was sunshine in Margaret Danser's life.

Kenneth J. seemed to grow with each stride.

They would walk to the park. He would run, beaming under a flawless blue sky, outshining blossoms in spring, laughing at the lazy days of summer.

Her son was truly the light of her life. She wondered how she had ever been able to see without him.

Little Kenneth J. Danser didn't look so much like his mom.

Sometimes, as she watched him, she couldn't help but think about the father: *Who was his father? and where was he? What did the father look like? Did he regret what he had done? Did he know what he gave up?*

Kenneth J. Danser—or K.J., as he was sometimes called—was an absolutely delightful child! As a baby, he hardly ever cried. Instead, he would sing to himself, gurgling excitedly—little baby

79

noises. And Margie would sing back to him—soothing, mama noises:

Your mama loves you, little one.

Your mama would move mountains for you.

That's what she would say to him. And little Kenny felt safe and secure. His mama loved him. His mama would move mountains for him. After all, isn't that what a mother does.

His eyes were blue, just like Margie's. But that didn't last. Soon they deepened to a yellow-brown, eventually settling on a brown-green hazel. A dark-haired little boy, his hair was much curlier than hers. Margie always envied people with curly hair. Kenny's complexion was fair and Margie felt sure he had inherited her pale, peachy skin. He would have to be careful to stay out of the sun. His ears were not like hers, thank goodness! She had always been self-conscious about her ears. They stuck out too far. Kenny's ears pressed flat against his head. Maybe his dad was a Vulcan like Mr. Spock. That would be cool, having Mr. Spock for a father.

On this day it was no wonder that Margie was thinking about Kenneth's father. It was *Father's Day!*

Everywhere Margie looked families were on outings. The whole park seemed to be celebrating. It was a very happy place.

Margie and J.J. had moved shortly after Kenneth J. was born. One of the reasons they chose this neighborhood was because it was so near the park. Today, looking out across the meadow, it looked to Margie like one of K.J.'s crayon drawings— all stick figures and trees.

J.J. was originally supposed to join them on their outing to the park, but lately things weren't going so well between the two women. Perhaps *lately* was not the right word. It had been building. It had been months since they last had sex. And the odd thing was, Margie wasn't upset. And therein lay the real rub. She knew she should be feeling upset. She wanted to, but she didn't. She also knew that J.J. was making an excuse when she said she couldn't join them that afternoon. Margie briefly wondered if J.J. was having an affair with another woman. But even that wasn't cause for concern. In Margie's mind, the world had been condensed down to the size of one small boy; all other matters were secondary.

That Kenneth J. might be part of the problem did not bear consideration in Margie's mind. She could conceive no downside to her darling boy. But, as is often the case when a child comes to a marriage, the father figure begins to feel neglected. It's almost as if there's only so much love to go around.

Margie made the mistake once of mentioning to J.J. that she was preoccupied with thoughts of Kenneth's father. This clearly aggravated the rift between them, and Margie made a promise to herself to never mention those thoughts to J.J. again.

But the thoughts were there and no amount of denial would make them go away. The occasion of Father's Day revived long-standing questions. What should she tell K.J. when he asks about his father? He was too young now, but he would ask. It was only a matter of time. Margie sensed it beginning, like the first small bubble in a slow-boiling teapot. He was aware that there was a difference between his household and those of other children. He would begin school soon, and that would inevitably stir the pot.

Meanwhile, mother and son splashed about the crayon-colored day, leaping at azure blue, tumbling in emerald green, bedazzled by lemon yellow, revved up by the radical red, and lulled by water-lily-white. They came at last to rest under the magenta shade of a friendly sugar maple.

"Look, Mommy, Polly noses."

Kenneth was right. It was definitely a "Polly noses" tree. Or a "whirlybird" tree, depending upon which application you choose. It had to do with the winged seeds. Left to dry out and fall, they spiraled down like whirlybirds. Or, if you got them when they were green, like now, the end could be opened, the seed removed, and the sticky end stuck to the tip of your nose. A perfectly splendid use for them.

But even "Polly noses" provided only a brief distraction. Soon K.J. was off again, to climb the "gummy" tree.

"Oh, no," Mama cried. "Not the gummy tree!"

And the race was on.

K.J. got off to a lead. Mommy had to stop and chase his straw sun hat, which fell off and rolled away. Meanwhile, K.J. was making a mad dash across the meadow to the dreaded gummy tree.

The tree's true name was the sweet gum, and it was a fine tree, with plenty of low branches, good for climbing. They were sturdy branches covered with a rough gray bark, fissured and

82

fragrant with the yellow balsam resin it exuded. A resin that was practically impossible to scrub off a little-boy's face and hands.

To someone watching, it might've looked like mommy was letting the little boy win. K.J. was just a few feet from the trunk of the gummy tree when suddenly a pair of lanky blue-veined masculine arms scooped him up—his little legs churning the air, surprise exploding into laughter.

"Hey, Sport, where are you going?" It was Paul. Paul Duberry from work. He flung Kenneth high in the air, better than a carnival ride.

The little boy was absolutely delighted.

And Margie was glad to meet up with a friendly face.

Paul was there with his family, picnicking in the park. His girls, Pauline and Rhonda, were big girls already. Several years beyond dolls, they eagerly offered to look after Kenneth J., to provide Margie with a breather.

"Come, join us for lunch." Paul put Kenneth down. His older girl, Pauline, quickly picked him back up. "Don't worry about Kenneth J., the girls will look after him. It gives them a chance to make believe they have a baby brother."

Margie eyed the two adolescent girls. "Or perhaps they're making believe they're mommies, with a baby of their own."

"Let's not get ahead of ourselves." Paul was pretending the thought never occurred to him. He was a protective father. "Don't you girls get any ideas. I'm not ready to become a grandfather for ten years, at least."

The girls blushed and giggled. And went running after their

new ward, who didn't seem to mind the attention one bit.

Paul's wife, Donna, was a heavy-set woman with an easy manner. She was busy setting the picnic table. "Margie, how nice to see you! You're just in time. We're about to put up some burgers."

At first Margie didn't notice the man seated at the picnic table.

And then, he was all she noticed. The rest of the scene faded into the background.

"Margie, allow me to introduce you to my brother," Donna said. "William Turner, meet Margie Danser. Margie works with Paul, out at the airport.... Willy's a cop, a detective with the Cincinnati P.D."

He had rugged good looks. He probably played football in high school and dated cheerleaders. He probably married his childhood sweetheart. Margie had the guy's life-script written, read, and rejected before "Pleased to meet you" left his lips. Why bother with conversation?! If there was a momentary spark, it was quickly rejected as nothing more than an aberration.

And it didn't take the detective long to pick up on the chill in the air. But he wasn't a man to scare off easily. He sat down across from her and prepared to weather the storm. Over plates of corn on the cob and potato salad, he did his best to keep up his end of the conversation. As well as hers.

Willy and Donna were half-brother and -sister. As Donna indelicately explained, her father ran off with Willy's mother when she was just a baby. *Men!*

84

"So, Margie... uh.... Are you divorced?" William wanted to know.

No was all the answer she offered. Just *No*.

He got a little flustered. "Oh... I'm sorry. That was dumb. It's just that so many people are divorced these days. It being Father's Day, and you and your son..." He wasn't helping matters any.

She took pity on him and decided to let him off the hook. "Kenneth's father and I were never married."

"Oh..." he said, unable to hide his relief, "Never married.... Me neither!" He was working on a ear of sweet corn, thinking of what to say next.

Donna was catching snatches of their conversation. She decided to chime in, "Oh, Margie dear, I must warn you, my brother is a bit of a lady's man, a bounder and a cad, if you know what I mean."

Margie thanked her for the warning, then fanned her hand in front of her face like she was hot. She gave a few short coughs, covering her mouth like she was stifling a laugh. Then, true to form, Margie burst out laughing. Right in Willy's face.

"What?" The detective looked hurt, self-conscious. "What's so funny?"

The others had all turned to see what was so funny. And they all started laughing. It was a contagious laugh.

"I'm sorry. I'm just being silly," Margie said. "Don't mind me, really." She wiped her mouth with her napkin and took a sip of her lemonade. "Go ahead," she dismissed the outburst,

"Don't mind me, eat your corn."

But as soon as William brought the corn back up to his mouth...

Margie's laugh bubbled back up.

He froze mid-bite.

"I'm sorry." Margie said, trying to gain composure. "It's really not that funny."

"What's really not that funny?"

"Your moustache," she said.

And he smiled at the sound of her laughter.

"It's your moustache," she confessed. "I told you it was silly. I'm watching your moustache and I find it funny. The way you eat your corn is very methodical, from side-to-side, like you're playing a harmonica. And your moustache is like a brush. It hangs over the corn just ahead of your mouth and sweeps the oncoming kernels. Then you turn the corn and start off in the other direction."

"She's right!" Donna said. "Now that you mention it, I've noticed that before. It's very amusing to watch Willy eat corn."

"Hey, Willy, can I see what they're talking about?" Paul asked.

"Me too," the girls chimed in. "C'mon, Uncle Willy, eat your corn."

And he did. He picked up his corn and he proceeded to eat.

And everybody laughed.

It wasn't *that* funny, but it *was*. Something about that moustache sweeping over the cob.

Rhonda suggested that he should butter his moustache instead of his corn. It might be better that way.

Then K.J. shouted "Whiskers! Whiskers!"

Willy lifted him up onto his lap.

And K.J. got to touch his first moustache.

Everyone was getting silly.

J.J. Twomey was having difficulty dealing with the changes in the relationship. She felt like she was losing influence, losing control. J.J. had always prided herself on being able to adapt without giving in, go with the flow and still manage to turn the tide. She was the misfit who fit, the odd man in. And now, for the first time ever, she felt apart, and she was having a hard time finding a way in. She knew she should've agreed to spend the day with Margie and K.J. She didn't know why she declined. Maybe it had something to do with Father's Day. Of course it did. That was part of it. How could they have Father's Day without her? She had wanted Margie to insist she come along. She wouldn't have had to insist vehemently. Just a little would have been fine.

But instead Margie said it was alright. She said it like she meant it.

That frightened J.J.

Maybe it was *alright* for Margie. But it wasn't alright for J.J. She could admit it to herself. She wanted them to make it *her* day. Father's Day—wasn't that supposed to be *her* role? Shouldn't it be *her* day?

It took a measure of surrender to follow after Margie and

K.J. She took off after them shortly after they left, but then she changed her mind. Then, about thirty minutes later, she swallowed hard and changed her mind again.

This time she took off with urgency. It was a short distance but she decided to drive.

J.J. worked for *Safest* Lock and Key, a locksmith company owned and operated by women. The ladies who worked there pronounced it *Sapphist.* The company logo—a rather butch-looking woman in a uniform holding an oversized key—was boldly painted on the side of the van. She finally found a parking spot, angled in, then jumped out and walked purposefully into the park.

Things had definitely gotten out of hand. She wasn't sure how it had gotten this far, but it was time to do something about it. She would tell Margaret how much she loved her, and how much she loved K.J. That was a good place to start. The moment she saw them she would hug them both. It couldn't wait. She needed to find Margie, to give her a hug. To be hugged by her.

"J.J.," she chided herself, "why do you always have to be so goddamn over-the-top?"

She was running along the outskirts of the park and looking in trying to glimpse Margie's green print blouse, or K.J.'s yellow straw sun hat. He looked so cute in that hat.

There were so many little kids in the park. Little kids with their parents—it made J.J. want to find them all the more.

She crossed the baseball diamond, checked by the bleachers, and over by the concession stand. She followed a path down behind the lake. On its surface, a flotilla of paddle boats formed a lively logjam. They were expending a lot of energy without getting very far. No sign of them there. J.J. was beginning to feel like she was spinning her wheels. She headed through a copse of trees, toward the open meadow.

That was when she spotted the green print blouse sitting at a picnic table. Her walk slowed, her heart raced.

What is Margie doing over there? Who are those people?

She recognized one of them. It was that guy from the dart team, Margie's friend from work, Paul. She never liked him. There was something about him she didn't trust.

Is that why Margie was so quick to go without her? Had she planned to meet up with them all along!

As J.J. drew closer, she noticed something else. *Who is that other man? Why are he and Margie laughing together?* Margie seemed very comfortable around him.

And then Kenneth J. ran up and sat in the man's lap.

J.J. couldn't stand to see any more.

They were celebrating Father's Day.

Her Father's Day.

Chapter 14

No one noticed the change in Lance Manly. Not Eunice Manly. Not daughter Lulu. Not that it was a particularly subtle change, because it wasn't. It was just that no one ever paid any attention to Lance.

Tracing the origins of this change, you would have to go back to the day Lance went on the Cave City Tour. It was about a week after his meeting with Otto Gothard. Lance didn't go to work that day; he called in sick. He hadn't planned on cutting work, but the prospect of having to deal with strangers was truly more than he could handle; he was making himself sick. His nerves were frazzled; his thoughts were jumbled and chaotic.

But once he told Nurse Johnson that he would not be coming into work, he started to feel better. The clamminess left his brow; the palpitations eased off. He was able to breathe more freely without the dread that came with being around people.

But what could he do? Where could he go?

He couldn't go home. Eunice was at home. She would want to know how come he wasn't at work.

So he drove around, not knowing where he was going.

It was the billboards that sealed the deal. Everywhere he looked there were billboards: Visit Kentucky's World Famous Mammoth Caves; Great Onyx Cave Tour Next Exit; World's Longest Cave—Open Daily.

So he ended up standing in line with a group of tourists, waiting for the next load of sightseers to be herded into the elevators and guided along the lighted passageways—"Mind your step and hold onto the handrails at all times."

As the oversized elevator started its gut-lifting descent, a docent dressed in a ranger hat and khaki uniform began the guided tour.

"Geologically known as the Central Kentucky Karst, this area is part of a huge limestone belt extending from southern Indiana, through Kentucky, and into Tennessee. Here, more than elsewhere, however, the surface of the Central Kentucky Karst is riddled with sinkholes and its underground is shot through with caves. Literally thousands of them honeycomb the landscape. Appearing as depressions on the land's surface, the sinkholes are prominent funnels through which water seeps to seek its hydrological base at the Green River. The caves range from the simple, containing one passage of no more than a few yards, to the complex, possessing miles of interconnecting shafts and passageways. Thus far, in the Flint-Mammoth System there are more than 300 miles of passages surveyed. Some geologists believe there may be as much as 500 miles. Historically and geologically, the most famous of these caves is Mammoth Cave, which has given its name to the entire surrounding region...."

The doors of the elevator opened up onto the floor of a colossal underground hall some 90 feet below the surface.

"...With underground temperatures hovering year-round at 54° Fahrenheit, these caves provided shelter and comfort against the cold winter winds and the hot summer temperatures above. You will see cave walls and ceilings that to this day remain blackened by the torches and fires of prehistoric men...."

Stepping forward into the murmuring vault, Lance relegated these facts and figures to the back of his brain. For once again he was seized by the smell of the Mother Earth. Wet earth, dry dust, ammonia fumes of bat urine, the fetid odor of guano decay, no plants, no pollen, only the action of bacteria within the cave soil—all contributing to form that special cave odor. He swooned in the musk of her nether region. He could feel his brain abandon evolution, throw off its higher centers, as one throws a switch.

To many on the tour it was a long scary ride down to a dark entombed realm of looming shapes, where a hideous fate awaited anyone unlucky enough to become separated from the group.

But not for Lance.

For Lance it was thrilling. It was lovely.

It was like going home.

Chapter 15

Otto Gothard really truly meant it when he said, "Lance, I've never known anyone to take to caving the way you have. The way you've immersed yourself in it, you've learned more in a month than most spelunkers learn in years."

The two men were moving along a narrow subterranean passage illuminated by the carbide lamps attached to the front of their helmets. Otto moved quickly and Lance was hard pressed to keep up. He had so many questions he wanted to ask, but the unfamiliar footing required his full attention.

From where Otto stood, he kept expecting to outpace his companion, to hear the plaintive cry of "Wait for me!" Yet each time he turned to check on the progress of the neophyte, he was surprised to find him right behind, his rubber lug-soled boots treading over the terrain with an almost familiar stride. If Otto didn't know better he'd have thought that Lance had been this way before.

"The place I'm taking you is only known to members of *the Grotto*," he impressed upon Lance. "I don't have to tell you, *Dedicated cavers are among the wor—*"

"The world's best keepers of secrets," Lance completed the sentence.

Otto was full of such sayings. And Lance had taken it upon himself to learn every one. He had learned the fundamentals of caving and the not-so-fundamental—the gear and the geology, the techniques and the terminology. Otto could not recall any other individual ever being sponsored for membership in a Grotto after only two months of caving.

A *Grotto* is what they call the local chapters of the NSS, the National Speleological Society. Lance was excited. He was also very nervous—he'd never been asked to join anything before.

Otto was really very reassuring. There was nothing to worry about. Like he said, Lance had learned more in two months than most learn in two years. And being an x-ray tech, trained in first aid, that didn't hurt any. The other members probably liked the idea of having a "medical" person along on expeditions.

"Are Albey and the others going to be there, or do they come later?" Lance inquired.

Albey Bunnell was the Grotto's most celebrated member. A world-renowned anthropologist and speleologist, finder of prehistoric animal fossils, he was the man credited with having discovered the famed Tennessee saber-toothed tiger. The bones were on exhibit at the Museum of Natural History in New York.

The passageway suddenly narrowed.

They got down on their hands and knees and began crawling through several inches of water and mud. The answer to Lance's last question would have to wait; Otto silently led the way. Somewhere in the damp hollow recesses a rivulet coursed its way down the limestone walls. Otto barely negotiated the squeeze, his bulk temporarily blocking off the barely perceptible movement of air in the tunnel. Lance could feel the stagnant void close in on him. Behind, he could sense the total darkness reclaiming its domain.

How he loved the caves!

The others had arrived ahead of them. Eventually, Otto and Lance reached the secret room. Gnarled calcite columns stretched more than 30 feet above, to the ceiling, where sprays of gypsum crystals festooned the chamber—beautifully delicate crystals that resembled asters, marigolds, larkspur, and lilies. Lance didn't see the others at first; they'd turned off their lights to conserve the battery packs on their belts.

Albey Bunnell, Jink Ray Cooney, and Jill Minter—these were the cadre, the Grotto. And of course, there was Otto.

And soon, there would be Lance.

Chapter 16

Friends can have a major influence on a man. Especially a man who's never had friends before. This was a new experience for Lance. Here was a group of people who accepted him. For the first time in his life he felt that he belonged. These people were different than other people. Something about caving made them different, *better*. The easiest way to explain it was to borrow a motto from Otto. Otto would say "Spelunkers are different from other people; spelunkers aren't surface people." That said it all, as far as Lance was concerned. Not surface people.

Otto Gothard was not an educated man, not in the formal sense. He was self-educated and could converse knowledgeably on the subjects of geography, world history, American literature and Greek mythology. But his strongest subject by far was—as might be expected—geology. He claimed to be a direct descendant of Stephen Bishop, the legendary slave guide and explorer of Mammoth Cave.

Jink Ray Cooney was always joking with Otto, saying how Stephen Bishop met Otto's great grandmamma when she was hibernating. That she was a cave bear. "It can get awful cold and lonely in them caves!" he'd say.

Funny thing, Otto *did* look a lot like a bear.

And when it came to Kentucky folklore, Jink Ray himself was practically a legend. He lent Cave City a touch of local color.

Or to be more precise, lack of color; you see, Jink Ray was an albino. The son of a coal miner who eventually succumbed to black lung, Jink himself had at one time worked for Consolidated Coal. His thin sharp face, pink eyes squinting from behind chalk-white lashes, and prominent gold front tooth made him look older than his forty-three years. About a hundred years older. Seldom seen in the daylight, he often walked along at dusk, wearing a woolen long-sleeve shirt, hobnailed boots, a copy of the Farmer's Almanac in his back pocket. Jink was one of central Kentucky's fabled cavers, a throwback to the bygone days when a solitary man would set out to explore the caves with only a coal-oil lantern in his hand and a can of beans in his pocket. By trade, Jink was a coffin maker. He was missing the tips off two fingers on his left hand, on account of an accident. He was no stranger to pain and death.

But nothing seemed to hurt Jink more than the destruction of his beloved Appalachian hills by strip miners. For generations the Cooney clan lived in those hills, in a place called—of all things—*Troublesome*. That was before the strip miners came. Then came the fires, and the floods, and the landslides. And in the end, they were forced to move.

So it was no wonder that Jink had become involved with ecological causes, even though he wasn't much of a joiner. He was president of the local chapter of the Southern Conference Conservationist Fund, the SCCF.

It was in that capacity that he enlisted the help of the others. They gathered at the home of Jink's longtime friend and fellow member of Grotto, Dr. Albey Bunnell.

Albey and Jill Minter were husband and wife, though she continued to use her maiden name. They both worked at the university, though Albey was retired now. He'd been a professor of anthropology. Jill too had her Ph.D. Ironically, she was a doctor of archeology. Not nearly as famous as her husband. After all, he was the man who discovered the Tennessee saber-tooth. Several times a week Jill commuted to the university where she taught a course in archeology. Jill and Albey—not surface people. Lance liked them both very much.

"Albey, it's starting all over again." Jink was yelling. "Only this time it's going to be in your backyard."

"I don't disagree with you, Jink, I'm merely cautioning against any action that might prove impetuous or foolhardy."

"Albey's right, you know." Although they were not in the caves at the moment, Otto maintained his air of leadership. When spelunking it is necessary for a group to have a leader, and though it was a tacit understanding, Otto was that leader. "You can't go off half-cocked. From what you've been telling us, the SCCF is fighting this... Elkhorn Mining Company. They may still be able to get a court order revoking their mining permit. What we have to do is gain a little time, delay the opening of the quarry to give the lawyers a chance." Otto lowered his oversized head and scanned the gathering. "We're going to have to plan this very carefully."

~ ~ ~

At issue was a strip mining site located less than thirty miles away—and only a quarter mile from an uncharted network of caves.

Lance learned early on that practically everyone involved in caving was an avid conservationist. Cavers routinely put themselves at great risk to prevent from damaging a stalagmite with the muddy print from a glove or a boot.

So it was not at all surprising that these same people were violently opposed to strip mining.

Lance himself was not familiar with the practice of strip mining or the disgraceful violation it visited upon the land. But that didn't matter. He had unwavering confidence in his new friends. If they said it had to be stopped, then it had to be stopped.

Jink Ray provided Lance with some background information. He spoke to the x-ray tech; all the while his rabbit eyes studied the new man. As Jink told it, this wasn't a new problem. For decades the poor people of the coal-bearing region of eastern Kentucky had watched as bulldozers gashed the earth and explosives tore the tops off miles of ridge line; huge rotating auger bits bore into their mountains. Rich topsoil, swift creeks, and uniquely varied forests once clothed the picturesque hollows of those blue limestone mountains. What had taken nature a hundred million years to create was turned into jumbled mounds of desolation, stagnant pools of yellow acid-water, a raw and ugly testament to the avarice of men.

And now these same villains threatened to encroach upon the sanctity of the caves. The delicate eco-systems of *his* caves. It was terracide, pure and simple—*terracide.*

~~~

Four days later the Grotto embarked on their expedition. It promised to be unlike any they had undertaken before.

They took Jill Minter's station wagon rather than Otto's Jeep; Otto's vehicle was too well-known around those parts. Besides, the wagon gave them more room for provisions and gear. After packing and loading—helmets, lights, shovels, rope, cable ladders, jammers, harnesses, carabiners, chocks, pitons and bolts for rigging—they realized they needed a second vehicle.

Lance offered to take his.

It was agreed—Jink Ray would ride with Lance; Otto would go with Albey and Jill.

They drove south with the setting sun at their backs. Otto was at the wheel of the lead car, the station wagon. Lance's brown Plymouth, with Jink Ray in the passenger seat, followed close behind. That was how they would proceed even after they had reached the caves; in spelunking you always want to position the two most experienced cavers—one in the lead, the other, trailing.

Lance was listening to the radio as Jink Ray sat reading the Farmer's Almanac. He claimed it forecast the weather "Better than any a' them weathermen on that damn radio station."

They stuck to the back roads. Watching the countryside roll by, it strengthened their resolve, reminded them of what it was they were attempting to preserve. Wrinkled ancient hills where life was hard. But at least there was life. They drove past one-room houses with tar-paper roofs, foundations of stones instead of concrete. In meadows best suited for growing wild flowers, small, family-owned farms struggled to raise a little corn or wheat, some garden fruits and vegetables—to put food on the table and maybe have some left to sell at market.

Family and neighbors—the two most important things in these upland valleys. Large families pulled together. In cold weather, the men still hunted, butchered their own meat, and cut firewood for the cast-iron stoves. During the tourist season, the women made quilts or baked pies to be sold at Mammoth Cave Hotel and to customers in Horse Cave and Cave City. They canned hundreds of jars of fruits and vegetables, some to be traded at the local general store for dry goods, sugar, coffee, candy and the like.

All this, the life and the lifestyle, was threatened by an industry that had perfected the art of being a bad neighbor to all living things.

The miner himself had become a paradox—an unemployed industrial worker in a rural wasteland. Surface mining no longer required hundreds of men to reach and remove a seam of coal.

If the mining companies got their way, there would be nothing left but a vast bleak mesa where nothing moved except clouds of dust on dry, windy days. The autumn rains would carve new creek beds across the dead surface. Without trees or leaves to impede its flow, the rains would be catastrophic. Enormous gullies would cut into the slopes and sheets of silt-laden acid-water would run red with iron or frothy white with sulfur. The

101

creek and riverbeds that had run clear for thousands of years would turn to mud.

Jink had seen it all before. The same kind of pollution had taken its toll on Hidden River Cave. A half-mile long exhibition cave and twenty miles of lesser passages became nothing more than a sewer. Contaminated waters from the surface flowed swiftly into the caves through joints in the rock. Instead of filtering slowly through purifying layers of sand and soil, the pollutants in the water entered the cave's delicate ecosystem with all their raw toxicity intact. The once-plentiful population of pearly blindfish disappeared. And vile odors drove spelunkers back to the surface.

That made Lance really mad.

Mad enough to want to kill.

Chapter 17

It grew dark. Not as dark as a cave. Nothing is as dark as a cave. But in the hills, a backcountry road on a moonless night is about the next closest thing. Lance followed the taillights of Dr. Minter's station wagon as they bounced along a winding strip of shale and gravel. It wasn't a real road, more like a narrow path that cut through the spindly forest of hickory and oak—to the entrance of an old abandoned mine shaft.

The entrance had the look of a badger hole, partially obscured by bush and vine that clung to the sandstone ledge.

They got out of the vehicles to take a closer look.

Jink Ray was getting a bit edgy; he was more talkative than usual. It was his way of dispelling the jitters. It seemed to work for the others as well, taking their minds off the dangers that lay ahead. And it was interesting to hear what he had to say. A little bit history lesson along with some, more pertinent information: "This mine has been here since the War of 1812. At that time a trapper observed a black funnel cloud that rose up from the ground. The cloud turned out to be an enormous swarm of bats erupting from the earth. And the place from where the bats emerged was a seemingly bottomless pit on this hill. After learning of this, a speculator by the name of Valentine Sims purchased the property. Then Sims brought in slaves, more than 70 slaves, to dig the shaft down into the bat chamber to mine the nitrate-rich deposits, which are used to make saltpeter, an essential ingredient in gunpowder.

"The property now belongs to a good friend of mine. He's the only one who knows we're here. No one else."

As Jink talked, Lance found himself staring, transfixed by the sight of the opening in the earth.

"In this light," Jink Ray remarked, "I'll be damned if your eyes don't glow… like a raccoon in a thunderstorm." He was looking at Lance as if seeing him for the first time. "Spookiest damn thing I ever saw."

"C'mon," Otto snapped, "we ain't got all night." He was already tying on his pack, securing it to his seat harness. "Not if we're gonna get there before those workmen.... Jink, I thought you'd be in there already, setting the belay."

Belay—that meant a safety rope connected to a caver when there's danger of falling. They would have to fix an anchor point to be used for rigging the pitches. By now, Lance was well versed in all the terminology.

There was nothing about caving that Lance didn't like. Only a few feet away now, the cave called to him wordlessly. Any time he would get near a cave he could feel himself slip into the mind of another person. Freer, less judgmental. But that didn't begin to describe it. He couldn't describe it—there were no words in the world of this *other person*. A younger world. A darker world.

He couldn't wait to be swallowed by the cave.

With these thoughts and feelings igniting his soul, Lance turned and noticed the albino staring at him. Not so much with his eyes—something else. It was as if he had *heard* Lance's rapture.

Whatever it was, however it had been communicated—the albino's nostrils flared and he snorted. It was an involuntary gesture. Territorial. He shook his head, the pink eyes taking on an apprehensive, knowing look. He let out a low, long *hiss*.

Notice had been given.

They moved on.

The entrance to the mine was shored up with rotting timber, shiny with wet patches of moss and lichen. A mine like this had all the hazards of a cave and then some. Floors could turn out to be nothing more than rubble held in place by rotten wood. The air could turn "bad"—gases given off by the rock itself.

As they advanced fifty or so feet into the mine, the floor began to slope downward and soon they entered into a wide corridor lined with chaotic slabs of rock. Lance became aware of an icy tinkling sound coming from the invisible ceiling above, like wind chimes.

Jink answered his question before it could be asked: "Bats... They're getting skittish, brushing against the stalactites. Sounds like sleigh bells, don't it?"

As they walked, their boots squished into mounds of powdery, foul-smelling guano. The ammonia odor was overpowering. They covered their mouths and noses. Coughing and gagging, they hurried after Otto as he led them past a junkyard of old guano buckets.

They wriggled past piles of shattered rocks.

105

They ventured further down the crumbling passage.

Then suddenly, there it was.

They were stooped over entering a small phreatic tube, roughly four feet high and four feet across.

They could feel the wind.

Not a breeze, mind you, but a wind. You could've clocked it at 30 or 40 miles an hour. It was escaping from a narrow slot in the passage floor.

They had reached the culvert.

Alongside, attached to the smoothly rounded cave wall, hung a rickety old ladder. No one could say how long it had been there. It was not to be trusted.

Jink chose a good natural belay for the descent.

Otto was the first one down. He had to chimney the narrow fissure until the walls of the shaft fell away, and he was suspended in mid-air.

Otto had been this way before. He had drilled the rock. A secure anchor lay just beyond his reach. The light from his helmet bounced off the walls and into the darkness as he swung to grab for the rigging bolt. As he clung to the small outcropping of stone. He wasted no time clipping the "cow's tail"—the name given to the security strap—into the re-belay point. Then, feeding the line through his rappel rack to control rate of descent, he slowly made the dizzying drop to the chasm floor.

One by one, they each got to take the plunge.

The netherworld acknowledged their incursion—with all-embracing silence.

Chapter 18

In the ravenous world of mining companies, Elkhorn Mining was a small dog.

Dig a little and you find out that it was bought out; it was actually a division of a ruthless conglomerate, American Carthage.

Frank Cur had a damn good job with Elkhorn, and he liked his work. The company had recently acquired the mineral rights to Cub Holler. He'd been put in charge of the operation.

Since the late 1800's, most of the mineral wealth in the region was the property of corporations headquartered in big cities. Sometime after the Civil War, purchasing agents descended upon the region. The people they found there were poor and isolated. So when the agents offered gold and greenbacks, the mountain people were quick to sign. Hundreds of them made their make signing over mineral rights. They were poor farmers who couldn't read, let alone the fine print. They affixed their signatures to covenants that bound the sellers and their heirs forever, conveying title to "all coal, oil, gas, stone, salt and salt water, iron ores and all minerals and metallic substances whatsoever," reserving to the seller the right to continue to use—and pay taxes on—its surface. Big city lawyers inserted clauses vesting the buyer and his successors in title with the right to do "any and all things necessary, or by him deemed necessary or convenient in mining and removing the coal and other minerals." And to be safe, additional paragraphs granted the owner of the minerals immunity from lawsuits for damages arising out of the extraction process. These became known as "long deeds," wordy documents that gave up all rights at the going rate—about fifty cents an acre.

Over the years, the Kentucky legislature, a long-time friend to mining interests, upheld the long deeds, smoothing the way for "development."

That's not to say that there wasn't some opposition.

Frank Cur was marginally aware of the "ignorant do-gooders and conservationists" who, in recent years, were making trouble for mining industry. But that wasn't his concern. He was paid to mine. He left the politics to the boardroom. Those white-collar bandits thrive on skullduggery: court papers to file, palms to grease.

Finally, after several months of waiting for permits, it was full steam ahead at the Cub Holler quarry.

Hard to say why it took so long—the site wasn't near any populated areas. Something about some caves. Some environmental group was up in arms. He couldn't understand what they were so upset about. The Cub Holler project was not on a grand scale, not by any stretch... Unlike the surface mining operations in eastern Kentucky, this wasn't even a coal mine. They were mining kaolin, a clay used in the manufacture of porcelain, and also as an adsorbent in diarrhea medicines.

Well whatever the reason, the delay was over, the operation

was ready to get underway. Everything was in place. In a matter of days they would begin to truck out several tons of the fine white clay on a daily basis. Soon the hills would shake with the thunder of explosions and reverberate with the rumble of heavy machinery.

Frank arrived at the site at five-thirty in the morning. He headed straight for his office, a large trailer at the base of the ridge. At that hour an eerie mist clung to the hillside, partially obscuring the earth moving machines, making steel cranes and shovels look even more like dinosaurs. They waded in the mist, clear harbingers of destruction.

He unlocked the trailer door and flung it wide. He'd have plenty of time to shave, have a cup, take a dump—all before the crew got there. He put up a pot. And while the coffee set about to perk, he went to the sink and lathered up. He was careful about how he shaved. When he was done, he ran a hand along his cheek to see if there were any spots he might've missed. Satisfied, he toweled off.

He went back, stood by the open door, and stretched against the chilly morning air.

Frank Cur turned his attention to the cloudless blue sky. Not a drop of rain on the horizon, not for weeks. That meant they were going to have to bring up another tanker filled with water; they needed to soak the hillside to keep down the choking dust.

The coffee smelled so good!

Frank had brought along a box of donuts. He picked out a jelly for himself.

It was so beautiful in the mountains. Pristine. Invigorating. Even his BM's were better up here. *Nothing like a good dump!*

He left his trailer and headed straight for the Andy Gump. All around, birds twittered in trees. But he wasn't one to notice such things. Besides, he was a man on a mission. *Must be this mountain air!* He quickened his step, practically jogging. The little green porta-potty was looking mighty good. He had begun to undo his pants. A few more feet... He reached the door just in time, dropped his drawers, swung his butt around—and let out a long low sigh of relief, from both ends.

He was so caught up in the moment that he didn't notice the mud. Not until a minute later.

MUD! MUD EVERYWHERE!

The outhouse floor was covered with it: slimy brown footprints, clumps of muck and mud.

Frank Cur was a fastidious man by nature. It bothered him that the outhouse was so filthy.

"If this is someone's idea of a joke..."

Outside, workers were arriving.

The site foreman stepped from the outhouse. He looked angry.

Where had all the mud come from? It hadn't rained in weeks; the ground was as dry as a bone.

He was looking around for someone to yell at when he spotted Clyde Estes.

He raced over, but before he could say a word, he saw what Estes was doing.

He was standing on one of the giant bulldozers, looking every bit as disgruntled. And he was clearing mud out of the cab. He'd taken up a rag and was wiping off the seat.

"Clyde! How'd that mud get there?"

"I don't know, Mr. Cur. That's what I was trying to figure out." Clyde Estes rubbed a clump of mud between his fingers, put it up to his nose. Clyde was a local and he'd seen this before—a gritty unadulterated soil, no slippery algae, no vegetation to bind the wet slop. Just mud—the kind you find deep in the earth. "I think it's... *cave* mud," he said.

Another worker came running toward them. He seemed distraught. He was shouting to Cur—something about hydraulics. Cur couldn't make out what the man was saying.

Clyde had started up his bulldozer to back down off the gradient.

"Mr. Cur! Mr. Cur!" the running man shouted, "Someone cut the hoses on the hydraulics on the steam shovel." The man came to a stop in front of Frank. He was trying to catch his breath—but there was more to say. "The dump trucks—the antifreeze has been removed from the radiators."

It took Frank Cur a moment for it to sink in. The roar of the bulldozer muddled his thoughts. *The bulldozer!*

The D-8 bulldozer is built by Caterpillar. It weighs almost twenty tons. The blade alone weighs three thousand pounds, rising five feet and curved like a monstrous scimitar.

"Get down off that dozer!" the foreman hollered.

But Clyde couldn't hear.

"Turn it off! Now!" Frank Cur waved his arms in the air.

But Clyde just smiled. Waving one of his arms in front of his face, "Yeah, sure is dusty!" he hollered back.

Just before the left tread came apart.

Chapter 19

The team reentered the cave system through a shaft dug in a sinkhole. Otto made certain to point out to Lance that he was the one to find this cave.

Over the years of exploring caves, Otto had discovered more new caves than anyone, except maybe Jink. Lance wondered how many secret cave locations he knew. But there was no way to know; he revealed the locations to no one outside the Grotto. Some locations, he told to no one; his own private caves. Otto had learned a long time ago that when you find a sinkhole and start digging, you're likely to find a cave. But when Otto discovered this linkup, some six -seven years ago, he never dreamed it would be used to steal away a small band of saboteurs. Less than a quarter mile from the Cub Holler mining site, it was ideal. A perfect trapdoor getaway. Otto felt like a kid at a game of commando.

And so far, everything had gone according to plan.

Or so they thought.

It wasn't until several hours later, they'd come out the other side and were loading gear back into the cars when Dr. Jill Minter turned on the radio:

One man was killed and another seriously injured early this morning at the Cub Holler kaolin mining site when a bulldozer overturned. The cause of the accident is under investigation... but according to Sheriff Doyle with the

Butler County Sheriff's Department, this does not appear to be an accident. In recent weeks, the Cub Holler site has come under attack by environmental groups seeking to halt the planned excavation. The mine was scheduled to begin full operations this week.... No word yet if this will delay the plans.

All eyes locked on Lance. *He* was the one tampering with that bulldozer.

Then just as abruptly, all eyes averted his; no one would meet his gaze. It was as if he was all alone. As if he had just been told that he'd lost his only friend.

He closed his eyes—squeezing the lids together hard. He wanted to scream, but he had no voice. He could see a huge blade, not unlike that of the bulldozer, only this one was wielded by a towering god-figure slashing great gaping wounds across Mother Earth. Blood was flowing everywhere. It filled his eyes, and his ears, and his mouth. And it was strangely nourishing. And it tasted like fear. Like mother's milk and orphan's tears. But mostly like fear. Fear of the father.

A hand on his shoulder shook him gently until his eyes opened. It was Otto Gothard who broke the spell. "Hey, Lance, take a deep breath.... It's not your fault. It was an accident. It could've happened to anybody." He didn't sound very convincing. "Besides, we're all in this together." He looked around at the others.

There was a momentary yet perceptible hesitation, after which they all acquiesced. One after the other, they nodded. Yes, they were all in this together.

So why wasn't anyone talking to Lance.

The entire ride home, no one said another word to him.

When Lance dropped Jink back at Albey's, Jink kept his eyes on the ground. He said goodbye, he didn't shake his hand, and he wouldn't look at him. None of them would.

They hated him; he could just feel it.

Otto said that it wasn't a good idea for them to get together, at least not for a while. He was speaking to all of them, but somehow Lance felt it was directed at him. They would never be his friends again. Albey patted him on the shoulder. He supposed it was meant to be reassuring, but it felt like he was being pushed away.

"We split up now," Otto said, "just like we planned... like it's supposed to be."

And a voice long denied echoed up through Lance Manly's brain: *LIKE IT'S SUPPOSED TO BE.... LIKE IT'S SUPPOSED TO BE!*

Chapter 20

When Lance Manly returned home his world was already spinning out of control. His head was pounding, and behind squinting eyelids a grindstone wore at fraying nerves, hot sparks of pain shooting behind his eyes.

He tried to hold on.

But when he stepped up through the screen door of his home-sweet-sanctuary, he crossed right into the path of a rampaging Eunice.

It seems someone from work called while he was away: "Mr. Manly's services are no longer required at the clinic."

"You slimy little worm!" She had murder in her eyes. But she didn't smack him.

He would've welcomed a smack. He certainly felt as if he had one coming.

But Eunice was too busy to smack him—too busy packing. "I gotta find out from some little piss ant receptionist that you've been missing days from work. She told me... you hardly show up there anymore. Where the fuck you been keeping yourself...? No, no, don't tell me! I can see... just by looking at you! You been crawling around in the mud again."

She grabbed Lulu by the wrist so hard the child yelped.

"Take a good look at your daddy, Lulu. Remember what he looks like—the muddy, disgusting, worm—'cause you ain't gonna see him any more after today."

"You can't mean that, Eunice." To the child: "Mommy doesn't mean that, Princess." Then back at Eunice, "I'll talk to them. I'll get my job back."

"You stupid slug!" She laughed cruelly. "You're too late. They've already hired someone new. Besides... they don't want you! Nobody wants you! Especially not me!"

That's when something snapped. Lance thought he actually heard something *snap*. Not just one, but a whole series of snapping sounds inside his head. Sickening sounds, like tendons and arteries being ripped. He stood there and he could feel his mind coming undone—undone from the restraints of civility.

But, as if to prevent the further unraveling of his psyche, a fat hand wrapped around his throat and began to throttle the life out of him. "And if you think you're gonna follow us and harass Lulu and me... or if you dare try to drag us into court... or make trouble for us in any way..."

He was turning blue when she released him. Eunice did have a way of getting her point across. He fell to the floor, choking and sputtering.

"But... but..." he was having a difficult time breathing. "You're my wife!" he blurted out. "She's my daughter!"

Eunice bent over, put her face up against his: "If I see you anywhere near Lulu... I'll crush you like a bug."

And she meant it—all two hundred pounds of her.

She went into his pockets and pulled out the car keys. With Lulu under one arm, a suitcase under the other, she stepped over him and headed for the car.

Half crawling, half stumbling, he went after them.

From under her mama's arm, little Lulu's wide eyes remained fixed on the silly daddy. Her eyebrows raised quizzically. She giggled mockingly.

She was looking more like her mother every day.

"Please, don't go," he pleaded. "Give me a chance..."

He was desperate to get Eunice to listen. He needed something, anything that might make her reconsider.

It came to him: "There's something I have to show you."

"I've already seen it, Lance in the Pants. Ain't interested."

Tossing his spelunking helmet and filthy overalls out of the car and onto the ground, she placed Lulu in the backseat. Her voice all sugar and song: "There... Does Mommy's little Lulu want to take a ride?"

Lulu bobbed up and down excitedly.

"Damn you, Eunice. Listen to me for a minute! I'm trying to tell you something important."

When she turned from Lulu, she was like a creature undergoing transformation. Her twisted snarl backed Lance up against the wall of the trailer. Her rotund protruding abdomen held him there.

"*Damn!*—you use such language in front of your daughter! I oughtta tear the tongue outta your head, you degenerate!"

He cringed like a worm on a hook. And he wriggled.

"Gold!" he blurted out. "I found gold." He was tearful, his voice wet with saliva and mucous and tears: "You can't go. I

118

have to show you the gold...."

Chapter 21

So Lance led his wife, his flashlight illuminating the way down a long subterranean corridor. Eunice took his helmet for herself, its head-mounted lamp flicking blotches of light along the crumbly "cornflake" rock walls. They waded through several inches of water. Thousands of years of the seepage from above had created a bristling comb of stalactites that ran the entire length of low-hanging ceiling.

Lance turned to check on Eunice's progress.

What he saw horrified him. Eunice was lifting little Lulu up so she could break off one of the stalactites.

"Icicles, Mommy, icicles."

"NOOO!" a panic-stricken voice echoed.

Then, as he watched, Lulu tossed down the broken speleothem and reached for another.

He raced back toward them. "No, you mustn't touch anything!"

A pudgy fist crashed into the side of his face, knocking him backwards. He tried desperately to regain his balance, his arms flailing shadows on the walls, but he was unable to stop himself.

He fell into the delicate flowstone formation. A million year old, transparent mineral drapery lay cracked and shattered on the cave floor.

He felt a dreadful sinking in his heart.

120

Eunice reached down and picked him up by the collar. "Now stop *fucking* around and let's see this gold of yours."

She released him, wiping her hand on her shirt. He was filth. He was scum.

Lance mumbled, "See, you curse in front of our child. How come when I say *damn,* I get the shit kicked out of me?"

"What did you say!?"

He bit his tongue and kept his eyes on the ground.

They proceeded on in silence.

Lance could tell Eunice was uncomfortable, maybe even frightened by the damp, dark world of the cave. But the lure of the gold was too strong. In the end he knew it would win out. She would follow him deeper and deeper into the twisted maze of tunnels, to become unborn—put back into the moist, dark womb of Mother Earth.

"We're getting nearer," he assured her, smiling to himself.

All the while the passage narrowed.

"We're almost there," he announced, as they approached a wedge-shaped crawlway. "It's just beyond this passage." Lance scrambled forward, and then, realizing he was going to need his hands free, he scrambled back and handed Eunice his flashlight. "Here, let me use the helmet, just until I get to the other side. Then I'll light the path and help lead you through."

"I don't know about—"

"It's the only way. Besides, it's easy! All you have to do is crawl on your side." Eunice started to say something, but Lance reminded her, "The gold is right there, just on the other side."

She was looking at him awfully hard.

"Just lie on your side and use your forearms. Slide your bottom thigh forward, like you're doing the sidestroke. It's easy."

Eunice was a good swimmer. The analogy helped put her at ease.

"Here, why don't I take Lulu with me!" he said, trying to sound matter-of-fact. "Would Princess like to play horsey-back with Daddy?"

"Horsey-back! Horsey-back!" she leaped onto his back, overjoyed at the chance to burden someone, especially the disgusting daddy-person whom Mommy was always debasing.

Before Eunice could object, he scrambled back down the mud-walls.

"Hold on tight Princess."

And Lulu laughed like any little girl at play. It was quite amazing the way the child exhibited no fear of being in the cave. Caves are dangerous places, scary even for adults. But she didn't know that. Besides, she was safe and secure with her parents. What could possibly happen?

Lance negotiated the passage on his belly. It was not the simple conduit he made it out to be. Keeping his helmet light aimed straight ahead he pushed outwards with his hands and feet against the sidewalls, bridging his way over the deep crevice in the rock. Mid-way through the tunnel the floor dropped away and blackness loomed below.

He had to stop several times and adjust Lulu's grip to keep her from choking him. All the while he spoke to her as if they were out for an afternoon stroll. He knew Eunice could see them, and could hear them.

He knew what she was thinking: *If he can do it with Lulu on his back, I should be able to do it, no problem.*

"Okay, honey, now it's your turn," he shouted. "Put the flashlight in your overalls. You won't be needing it for now. It's more important that you have your hands free." He was beginning to feel excited, but he tried not to let it show in his voice. "I'm going to keep my light shining directly at you. You just come toward the light, okay, honey."

The beam skittered along the solid bedrock sides and ceiling. Sweating profusely, he steadied the lantern in his hands. He needed to make sure to blind her to what was below. Or more exactly, what wasn't.

"That's it, honey, you're doing fine!"

Experienced spelunkers know to never descend a tight crawl headfirst. You must lead with your feet. What if the squeeze ends in a cul-de-sac? It can be difficult to go back feet first. It can be impossible. It's also important to keep your arms out in front of you. You don't want them jammed between your body and the wall.

"Keep coming, pumpkin, you're almost there"

"Just shut up, Lance, and shine the light down a little lower."

As she spoke, Eunice's right shoulder slipped down into a V-shaped notch. She tried to push off from the wall. Her hand found a jagged protruding rock. But it wouldn't hold. Small pieces broke free, crumbling under her weight. She toppled forward and down. The flashlight came out of her pocket, clattering off the walls as it fell, end over end, down, and down, and down...

It was just as Lance had envisioned. Her arms were wedged at her sides. Her large breasts had squeezed through the tight spot, but her hips and butt became stuck. Those great big hips! That magnificent round rump of hers!

Lance shined the light down at her. She couldn't roll over. She was lying on her right side at an angle of about thirty-five degrees. Her right arm was pinned under her, her head turned uncomfortably upward, her left cheek pressed against the rock. Eunice was in a stone straitjacket.

The light went away. Out of the corner of her eye she could see him holding the lamp. He was shining the light under his face, illuminating an eerie smile.

Panic seized her.

She kicked uselessly, her feet banging against the walls, raining down fragments of rock and dirt. She became more tightly wedged.

She screamed...

And screamed...

For God knows how long.

Until her voice gave out.

Over the frantic beating of her heart, she could hear the soft rivulets of sand sliding downward. Every movement was making things worse.

Then suddenly, things got much worse. The light was gone.

124

She was plunged into total darkness unlike any she had even known.

And again she began to scream.

Chapter 22

Lance raced through the murky labyrinth of tunnels, his chubby little girl in his arms. She cried and wailed, he laughed maniacally. This blended with the sound of his fleeing footfall, and bounced around inside his cranium like an auditory hallucination.

Running with his head bent low, he entered into a long keyhole passageway.

He wondered why he was laughing so hard. He couldn't explain it. Was it elation? He felt terribly distraught and yet incredibly alive. The great weight of sanity was being lifted from his mind. He would miss dear Eunice but, for the time being, he reveled in newfound virility. It was a victory for the caves. A triumph of *devolution*. A win for Lance Manly. Somewhere within the twisted strands of his DNA he'd found a forgotten trait. An ancestral mandate. A killer instinct.

His senses were growing keen. Sharper than he had ever known. Down through the cavern and echoing within the growing hollow of his heart, he could hear Eunice's vain screams draining her strength. While a part of him grew strong—a part he liked very much.

"Don't worry, Princess, don't worry. Daddy is—"

She struggled like a little wild animal.

He was trying to hold her hands and feet, but one arm got

loose and hit him hard in the nose. *Mommy's little girl!*

In his haste, Lance had failed to secure the helmet strap under his chin; the power of the punch knocked the helmet completely off his head.

It rolled away down the cave, taking the light with it. The carbide flame dimly illuminated the rubble-strewn trench into which it had fallen.

Lulu hit the ground running.

Her daddy made a grab for her, but all he got was a hair ribbon and *"Ouch!"*—strands of thin red baby hair still tangled in its dainty clip.

"Mommy! Mommy!" her cry flew into the honeycombed blackness.

The light!—it was failing. Weakening... Flickering... Gone!

A soft radiance from sulphate crystals within the walls held onto a fading afterglow.

Then it too was gone.

Lance stood in the blackness. At home in the blackness.

Yet he knew he had to retrieve the lamp.

Any spelunker knows, you should always have at least three sources of light. Lance had a flashlight—but he gave that to Eunice. He had a carbide helmet lamp—but Lulu took care of that. He couldn't very well hunt for it in the dark. And once he found it, it was probably going to need some repair. That would take light. So he was down to source number three: a candle.

In a small pouch at his side was a waterproof container. Carefully he removed first the candle, then the matches. He hesitated, then he struck the match, pushing back the enveloping blackness.

Lance found little Lulu at the bottom of a steep drop. She was broken beyond repair. Her little skull had been fractured by the fall, blood forming a blue bruise behind her right ear. Lance, having made his way to her side, sat motionless before his child. His *only* child! *His only child! His only child?*

He could not bring himself to move. His muscles would not take instructions from his brain. And his mind was madly spinning off images.

Staring at his Princess, he flashed on an image of an ancient Indian mummy. He was aware that the remains of two such Indian mummies had been unearthed somewhere in these very caverns. Preserved in the environmentally constant world of the caves, desiccated by the effects of the guano, the shriveled apparitions were found sitting upright in their stone coffins, several feet below the cave floor—just like baby Lulu—amid an assortment of feathers and beads, snake rattles, and a deer-foot talisman.

Then the image melded to one of another baby, on a porch—a long time ago.

THIS IS HOW IT'S SUPPOSED TO BE!

He was hallucinating freely now. It was all beginning to come together.

THIS IS HOW IT'S SUPPOSED TO BE!

It was beginning to make sense. It was a man's place to

bestow life... to enshrine descendants away from the light. The child must be put back inside... back inside the mother, the mother earth... Only then...

It wasn't so much a solution as it was a matter of faith.

The important thing: he knew what it was he must do.

~~~

Margie Danser and her son, Kenneth J., spent the day at the amusement park. The sun was shining and the only clouds in sight were white and fluffy. They loved the rides and the cotton candy. They loved spending time together. They especially loved being outdoors.

Chapter 23

The call came in early in the morning. Detective William Turner was running a little late—not all that usual. His partner was already at scene. Turner grabbed an unmarked car off the lot and got there as quick as he could.

It was not the usual crime scene location—if there even is such a thing.

As he made his way past the yellow tape that roped off the Women's Health Center, he was reminded of a joke: *A woman gets in line at a sperm bank. The man in front suggests that she's in the wrong line. She ignores him. When she doesn't say anything, he lowers his voice and explains that it's a sperm bank. She nods and continues to stand there. "I don't think you understand," he says. "This is the line for deposits. The woman mumbles, "I can't talk right now..."—Her mouth is full.*

"Hey, Detective, good of you to drop by..." a voice called out.

It was his partner, Lou Taber.

As Willy walked up, Lou leaned in: "You hear the one about the crook who robbed the sperm bank?"

Turner decided not to tell his joke. He wasn't very good at joke telling.

"Save the humor, Lou. Tell me, what do we have?"

Lou was only recently assigned to work with Willy. It seemed to be working out.

"We have a couple of terrified females. One was just taken away by RA to White Memorial. The other one's doing a little better. You should probably talk her while she's still here. We'll give her in a minute. Let her calm down a little. This is a crazy one. 'Sounds like we have a real sicko on the loose."

"One suspect?"

"One suspect—male white in his late twenties—he was waiting for her when she came to work."

The two men went around back. Taber took him through it, step by step.

"The guy parked here."

Turner knelt down. He made a mental note of the time and the weather conditions, and the lighting. Going slow, he ran his eyes over the asphalt—no cigarette butts, no litter, some muddy tire tracks.

"We got a witness says he saw a muddy, brown Plymouth sedan parked here," Tabor told him. "Eight- ten-years old, a four-door, maybe; Kentucky plates. The witness was very specific, the car was muddy. Covered with mud. Like it had been traveling off road." Anticipating the next question: "No, he didn't get the plate. Not even a partial."

"Anyone actual see the suspect in the car?" Turner asked.

"No, but according to the witness, it was the only car back here this morning, not counting the two that belong to our victims." Tabor pointed to the only cars parked within the outer perimeter crime scene tape.

The two detectives walked slowly, picking up their feet as

they stepped.

Turner envisioned a grid and superimposed it on his visual field. He systematically scanned each quadrant of ground as they walked, still listening to Taber as they approached the rear door. Yellow tape held it open.

Turner bent down to look at the lock and the doorknob. He observed no marks on either.

"Is this the point of entry?"

Taber nodded.

"Who let him in?"

Taber's eyes looked up in his head, like he was thinking."That would be the nurse."

Willy stood up.

"Some time around seven this morning. He knocked, the nurse opened. She thought it was one of the medical students. The clinic hires medical students, pays them to whack off. Don't that just beat all!—No pun intended." Tabor couldn't resist.

"Really! Lou."

Lou shrugged. He chuckled a little and added, "If someone had given me a nickel for every—"

"How come they don't use the front door?"

"Who?"

"The medical students! How come the medical students don't come in the front door like everybody else?"

"Oh, that's easy. The clinic don't want the donor to possibly bump into the recipient, and vice versa. No contact at all. It's the latest thing—take the *bump* outta the hump." Lou did a mini-pelvic trust.

"Jeez, you're a laugh riot this morning." In a mock-aside: "So, you sign up to be a donor yet...?"

Lou snorted, "I gotta run that by the wife. Besides, the nurse says I'm too old. They don't take anybody over thirty-five. Can you believe that?" He did his best *hurt and disappointed* expression.

Turner smiled and shook his head.

"How 'bout you, *Tomcat*...? How old are you? Thirty-three, thirty-four?"

It had been a while since anybody called him that. Willy "Tomcat" Turner. That was his nickname back in the day. He was a wild man when he first came on the job.

"Thirty-eight, Lou, I'm thirty-eight. Too old to donate. But that's okay. It so happens I like the *bump* in my hump."

"Me too! Hey, me too!"

The two men entered the clinic. Taber led the way. They passed a uniformed officer in the hall; he nodded and stood aside. A second officer was with the victim, a gray-haired woman; she had a blanket wrapped around her. As the detectives approached, Taber wordlessly dismissed the officer.

"Dr. Shirley Powell, I'd like you to meet my partner, Detective William Turner. Detective Turner's going to be asking you a few questions."

"Detective..." As the doctor went to extend her hand she began shaking uncontrollably.

Turner still didn't know what this was about. Taber hadn't said anything about the actual crime; that was on purpose, to let

the victim tell it, so Turner could get an untainted first-hand....
Now even before Dr. Shirley began, the hairs on the back of his
neck were standing up; *this was going to be something bad!*

He waited for her to regained her composure.

Unexpectedly, after only a moment, she bravely girded
herself and informed him, "Okay Detective, I can answer your
questions now."

He studied her an instant. "Okay, tell me what happened, in
your own words, in the same order as it occurred.

And then he leaned forward and he listened. Occasionally he
asked for details, but he tried not to interrupt.

Her voice was laced with outrage and fear, and even a little
sympathy as she told him about the strange, misguided man who
burst into her office and held her prisoner for over an hour. It
was as strange a story as any Turner had ever heard.

Armed with what she described as "some kind of hammer-
pick," the suspect barged into the office. She described the
weapon: a foot long wooden handle with a hole through the base
and a nylon strap running through the handle, wrapping around
his wrist. In due time, Turner would learn that it was a piton
hammer—commonly used in mountain climbing, or spelunking.
Shirley showed him how the suspect held the hammer. In his
right hand. His fist gripped the tool like an extension of his arm.
On the business end—black steel shaped like a block on one
side, coming to a point on the other.

"He seemed quite delirious," she said. He kept asking, *Where
was his Princess? Had they seen his Princess?* He tied them up with

rope. He came prepared with a great deal of rope. Then, he proceeded to rummage around the office, searching through the files. In search of what?—he would not say.

According to Dr. Shirley: "I knew I'd seen him before, but I couldn't be sure... He was so totally distraught, nearly incoherent." Nevertheless, from his rambling she was able to surmise that the poor man had recently lost his family, both his wife and his daughter. *Princess*—that was apparently a pet name he called his daughter.

Early on in the ordeal, there was a very tense moment; Dr. Shirley and the nurse were both tied up, the man was ransacking the office, and someone began knocking on the back door.

He raised his hammer-pick and froze, staring at his two hostages. Sweat stood out on his brow. The doctor was *not* gagged. Neither was the nurse. One yell for help, a scream, and *some*one would know. The knocking continued, louder. At that instant, Dr. Shirley was sure he was going to bludgeon them both. Recounting the moment, her head cycled in a series of short twitches: "I mouthed, in a whisper, 'No, we won't say anything. Please, don't hurt us. We won't say anything.' Then— thank God!—the knocking stopped."

They could hear the sound of footsteps going away.

As soon as the person left, he put down the pick-hammer.

He grabbed a marker-pen from the front desk and made a sign to post on the door. In block letters he wrote: CLINIC CLOSED DUE TO A DEATH IN THE FAMILY.

When she saw what he had written, she went to pieces and

began to cry.

And then... *he* began to cry.

If her hands weren't tied, had she been free, she probably would have gone to him, to comfort him. To think that she would have tried to console that monster. It made her so mad.

Taber found a box of herbal tea on one of the shelves in the office, next to the microwave. He didn't bother to ask; he just brought her a cup. "Try and relax. You're safe now."

She appreciated the gesture.

And after a few sips, she was ready to continue.

When the suspect began to talk of his tragedy, Dr. Shirley's heart went out to him. His wife and his daughter—both dead. Without explaining how they had died, it was clear only that it was sudden, and very recent.

It became obvious to the doctor that the man was in a state of grief, slipping in and out of denial as again he began calling for 'Princess' and tearing through the files. At that point, she wondered if he even knew where he was or what he was doing.

After several more minutes of ransacking, he sat down exhausted.

He had stopped crying. In a flat, cold voice he said, "Doctor, I want you to tell me where you keep the files on the A.I. donors."

She stared at him, her eyes growing wide. *So that's what this was about!* That information was strictly confidential.

He repeated himself.

She didn't say a word. *She wouldn't!*

Then the silence cracked as his laughter broke through. A mean, crazy laughter that erupted—laughing and blubbering at the same time.

He was back standing, bending over her, piton hammer in hand.

An A.I. donor! That was it!

She looked up, past the weapon, to the pale face with its shiny eyes. That's when it hit her. Not the pick-hammer. The recollection! She knew where she had seen him before. She knew.

In all her years of doing artificial inseminations, Dr. Shirley never dreamed of this situation. It never occurred to her that something like this could happen. The man wanted the names of all the women inseminated at the clinic during the end of 1988, the beginning of '89.

He wanted the files identifying donors and recipients.

He was looking for *his* children.

Chapter 24

As far as Detective Turner was concerned, this was the most insidious crime he'd ever come across. No one was bloodied. The victim didn't feel a thing. It left no marks.

He would prepare a crime report for false imprisonment, theft of medical records, and assault with a deadly weapon.

A most unusual weapon—an x-ray machine.

He had tortured the doctor with the x-ray machine.

She was still unable to recall his name. But she would not be able to forget what he did to her. While it was being done, and long after, she would ponder the extent of the damage inflicted.

The suspect obviously knew how to operate x-ray equipment. She described how he tied her to the x-ray table using very intricate knots. She couldn't move at all. He rolled the x-ray tube along its track, positioning it directly above her. He leaned over and adjusted the collimator, spreading the focal spot over her entire body. All the while he was cackling and crying, not bothering to wipe his nose. When he stood behind the lead barrier, he called out the settings: milliamperes and kilovolts. Starting off with relatively low exposure: 50 mA, 40 kV for a tenth of a second. No more detrimental than the ultraviolet rays of the sun at high altitudes.

"Where are the files on the donors? Give me the names of the women you inseminated in 1989?"

100 mA at 50 kV for two tenths of a second. According to the Department of Health Services, an occupationally exposed individual over the age of 18 may receive a maximum whole-body dose equivalent of 1.25 rems per calendar quarter. Stated in terms of the acronym *Rem* for Roentgen Equivalent Man, a normal chest x-ray taken at 200 mA, 70 kV for a tenth of a second generates less than .01 rems. Dr. Shirley told herself that she was in no immediate danger. Thank God she was past child-bearing years. From behind the partition, a torrent of laughter. Her captor increased the factors: 200 mA, 60 kV, for one half second.

"Where are the files on the donors? Give me the names of the women you inseminated in 1989?"

She heard the repeated click of the button, the exposures adding up, the constant grim whirr from the rotating anode within the x-ray tube.

The click. The whirr. The pounding of her heart trying to get out of the rib cage.

His incessant bawling and braying.

The click. The whirr. The pounding...

The click. The whirr. The pounding...

At doses exceeding a thousand rads, death will occur within hours of exposure. This is due to the breakdown of the nervous system. At lower doses, usually above 600 rads, death occurs within 15 to 30 days and is associated with destruction of the gastrointestinal system. At even lower doses, but greater than 100 rads, death may occur due to hemorrhage of blood-forming organs. Typically, at 50 rads or less, there are no outward signs of permanent injury. In fact, at 100 rads, most individuals will show no symptoms. It's the long-term effects that are the far greater concern. Ionizing radiation causes increased incidence of skin malignancies, leukemias, and other forms of cancer. These effects are not experienced until years later.

200 mA, 70 kV, six-tenths of a second.

The click. The whirr. The pounding...

"Where are the files on the donors? Give me the names of the women you inseminated in 1989?"

200 mA, 80 kV, eight-tenths of a second.

The click. The whirr. The pounding...

"Where are the files on the donors? Give me the names of the women you inseminated in 1989?"

300 mA, 90 kV, one second.

The click. The whirr. The pounding...

God forgive her—she gave him what he wanted.

~~~

"I'm telling you, Lou, something bad is going to happen. I can feel it."

"So what are we supposed to do?"

Taber was driving; Turner was spinning his wheels.

"We need to go all out on this. We should be tracking down all the women that went to that clinic in 1989. At the very least we need to put out some kind of warning. Why do we have to wait till someone's dead before we do anything?"

"Now c'mon, Willy, the captain said no publicity. It'll just panic people unnecessarily. I think he may be right. The suspect took the files, and without the files... Besides, most of those files don't have the names of the donors in them anyway. Dr. Shirley said so herself. Just the recipients. So he doesn't even know which of those women got his man juice."

"All I know is that *some* of those women are in serious danger."

"You don't *know* that! You don't know that at all. Don't get me wrong; I'm not saying the guy ain't a nut. But really, Willy, you can't be sure that he's going to hurt anybody? For all we know he might've had the x-ray machine turned down. He may have just been trying to scare the doctor."

They were stopped at a light.

"You know, I've been thinking about this too." It was Louis Taber the family man speaking. He faced his partner and said, "Don't you think a man has the right to know who his kids are?"

Chapter 25

In the end, Mandy and Howard Greenleaf decided not to tell Howard's parents about the procedure. There was some discussion, much brooding, and ultimately, it fell to inertia. By doing nothing, the decision was made. What was there to be gained by telling them about the insemination of their son's wife with another man's seed? Surely they wouldn't love little Brad any less...? But why trouble them with such details. The important thing was that they have a grandchild. Bradley Vincent Greenleaf was a beautiful baby boy.

And his grandparents were so loving, and helpful.

Shortly after Brad was born, Howard's father, Howard Greenleaf Senior, helped them out so that they could afford their own home. It was a beautiful split-level ranch, a three-bedroom, two and a half bathroom, with a two-car attached garage and a fireplace. And, there was a nursery. When Howard and Mandy first got married, Mandy had the feeling that Howard's parents didn't really approve of his choice. But now, with the birth of little Brad, all that changed. Granddad Greenleaf said the down payment on the new house was "a belated wedding gift." And Grandma Greenleaf was only too happy to lend a hand with whatever she could.

So why wasn't everything perfect?

Was not telling them the same as lying to them?

It was as if *The Lie* had become a fourth person living in that house with Mandy and Howard, and Brad. A moody boarder whose presence was always felt. An instigator who pitted them against one another. The Lie was a stranger who went to bed with them at night. And woke up with them in the morning.

It was a Sunday morning and Mandy sat in her kitchen: solid oak cabinets, Solarium floor, built-in dishwasher and microwave. She sat at the ceramic tile countertop, white with mauve. She sat looking out the white-anodized aluminum greenhouse window. She desperately needed a pick-me-up from her morning cup of coffee. All last night she and Howard were arguing. In her mind she couldn't stop replaying the tapes. The whole thing didn't make any sense. Something to do with the baby-sitter.

They'd been planning all week to get together with Richard and Joy. Mandy made a special trip to the beauty parlor; she had her hair and nails done—Howard had this thing about women having nice fingernails. They made reservations to go to a trendy new Indian restaurant. It was supposed to be a pleasant, relaxing night out.

But as soon as the baby-sitter got there...

Howard was in one of his moods. At first Mandy didn't make the connection. Lynn, the baby-sitter, was a lovely girl, a single girl, a few years younger than Mandy. She came highly recommended. Mandy didn't think it was a problem that Lynn was pregnant and just beginning to show; it didn't seem relevant. But Howard took Mandy aside and told her that he didn't think it was right to have an "unwed mother" baby-sitting *his* child.

143

Mandy did her best to deal with it. No point discussing it right then. For the evening at least, they had no choice; there wasn't time to find another baby-sitter.

Howard made it clear, in the future he wouldn't have it. Not in *his* house.

Throughout dinner he obsessed. He wouldn't let it go. He tried to engage the other couple in a discussion of family values. Carrying on about how "the family" itself was under attack, and how good Christian values were in a disgraceful state of decline.

All because of a pregnant baby-sitter!

Richard and Joy couldn't see Howard's point either.

In the end, he succeeded in ruining a perfectly lovely evening by making everyone uncomfortable. Especially Mandy.

She wanted to yell, to bring it out into the open: *Howard, you're acting this way because you're having difficulty accepting responsibility for another man's child! You can't handle that Brad isn't your flesh and blood! Seeing that pregnant baby-sitter stirred up resentment. All the feelings that you work so hard to keep down....*

But of course she wouldn't do that. It was a secret. Not even their best friends could know. Richard and Joy didn't know. Just Howard and Mandy—and The Lie. They didn't dare say it aloud, not even to each other.

They said goodnight to Richard and Joy, and they took The Lie home with them.

In the privacy of their split-level ranch house, *he* lay in bed with them. *He* stood vigil over their restless night's sleep.

And then, after eating away at their innards, this stranger in their household awoke bloated, and his shadow spilled beyond their single-family dwelling. The Lie seemed to seep into the morning sky, flat and gray beyond the windowpanes.

As far as Mandy's eyes could see: the all-pervasive Lie.

Sometimes it felt like she'd been caught cheating. *What price was Howard extracting from her? from himself?*

He was already out in the garage. His Sunday morning ritual: to bury himself under the hood of his Camaro. A TransAm IROC.

The car had been a gift from his dad. Howard would work on it all day long.

What could he possibly be doing? she wondered. *The car ran fine!* It was just another distraction. Always some distraction. Either the TV, or his work, or that damn car.

On the counter in front of Mandy was a baby monitor. Little Brad's respiratory condition wasn't improving as quickly as the doctors anticipated. In fact, it wasn't improving at all. Howard put in the *Medic Alert* monitoring system when Brad came home from the hospital. The intercom was installed so Mandy could hear Brad if he started to wheeze or cough.

"Mommy! Mommy!" There was no getting away from being a mommy. She was bringing the cup of coffee to her lips as, she heard the cough and the cry, "Mommy!"

Down went the coffee cup, up went Mandy. She rushed through the house and into the bedroom, where little Brad sat... laughing: "Mommy! You run funny, Mommy."

Anger. Frustration. Resentment. It had been building.

Because of Howard's neglect. Because of The Lie.

She picked the child up roughly in her arms; he began to howl loudly—more out of fear than pain. She shook him hard and threw him down, back onto the bed. He bounced off the mattress, eyes fixed on Mommy—*not laughing anymore!* The little boy recoiled back away from the raised open hand.

"One peep out of you, you little bastard, and I'll smack—"

He managed to stifle his tears down to a soft snivel.

But the moment the hand was lowered, he started back to hack and wheeze, and then, to wail. Like a siren it went up, loud and grating against her frazzled nerves. Mommy was crumbling fast, her hold was slipping.

Just then, ringing through the cheerlessness, the phone intervened. The phone was ringing.

Mandy jumped. Grabbed the receiver.

The voice at the other end: "Mrs. Greenleaf...? Mrs. Mandy Greenleaf...?"

"Uh-huh..."

"You don't know me... but I know you have a child by artificial insemination."

A loud buzzing started somewhere inside her head. Someone—she didn't know who—just spoke her secret. Words she was too afraid to speak—he had just said them, aloud, on the phone.

In an almost apologetic tone, he continued to talk: "That was over three years ago. Nine months before that I made a donation at the Women's Health Center." The voice paused.

"...A sperm donation."

This was not supposed to be happening. No one was supposed to ever know. They said it was totally confidential. He wasn't supposed to have any way of finding out...

He read her mind: "I know I'm not supposed to contact you ever."

Mandy started to hang up, but couldn't. She had to listen to what he had to say.

He knew that. He said it: "You must listen."

His words were playing tricks with her mind. She got lost for a second, thrown for a loop. She heard only snippets of his words, but the meaning came across. She sat down on the floor. Her knees folded, her body lowered, and there she was—sitting on the floor. Listening.

"A terrible, terrible accident... My wife... my daughter... both. She was my only child... So difficult to talk about.... A life lost... so lost... so difficult to go on... But then..."

And in a zombie voice, his words came right through the phone and socked her in the gut: "I realized that somewhere there was a reason to live... That I hadn't lost my only child... That a child of mine was in the world."

She didn't remember finishing the conversation. She didn't remember hanging up. It had only been two or three minutes that she was on the phone. One minute she was having coffee, sitting in her kitchen, looking out the window at her husband, the man she married, but *not* the father of her—

147

Brad!

She'd forgotten all about the child. The child was still crying.

Mandy got up off the floor quickly.

She held her son in her arms and she trembled.

It scared the boy to see tears streaking Mommy's cheeks.

It scared him the way she held him so tight.

Chapter 26

Howard Greenleaf prided himself at being good at maintaining things in good working order. He was looking forward to changing the oil in his car. It had been 3,000 miles since he'd last done it. Might as well check the brake pads too—discs, linings. and drums. What the heck!

This was *his baby*.

"Honey...? Can I talk to you for a minute? Honey...?" Mandy stood a measured distance away, in the driveway, careful not to infringe on *his* space. His *car* space. His domain of *male*ness. Her hair was still messy from sleep, pressed in several directions. Her housecoat was tugged snug against the chill.

"Honey, there's something I have to talk to you about.... There's something we have to talk about."

"Not now, Mandy! Can't you see I'm busy!"

She didn't leave; she stood her ground. Her mouth stayed open, lower jaw set forward, breathing heavier than normal. This was urgent. She needed to be heard.

"Didn't you hear me! I said *'Not now!'*"

She hesitated. Then she turned and walked back into the house.

The Chevy Camaro perched at an angle, held aloft by a pair of jacks, each positioned along the underbody just behind the front wheel wells. The two front tires were pulled off, stood up against the garage wall. The hood stood open, the fenders draped with polishing rags. Tools lay spread out on a drop cloth that disappearing under the chassis. Howard lay on his back—head, arms and shoulders working away under the 350 V8 fuel injected overhead cam. An extension cord snaked along the floor to a work light; its harsh bright light—a contrast to the overcast day. A radio on the workbench played country western songs to fill the silence. Howard wasn't a fan of silence.

He always had to have some kind of noise in the background. At work, the radio played constantly. At dinnertime, the TV was always on, and kept on until bedtime. He fell asleep with the TV on most nights, and Mandy had to shut it off. Howard definitely avoided silence, but he never thought anything of it. Lots of people were that way.

Suddenly the radio went quiet, like someone lowered the volume.

Looking out from under the Camaro, Howard could see pant legs. Shimmying along the floor on his back, he edged part way out.

"Can I help you with something?"

The man standing in his garage took a step back, bent at the waist, and turned his head to the side so he could see Howard. And Howard could see him. He was a thin man, and he looked utterly miserable and exhausted. He said something, but he spoke so softly that Howard couldn't make out what he'd said.

"What do you want?" Howard allowed a degree of

annoyance in his tone . He wasn't particularly annoyed; that was just his way.

"...Princess. Have you seen Princess?"

Howard eyeballed the stranger. He still didn't quite hear what he was saying. Something about a *Princess...*

"I can't hear you. What did you say? Princess...? Who's *Princess?*"

The stranger tried again to make himself understood. He spoke louder. But at just that moment, a plane passed overhead. The Greenleaf house was in the flight path; it happened all the time. Howard didn't mind. As the jet moved away, Howard caught the tail end of what the guy was saying. He said something about Princess being a *pet* name.

No wonder the guy looked so miserable. He lost his dog.

"Hey, that's a tough one." Howard got to his feet. "That's a tough one... What did you say your name was?"

"Lance. My name's Lance."

"Lance. I always liked that name." Howard extended his hand. "Howard, Howard Greenleaf."

The stranger stared, blinking a lot. He went to shake hands.

Howard, suddenly realizing he was all greasy, pulled his hand back and wiped it on his overalls.

"Greenleaf," the stranger repeated, nodding to himself.

"Lance, I know how you must feel. I had a dog. He ran away. It was a terrible. The pits.... Hey, you want a beer?" Howard spun around and opened a fridge. It was an old paint-splattered Frigidaire filled with nothing but beer. "What kind was she?" He spun back around, popped the can open, and put it in Lance's hand. Then he took one for himself.

"Red hair." Lance stared flatly at the can in his hand. "She had red hair."

"Irish Setter," Howard nodded. "Must've had some Irish Setter in her...? How big was she?"

Lance switched hands, putting the can of beer in his left. He held out his right, palm flat, about three feet from the ground.

"Yeah, sounds like she had some Irish Setter in her."

They stood there for a minute without another word. Both men with their heads held low, bemoaning the plight of poor missing Princess.

However the radio still played low. Randy Travis was crooning in the background.

"You live here?" the stranger stuttered.

"Yeah, sure...."

"With your wife and children?"

"You know, you don't look so well, my friend." Howard leaned in, and stared into the pale, pinched face. Lance's face was frozen in a grimace; he was squinting so much, his cheeks were all balled up and his top teeth were showing all the time. He reminded Howard of a gopher. Howard tried to peer in the shiny slits for eyes, but they started blinking in a twitchy kind of reaction.

"I haven't slept much." Lance said flatly. "I've been looking for my—"

"Maybe you ought to sit down for a while." Howard pulled

over a low stool, dragging it across the floor, making a chalk on chalkboard scraping sound.

Lance sat down.

After a moment, Howard went back about his work. He continued to talk to Lance as he slid back under the car. "So Lance," he said loudly, "are you from the neighborhood, huh?"

Lance sat silently, though attentively as Howard prattled on. "Me, I live with my wife and son. You married, Lance?"

"Married? Yes."

"Well, then I don't have to tell you..." Howard shimmied out from under. He pulled a big metal basin after him. It was filled with used motor oil. "You got any kids, Lance?" He asked as he carefully carried the oil out to the curb.

Lance followed.

"You can't dump that into the storm drain! It'll seep into the underground water and—"

"Nah, don't be silly, I do it all the time." Even as Howard spoke, it was too late; he poured the five gallons of oil into the sewer. "Don't tell me you buy all of that environmental hooey!"

"It'll pollute the caves." Lance's voice dropped as he watched the oil go down the drain.

"Caves? What are you talking about? There are no caves..."

And again Howard put his face right up next to Lance, to scrutinize this odd stranger.

The sun was burning off the morning haze. Outside of the garage, in the daylight, this Lance person didn't hardly look like a man. Not 'his kind' of man. Suddenly Howard didn't want to have anything to do with him.

"You know, Lance, maybe you ought to get back to looking for that dog of yours. I'm kind of busy. I got a lot of work to do. I can't stand around jaw jacking all day." He slapped Lance on the shoulder, leaving an oily palm print. "Maybe I'll catch you another time." And he walked away, leaving Lance standing on the fringe of grass at the side of the curb. "Don't you worry," he hollered over his shoulder, "I'll keep an eye out for Princess." Without looking back, his hand waved once in the air.

Once back in the garage, the radio's volume went back up. Way up.

Howard Greenleaf gave no further thought to the freaky little man. He crawled under the car to replace the filter. Not a thought at all to the strange encounter. He screwed in the drain plug and tightened it down with a small wrench.

He didn't hear Lance reenter the garage.

It didn't occur to him that he might have a problem with the mopey little oddball.

Not until he heard the jack being released.

Chapter 27

J.J. walked up the street. It was a studied gait. Her feet
strode parallel a shoulder's width apart; her arms were bent
slightly and swung forward and back. Through consistent effort
it had become automatic to check any unnecessary swivel in the
hips. To the casual eye, she affected the physical bearing of a
male.

She took the front steps two at a time and knocked twice on
the door.

It felt funny standing there. It felt funny coming over *to visit.*
She jingled the keys in her pocket, but decided against it.

She knocked again. This was going to take some getting used
to.

The door opened. Margie stood there. In a dropped beat,
both women felt a sensation like an undertow. Margie held her
breath. J.J.'s heart was racing. They were both resisting...

"J.J! J.J!"

Looking down the hallway, J.J. could see Kenny sitting at the
dinette table having his breakfast.

"J.J! J.J!" he repeated excitedly.

The tide ebbed.

J.J. knelt down and K.J. came running into her arms.

"How's my favorite boy in the *whole world?*" She rumbled the
words and shook her face "...in the *whole world!*"

It was the truth. In the whole world, he was her favorite. He was her only. She hugged him to her heart. She loved him with a fierceness.

"Animals! Are we going to see animals today?" He nodded a hopeful anticipation. "Are we? Are we?"

She held him out in front of her and looked him in the eye. "Did I say we would go see animals today?"

He nodded yes, yes.

"Then that's what we'll do. We'll go see animals."

J.J. knew to keep a promise to a child. Adults aren't always honest with each other, With a child, it's even more important. She raised her eyes slowly to look at Margie. It felt bittersweet.

It had been two weeks since she moved out. The days were stacking up like a wall. Each day, another brick. Soon there would be no getting over. She and Margie would get more and more distant. A beautiful thing would be lost.

But right now there was something else she needed to do. It too involved a matter of the heart; in this case, the heart of a small boy. How do you explain to a three year old that you're not abandoning him? That sometimes parents need to be apart from each other. And even though you're no longer living with him, you're still there for him. You will always be there for him. You just say it and hope he understands.

She took his little hand in hers.

She told Margie, "We should be back sometime around three.

Margie knelt, gave Kenny a hug and a kiss.

"J.J." she asked pointedly, "Did you take your meds today?"

A look of annoyance was conveyed behind J.J.'s narrow glare. *Who does she think she is? She's her ex-, not her mother?*

But then she felt the tug of K.J.'s little hand in hers, and she thought differently.

She motioned for him to be patient: "Just one more minute, darling. I have to finish speaking to your mommy." The last thing she wanted was to get upset. The last thing she wanted was for Kenny to see her upset. "Yes, Margie, I remembered to take my medication. Thank you."

Margie had removed the child-seat from her car. She handed to J.J. to use in her van.

They smiled short matching smiles.

J.J. quickly turned away.

Margie watched the two of them, hand-in-hand, off to the zoo.

As the Safest Locksmith van tooled down I-75, J.J. sang the Simon and Garfunkel song:

It's all happening at the zoo.

I do believe it.

I do believe it's true....

J.J. had timed it so that they would miss the morning rush. The day shimmered on the windshield. K. J.'s little face beamed all shiny and new.

Exit 6: the CINCINNATI ZOO AND BOTANICAL GARDENS.

157

A series of signs guided them to ZOO PARKING.

It being a weekday, the lot wasn't very full. J.J. had her choice of spots. Several yellow school buses waited near the entrance. J.J. pulled in under a tree, got out and went around to the other side. K.J. was already out of his seat and ready to get going. She lifted him down. They hurried up the path to the ticket window.

Lions and tigers and bears, oh my!

Lions and tigers and bears!

There were no lines at the turnstiles. Above the gate, the blue sky was decorated by a rainbow of streamers. No balloons. A vendor outside the gate had spinning wheels and banners, but no balloons. J.J. was all set to buy Kenny a balloon, a big squiggly one. It hadn't occurred to J.J. that they wouldn't have balloons.

Then she saw the sign:

No balloons allowed in the zoo.

Animals sometimes mistake them for food.

Swallowing balloons can harm animals.

Children and animals! – They required special care. Sometimes, without ever meaning to, we hurt them.

That was what J.J. was trying to avoid. She knew that people don't usually remember the things that happen when they're Kenny's age. But she hoped he would remember this day in his soul. That he would remember the fun. J.J. understood, things that happen when you're too young to remember can still make a difference.

They went straight to the gift shop.

A quick search of the shelves, and soon they were three.

J.J. forked over twenty-five bucks for a stuffed monkey. A monkey named "Monkey." And she marveled at the way Kenny immediately began to talk to it, the way he held onto it. Someone to care for. It's so important to have someone to care for. She smiled past the lump in her throat. She watched the little boy give his new friend a hug. Money well spent.

Next stop, real monkeys.

J.J. never realized there were so many different kinds of monkeys. The woolly monkey came from the Amazon. He looked a lot like K.J.'s new friend, furry with a curly tail. A classic monkey face.

The silver langur monkey of India and Southeast Asia did look Asian. They had tiny noses. One of them became very interested in K.J.—or perhaps it was Monkey that got her attention. She peered out from under a fringe of straight hair that bordered her face like the hood. Whatever the fascination, it didn't last; the Langer grew turned her back. It would seem three year old Kenneth J. had the longer attention span. Which wasn't saying much for the Langer. Then again, J.J. may have misread the behavior. For all she knew, monkey body language could be entirely different than people body language. But she doubted it.

Noisy baboons anxiously walked back and forth on branches, looking every which way. Smaller baboons playfully chased one another across the upper reaches of the cage. Small sparrows from outside passed freely through the fence and into the cage. They pecked away at unseen morsels of food on the

159

cage floor.

J.J. read the names of the animals off the small plaques attached to each cage. Some of the names were clever. There was a baboon named "C.U. Soon."

There was a Siamang ape whose name was Wallender Caruso. He had a pouch in his neck called a throat sac. It was like an echo chamber. It puffed up and—*Boy! Was that monkey loud!* Every time Caruso would scream, K.J. would scream and laugh, and run around in a circle.

What a wonderful monkey!

And the afternoon went by like a carousel—a whirl of animals and laughter.

It felt like they had the zoo all to themselves. Once in a while they'd see a family, a mother and a father with two or three little ones in tow or in a stroller. They passed several groups of preschoolers in neat lines, with colored name tags pinned to their shirts. Perhaps they were from a church group. They probably came from those buses out front.

J.J. and K.J. just finished looking at the giant orangutan. He lived behind a moat, with a large tree trunk and stone caves. There was a daddy orangutan playing with a youngster.

J.J. had been waiting for the right opportunity. There was so much she needed to say.

Finally, K.J. was ready to sit down.

Just ahead, a little off the main path, were some swings. He'd stop running around. They would be able to take a break.

She could push him on the swings. And she could try to explain why she moved out of their house.

"K.J., I have to talk to you about something, something that's very important."

The little boy held onto his new friend. "And Monkey…?"

"I have to talk to the both of you actually."

He smiled. He liked that. She was going to talk to Monkey, too.

Maybe it would make it easier, talking to the stuffed animal. She could already feel herself well up. So she concentrated on Monkey, looking into its face, its shiny eyes.

"You see, Kenny, sometimes adults—"

"Are you and Mommy going to sleep together anymore?"

Children can surprise you. For a second, she wondered if he actually understood what he'd said. Of course, she knew he didn't. But children can seem wise. Once they learn a thing or two, they become foolish like the rest of us.

She recovered from the question and said, "That's hard to say. Are you going to sleep with Monkey tonight?"

He nodded vigorously.

"And are you going to sleep with Monkey forever? Even when you're all grown up?"

He nodded again, with enthusiasm and certainty.

So much for that...

"Well, Kenneth, and Monkey, things don't always work out the way we want. And sometimes, with adults, even though they love each other very much, they grow apart." She had to stop and take a deep breath. "Your mommy and I both love you very much. And nothing can ever change that. Right now, I'm not sleeping in the same house, but I will always be here for you." She was afraid she might be scaring him, biting apprehensively on her lip, staring into his young eyes. She turned away.

"We love you, J.J." Little arms wrapped around her neck and gave her a big hug. The kind of hug she wished she could feel for the rest of her life. She sniffed back tears, and held Kenneth J. to her heart. She rocked him gently. He rocked her to her core.

A monarch butterfly lighted upon Monkey's shoulder. The child's face lit up. In his eyes, this ordinary insect was every bit as magical as the rare snow leopard. And the flutter of orange and black sent him running.

J.J. stayed close on his heels.

Into the air, the wings floated high before coming once again to light. This time on a water fountain, next to a cage, like a huge birdcage. Only inside weren't birds. A thin mist sprayed over the top to simulate a rain forest. In the middle, a large tree stood completely stripped of bark. And hanging from its branches like so many exotic fruits—bats. A colony of bats. There must have been a hundred of them. Noisy, squabbling, roosted upside down, with their wings wrapped around their little bodies like pods. Like mummies. Like droplets of evil. Their faces were like snarling dogs. It was very unsettling to see dog faces on bats. Wings and no feathers.

But there was something else about the bats, something completely unexpected. Something that J.J. found to be far more disconcerting.

The bats had human-looking genitals!

The boy noticed it right away. "Look, his pee-pee!"

J.J. couldn't help but notice. It was just there.

Disproportionately large, compared to their little bodies.

Hanging, upside down—a penis and two balls!

Chapter 28

Your daddy's rich and your momma's good looking...

Summertime – every day felt like summertime for Monty and Becky. And little Max Mandell, he had no reason to cry.

The nanny got him ready for bed. There were hugs and kisses from his Mommy.

And after he got through saying goodnight to his mommy..."Hey, don't I get a goodnight hug from my big boy?"

The nanny lifted the sleepy little boy into his daddy's arms. "Mr. Mandell, we were just about to go look for you, weren't we, Max?"

Max didn't have much energy left. He'd played hard all day and was fading fast. He mustered a mighty hug for his daddy and a kiss on the cheek.

Monty Mandell held onto his son a little longer, feeling the love in his veins. He marveled at his capacity to love. Not the reckless love of a young man, but every bit as sweet. He hummed softly and rocked the child.

He noticed the nanny waiting patiently. He deposited his son back into her arms. He could hardly take his eyes off the boy. The nanny—a gentle woman from Sweden—smiled sweetly. He nodded, dismissing her. She hurried away to tuck the child into bed.

Becky Mandell reclined on a couch full of pillows, chatting long distance on the phone like a schoolgirl. With no makeup, wearing jeans and a halter top, she could have been a schoolgirl.

On the other end was her girlfriend from Vegas, Heather Darling. That was her stage name, of course. Heather would always introduce herself saying "Hi, I'm Heather..." and then she'd pause before saying her last name. Fellas always thought she was talking to them, calling them *darling*. Heather was so much fun!

Monty came out on the veranda. He had his gardening clothes on. He placed a cool drink down beside her.

"What a sweetheart!" She took a moment to look up at him.

Bending forward, he moved the phone aside and planted a peck on her lips. She tried to lock him into a longer kiss, but he pulled back, making her stretch up out of her chair. He smiled mischievously. She ran her tongue slowly across her upper lip and smiled.

"Say hello to Heather for me," he said, as he walked off to take his seat in the garden, where he would sip his coffee and watch the sunset. He'd only recently taken up gardening. He said he never had time for it before. They still kept their gardener, Toshi. He came once a week. But one section of garden by the fountain—that was strictly Monty's.

Which was why Monty was puzzled when he noticed footprints in his tomato patch. They didn't belong to anyone in the house. They were too big to be the nanny's, or the housekeeper's. Besides, none of them would stand in his garden.

Becky hung up the phone and sat up. From her seat on the terrace, she could see Monty in his garden below, his gray head beginning to show a little scalp. Still, he was so handsome. She thought back to when they first met. She was working at the Aladdin. She didn't notice him right off. He didn't have that kind of appeal. He grew on her. And now, she didn't know how she didn't see it all along. So she could understand why Heather and some others sometimes acted like they did. They thought, *Poor Becky, married to that old guy*. Or they thought, *Lucky Becky, married to that rich guy*. But none of that mattered. They could think what they wanted to think. Monty was the love of her life.

"Hey, doll, you weren't going to watch the sunset without me, were you?" She came up behind him and put her arms around him.

"No way! We were both waiting for you, me and the sun. Now that you're here..." He pressed his lips against her forearm like a gourmet sampling a delicacy.

At that moment the sun began to slip behind the horizon. She felt a breeze on her skin, gently lifting up her silk dress.

"Oh, daddy, you thrill me!" Becky kissed the top of his head. "Let's go upstairs."

She didn't have to ask twice.

The bedroom was dark and fragrant. From the master bath, a sliver of soft light fell.

Out beyond the patio doors, below the veranda, an eight foot wall stood guard over the two and a half acre estate. Nestled in the snug harbor of *suburbia*, amid the cozy twinkle of good fortune—no other security measures were in place.

Monty stood before the mirror in the bathroom. A younger man might have preened after a performance such as his. Monty washed. His body was surprisingly firm. Even there. Even after. She was that exciting—his Becky. If there was credit to be given, he gave it to her. He gave everything to her. The water ran lukewarm. He lathered a washcloth.

Becky lay on their king-size bed. Her whole body *'thrummed'* with satisfaction. *Thrum*—that's a combination of throb and hum. Waves of heat radiated from her naked body. She could feel the cool night air against her skin, drifting in the open patio doors, with scents of flowers and fresh-turned soil from Monty's garden.

Then suddenly she shivered. A chill ran through her. From somewhere deep in her central nervous system, a forgotten area of the brain—a sixth sense tingled.

Monty returned with the warm washcloth for her. He knelt by her side.

"What's wrong?" He was quick to tune in on her; something wasn't right.

She didn't answer. He followed her gaze.

Standing wordlessly, he went and closed the patio doors. He looked back at her. She was breathing evenly now, the color returning to her cheeks. He drew the curtains; she let out an audible sigh of relief.

"What was it, Becky? You look like you saw a ghost."

"It's nothing," she snapped. "I mean, no, I... I don't know... I'm not sure. It was the strangest sensation. I can't explain it. Monty, you know I'm not the type to imagine things." She looked to him for reassurance.

He was unconditional. "Sure, baby, I know that."

She held her hand out to him. He went to her and took her hand in his. It took a moment for the calm to pass between them and displace the mysterious dread.

"That's not the first time that's happened," she said. "Yesterday, when we were at the movies, sitting in the theater, I had the feeling that someone was watching us in the dark. Someone that could see in the dark. And just now, outside, in the garden..."

He reached over to the nightstand and turned the light on.

~~~

Monty Mandell was an incredible man. Becky could hardly believe her good fortune. He was kind and funny, generous and passionate Not to mention spontaneous.

Two hours after his kooky young wife has some weird anxiety attack, he has her and Max and the nanny all whisked away on vacation. He wouldn't even let them pack.

"There'll be stores where we're going," he said. "If there's something you need, you'll get a new one."

Just like that! He picked up the phone and made the arrangements. It had been too long since Becky'd seen her girlfriends in Las Vegas. After a couple days there, they'd fly down to the Caribbean. Becky had never been to Antigua and the

West Indies. Monty loved introducing her to new places. It was one of his favorite things to do.

As they boarded the plane, they were unaware that they'd been followed to the airport. They took their seats in first-class feeling worry-free and grateful to be alive.

They were right to feel that.

The muddy brown Plymouth sat stymied, like some creepy thing crawled out of its hole to chase a bird, but couldn't fly.

Chapter 29

Detective William Turner learned of the death of Howard Greenleaf in the paper. He arrived at work early for a change, so he sat down at his desk with a cup of joe. He was thumbing through the local news when the story caught his eye.

The body had been discovered by Howard Greenleaf Senior, the dead man's father. He had been dead for several days, crushed under his Chevy Camaro. In a statement released by Sheriff Boomer of Milford County, the circumstances surrounding the death of Mr. Greenleaf were called "suspicious." Boomer went on the say that the investigation was focusing on the disappearance of the dead man's wife, Mandy, and their three year old son, Brad. The sheriff stopped short of naming Mandy Greenleaf as a suspect, saying only that investigators needed to speak to her.

There was something they weren't saying. Willy read into the omission. They probably collected some evidence at scene; whatever it was, the sheriff didn't seem particularly worried that Mrs. Greenleaf had fallen victim.

But then he didn't know about the women terrorized at the Health Center. He didn't know that Mandy Greenleaf had been a patient there and had conceived there. He didn't know about Lance Manly, out there, calling on his flesh and blood.

The weather section was forecasting a storm sometime

during the next twenty-four hours. That was how Turner felt, too.

"Morning, Detective." It was Detective Lou Taber arriving for work at eight A.M. "You're here early. To what do I owe this—"

He didn't get to finish the sentence. No sooner had he put his coffee down than Turner picked it up, and used it as a carrot. "We gotta go" was all he said.

Playing along, Tabor held his hand out for the cup and was soon following Turner out of the building, where he got his cup back.

He took a sip. "Oh well! If we gotta go, you're driving!"

Turner got behind the wheel. He threw it in gear and sailed over the speed bumps. A moment later they were on the interstate.

Taber continued to sip his coffee while eyeing his partner. "You seem a little uptight, partner."

Turner was leaning forward as he drove with his face up close to the steering wheel. He was like a man trying to outrun a storm. The barometric pressure may have been dropping outside, but the pressure inside was way up. He expected raindrops on the windshield at any moment. He half-expected them to splat blood red. That was the kind of clouds rolling across his mind.

Eating up miles of road, he continued to steer the government vehicle intently.

From the passenger seat: "So, you gonna tell me where we're going?" Taber had his head tilted down; he was looking out from under his eyebrows. "No, don't tell me." Taber toyed. "I'm such a good detective, I already know."

"You do...? And how do you know that?"

"You know, it might not even be the same Mandy Greenleaf. Ever think of that? There could be more than one. It's not that unusual a name."

"Okay, so you read the paper. Tell me this, how many Mandy Greenleaf's do you suppose happen to have a child who just happens to be three years old? Huh?"

"Actually, I didn't read about it. My wife told me. She said they had it on the news last night. She and I have been having this 'discussion' about the clinic. About this whole business of artificial insemination and, well, she agrees with you. Thinks we should've called every mother on that list to warn them. She'd have done it herself if I gave her the list. If she thinks a child is in danger..." Lou paused and shook his head; it was beginning to sink in.

"She's a smart woman, your wife. Right now I'm sorry she's not running the department."

The first few drops of rain dotted the windshield.

Next exit: Milford.

~~~

Sheriff Boomer of Milford County said he appreciated their interest in the case. He welcomed any information that might have that could shed light on the mysterious disappearance.

"Honestly, boys, I don't see that your irate jizz donor makes a whole lot of difference. Either way, we still got to find Mandy

Greenleaf. She's the key. If we keep circulating her picture, someone's bound to recognize her. Once we find her..."

"I'm sorry to have to disagree with you, Sheriff. I think maybe Mandy was abducted." Turner looked at the picture of mother and child. "If it's the same suspect from the clinic, she's in a lot of danger. She may already be dead."

"Well, I hope you're wrong." The sheriff scratched the back of his neck and bit at the inside of his cheek. "Did I mention to you that we interviewed a couple who had dinner with the Howard and Mandy the night before he was killed?"

Taber nodded. "Yeah, you told us. They said they were having marital difficulties. I think you're going at this all wrong, Sheriff?"

Boomer was a head taller than Taber. He didn't appreciate big city police telling him how to run his investigation. But he knew he should cooperate on the off-chance that these dicks were right.

"What about the stuff you found in the house?" Taber asked. "You said there were signs of a struggle. Traces of blood, a broken fingernail..."

"Okay, okay, tell you what I'll do. I'll have our guys send you a copy of everything we got from the house: prints, fibers, the whole nine yards. You can compare it with what you got from the Women's Clinic, maybe we'll get a match. Meanwhile I'll ask around and see if anyone saw a muddy brown Plymouth in the area around the time of the murder."

Turner was relieved to hear the sheriff use the *M* word.

Chapter 30

It was cold and gray with a storm on the way. A perfect morning to sleep in.

And it so happened to be Sigreid Calhoun's day off. She was taking full advantage of it, staying curled under the covers a little longer. She had a new comforter and it was so cozy. Normally, from her bed she could see out the window to a patch of blue sky. But this morning, gray clouds hung like a drop cloth. She rolled over and hugged her pillow, listening for the distant roll of thunder, waiting for the sound of raindrops. She expected to hear it at any moment, hearing it already in her mind's ear. But no thunder came, and no raindrops. So finally, she got up out of bed.

It was a laundry day. A hot chocolate and cinnamon roll day. A pair of old sweatpants, a flannel shirt, and a bedroom slipper day.

She loaded up her laundry, detergent, bleach, and fabric softener.

Doing laundry made her think of when she was a kid; she'd go with her mother to help fold. She would bury her face in the warm, clean towels. Her mother was long gone, and she was all grown, but she still loved the smell of dryer-fresh linen.

She wheeled the cart through the foyer, out of the apartment and to the elevator.

She waited for the gears to mesh. It was a noisy lift, but she'd gotten used to its slow clamor. It arrived empty. She got in and pushed 'B' for basement.

One thing she hadn't gotten used to: She hated having to go to the basement to do her laundry. She thought about going to a Laundromat outside the building. But that didn't make any sense, not with the weather like it was.

She came to a shaky stop on the bottom landing, pulled the laden wire basket from the elevator, and then pushed it. The wheels squeaked along the corridor. There were no windows, and it never failed!—there was a bulb out.

Behind her, she could hear the elevator door close. The car rattled upward, leaving her alone in the basement.

She opened the door to the laundry room. The air was stale. The light was dim and fuzzy, like a veil of lint. The room was empty, no one else using the machines. It was a narrow room, machines against one wall, a bench and a small table along the other. The far wall was bare and made of gray brick, which made it seem a little like a dungeon, complete with cobwebs in the corners.

She unloaded her things quickly, not wanting to spend any more time there than she had to.

What was that noise? Her head jerked in the direction of the hallway.

It was just the elevator coming back down. Someone else must've decided it was a good day to do laundry.

She separated out the whites, selected the temperature and

fabric setting.

A minute had passed since she'd heard the elevator. Yet no one had come down. Strange! Someone must've pushed all the buttons. That happened sometimes.

She retrieved her change purse from the bottom of the basket and proceeded to count out her quarters. She thought she had enough, but she was a quarter short. *Damn!*

She decided she'd leave everything as it was, rush upstairs, and see if she couldn't find another quarter.

She was reaching for the doorknob when it suddenly pulled open from outside.

"Oh, excuse me.... Oh... ah... I'm sorry," an apology was hastily offered.

Sigreid clutched her chest with one hand, her eyes blinking in the dim light. As the man in the hallway came into focus, her heart slowed back down in her chest. The even rhythm of her breathing returned.

"You really frightened me," she said. "I wasn't expecting—"

She felt a little foolish at having taken such a fright! The poor man seemed equally startled, maybe more. His eyes were wide... and kind of shiny.

"I'm s...s...sorry. I didn't mean to scare you," he repeated.

She heard herself laugh—a short, nervous laugh. It was an awkward moment. They both stood there without moving. Then she remembered: "Hey, would you happen to have a quarter?"

"Let me check.... Yes, here you are. I have two quarters."

"No, that's okay. All I need is one." She picked the coin up out of his palm, replacing it with two dimes and a nickel. "Thanks. Thanks a lot," she said and started to turn.

Until that point, she hadn't noticed anything out of the ordinary. More accurately, it hadn't registered yet. She'd been startled. The light was dim. All she wanted to do was put her coins in the machine and leave as quickly as possible. She hadn't noticed *the wounds*. The young man's face was thin. There was the beginnings of a beard. But it was too sparse to hide the tears in the flesh. They were deep scratches that bore testament to a very recent fray.

Sigreid could envision the fingernails trailing across his cheeks, set in motion by fear and self-preservation.

She froze.

Turning back very slowly she saw the piton hammer in his hand, dangling at his side.

"Your name is Sigreid, isn't it?" he said. "Sigreid Calhoun."

When he said it the second time, it was no longer a question. It was an accusation.

"My name's Lance," he proclaimed. "Lance the Father."

Chapter 31

Turner scanned the heavens. Brooding storm clouds continued to press down on the city. The called-for rains hadn't materialized as yet. But that didn't mean anything. This was one storm wasn't going to blow over.

He and Taber set out to warn the women on the list. He took half the names; Taber took the rest.

They needed to handle the notifications in person. There were plenty of reasons. This was an end-run around their supervisors. They'd been told: The Department isn't ready to go public. It'll only serve to panic the community unnecessarily. There's not enough evidence to make that call.

Turner wasn't waiting. He knew they couldn't just call these women on the phone: *Excuse me, ma'am, but a homicidal maniac is stalking your three year old.* No, they needed to talk to each one, in person. Luckily, most were local.

He did phone ahead on one name: Becky Mandell. Mrs. Mandell lived far outside the city in a wealthy suburb. He wanted to make sure someone was home before going out there. It turned out that she and her husband were away on vacation.

Turner spoke with the housekeeper: "Mr. and Mrs. Mandell are not expected back any time soon.... Yes, they took their son Max with them."

So much for that one, he thought. *She should be out of harm's way for the time being.*

"No," he told her, "There's no need to contact them in Las Vegas. Nothing urgent. If you could just be good enough to give Mrs. Mandell my number...? Have her ask for Detective Turner." He thanked her, and went on to the next name on the list.

Margaret Danser. Detective Turner didn't know where he'd heard that name before. It sounded very familiar.

A modest row house in a good, working-class neighborhood. He checked the number against the address in his notepad. It was the right house.

He knocked on the door and waited.

He could hear voices inside. It sounded like singing. A woman and a child:

Rain, rain, go away.

Save it for another day...

He could hear someone coming to the door.

"Who's there?"

"Police." He held his badge in front of the peephole.

The door opened.

Turner was faced with a pleasant looking young woman. Her hair was short cropped, chestnut brown. Her facial features were sharp without being hard. A soft roundness beneath the denim work shirt went a long way in adding to an impression of warmth and comfort.

"Yes, can I help you?" she said.

Turner couldn't be sure, but for a split-second, as her eyes rose up to meet his, he thought that he saw a reaction, a hint of recognition. Then all the warmth and congeniality just drained away, leaving only frosty contentiousness.

"So, what is it? What do you want?" she asked again, this time with a chip on her shoulder.

"May I come in?" he asked. He pulled the collar of his coat close to ward off the damp chill. "This will only take a minute."

"Okay, but only for a minute. I have things to do."

Turner introduced himself. No hand shake was exchanged.

He took a hasty inventory of his surroundings. To his right was the living room. A staircase was on his left. There were probably a couple of bedrooms upstairs. Down the hall, he could see into the kitchen. There was a small dining area there where a small boy sat at the table with crayons and a coloring book. Sitting next to the boy, in a high chair, was a stuffed monkey. There was a rear door at the back of the kitchen. It probably opened onto a backyard.

He followed her back to the kitchen where she sat next to the boy. She tousled the boy's hair. "Kenny, you go right on coloring while I talk to this policeman."

Turner remarked, "Wow! That's a spaceship you're drawing, isn't it?" He tried to get the child to look up. "You're really a very good artist, you know that?"

The boy was shy; he nodded but kept his head down, buried in the book.

Again, Turner had the feeling he'd met this child before.

"Officer...?" With no pretense at cordiality, "Get to it! What brings you here?"

He reverted to a strictly profession demeanor. "Can we start with your name? Who am I speaking to?"

For a moment it seemed like she wasn't going to answer.

"J.J. Twomey."

Something was going on here.

"Is this the home of Margaret Danser?"

Again she hesitated. If Turner wasn't mistaken, the hesitation was filled with hostility.

"Yeah, she lives here."

"Is she home?" He gestured upstairs.

"No, she ain't here."

"Do you live here also?"

Now there was no mistaking it. He was getting the evil eye. It was as if he'd said something bad about her mother, when all he'd asked was, *Do you live here?*

"No, I don't live here. I'm just baby-sitting."

As J.J. Twomey grew more irritable, the boy pushed down harder with his crayon.

"Is there something wrong with that?" she demanded.

"No, of course not.... Is this Mrs. Danser's—"

"*Ms.* Danser. And yes, this is Margie's boy. You still haven't said why you're here asking me all these questions."

"No, I haven't. But I assure you that Ms. Danser isn't in any trouble with the law. At least not that I know of."

He tried to smile, to lighten things up. It wasn't working.

"Do you expect her back soon?"

She looked over at the clock.

"No, I don't expect her back, not for several hours."

"Would you happen to know where she is?"

Her eyes flashed daggers. "No, I don't know where she went."

"When she returns, could you give her this?" He handed her his card. She didn't move to take it. He just left it on the table. "It's very important," he said. "Tell her that she should contact Detective Turner as soon as possible. Will you do that for me?"

"Yeah, I'll tell her. She should call you as soon as she gets in." J.J. was clearly mocking him.

"Ms. Twomey, this is official police business. Interfering with a police investigation is against the law."

She seemed underwhelmed.

He headed for the door. "That's okay, I'll show myself out."

She made no attempt to get up.

The exchange left Turner with a peculiar feeling. It was as if his words had alternate meanings. He had no idea what triggered that reaction. He didn't like that. And there was something else, something skirting the edges of his memory.

He was glad to be getting out of there.

He stepped out onto the doorstep, into the gathering cold gray night.

As he closed the door behind him, he heard the child's voice call out, "So long, Whiskers."

Chapter 32

Faced with her potential demise, Sigreid Calhoun showed remarkable composure. Truly remarkable.

Predators hone in on the vulnerable, the victims. Never show fear. Don't run. They can smell it on you. They will chase you down.

Sigreid walked calmly over to the wooden bench along the wall opposite the washers. She sat down.

"Would you like to sit for a while?" she suggested. She moved closer to the end of the bench, making room for him to sit. Which also put her closer to the door. "Perhaps there's something you'd like to talk about?"

It was a wild gambit, disarmingly so.

Lance sat down, and things got even more surreal.

Sigreid didn't look up; her eyes shifted from the floor to the hammer in his hand, to the door, and back again. "So, do you come here often?" she said.

If he thought it was a stupid question, he gave no indication. He seemed pleased, and only too happy to go along with the charade.

"No, this is my first time here, and you? Oh, how silly of me! You live here."

She tried to breathe evenly, naturally. "Do you live around here?" she asked.

This was a cruel nightmare. They just sat there and he talked.

All soft-spoken, and timid, he told her that he was living in Kentucky. He talked about the weather. He said he liked this kind of weather, cloudy and overcast.

Her right hand slid over the side of the bench. An inch from her fingertips was a bottle of bleach. She could feel the bottle top. She pressed down on the cap, turning to open. Sigreid was super-aware of his slightest movement. She couldn't seem to focus on what he was saying; his words began to lose their shape, his meaning lost in sounds.

Then, from out of nowhere, he said something, something that twisted in her gut like a knife: "I am the father of your baby. It was *my* sperm in your womb."

She was caught off-guard. An emotional ambush of an open wound.

With his breath close to her ear, he said, "Where is our baby?"

It had been over three years. She went about her business and tried not to think about it.

"Our baby belongs with me, underground," he said. Barely a whisper, but in the basement his words reverberated.

Had she heard correctly? Could she bear to hear it again? She faced him without fear or hesitation, just grief and anger. "What did you say?"

Eye to eye—he had to blink, to look away.

Again, "What did you say?" she demanded to know. "What are you saying?"

His mouth was moving but no words were coming out, only

184

a long string of slimy noises. She was repulsed, but riveted. She watched Lance Manly's face contort through each incoherent syllable.

As he mumbled, Lance slowly and steadily raised the piton hammer.

"My baby never got to be born," she said quietly and sadly, as if to herself. "I had a miscarriage in my sixth month."

The hammer paused. It wavered atop the arc; then slowly, it started back down.

Splash!—a wave of bleach broke across his face.

Instantly there was burning in his eyes. The angry red lacerations that streaked his cheeks began to sting.

Sigreid Calhoun did not run from her would-be captor. She walked out the door and into the hall.

She could hear Lance screaming on the other side of the door.

She ran to the elevator. She was in luck; it was there, on the landing. She got in and started pushing the button. "Hurry up! You piece-of-shit elevator!" she pleaded. "Move!"

She stuck her head out to check down the hall.

The laundry room door flew open.

She went back to pushing buttons. "C'mon! Hurry! Close. Please close."

There were footfalls down the hall, growing louder, drawing near.

A metal arm unfolded, and the door began to slide. As it closed, a few tears rolled down her cheeks.

She breathed a laugh. "I'm sorry, Mr. Elevator, I didn't mean to say bad things about you. You came through in the nick of time."

Lou Taber and William Turner were seated outside the captain's office. They were being called on the carpet.

While Turner was at Margaret Danser's house receiving an icy reception from J.J., Sigreid Calhoun was being terrorized by the suspect. It so happened, Lou was en route to Sigreid. He had just entered her apartment building and was standing in the lobby waiting for the elevator. The door opened, and a woman came tumbling out. He steadied her, his hands on her shoulders.

He would later tell Turner. "I knew instantly that it was her, the woman I'd come to see. She grabbed onto me like a life preserver. She kept saying, 'In the basement! In the basement! I'm sure he was going to kill me. Call the police.' Then she said something about a baby, and a hammer. As soon as I heard the word *hammer*, I knew it was our guy."

Lou held his thumb and index an inch apart. "I came this close, this close to getting the bastard."

"It was a judgment call. Stop kicking yourself." Turner knew what it was like to go over an incident again and again in your head and have it never come out right. "I think you handled the situation okay. We shouldn't have split up. That's what they'll ding us for."

"If I took the elevator, he could've taken the stairs. If I'd have taken the stairs, he could've taken the elevator. I made a big mistake; I told the Calhoun woman to stay there, to hold the elevator on the first floor. 'Don't let it move.' I should have stayed in the lobby. Instead I drew my gun, and proceeded down the stairs. I didn't know if there was another way out of the basement."

"It could've turned out a lot worse."

"I tell you, Turner, when I heard that scream, I was never so scared in my whole life. I raced up from the basement. I expected to find her with her skull bashed in. I'd have never forgiven myself." Lou shook his head. "That son-of-a-bitch! He went up to the second floor. When I get down to the basement, he comes waltzing out of the stairwell. That poor woman, I left her holding the elevator. When she started screaming, I thought for sure she was being done."

Turner wasn't listening anymore; his eyes were fixed on the door to the captain's office.

"You think the captain's going to pull us off the case?"

Lou gave him a puzzled look. "I don't remember the captain ever putting us on the case."

Chapter 33

It was astounding—J.J. Twomey in love with a man. A male of the species.

J.J. Twomey, who never wanted to have anything to do with men.

But she opened her heart to this man. A very little man.

And with the love she felt for Kenneth J. came an acceptance of the duality she had denied. How could she dislike men and at the same time emulate them. How could she resent a part of her?

She loved her little man.

"Okay, K.J., it's time for you and your monkey friend to get ready for bed."

He was already half asleep on the couch. She scooped him up in her arms, and brought Monkey along too. Together they climbed the stairs.

"We need to get you all washed, in your pajamas, and in bed by time your mommy gets home."

"Mommy," the child said. Nothing more, just that. He looked up at J.J. and said *Mommy*.

J.J. looked back at him adoringly.

She and Margaret told him that he was a special boy so he got to have two mommies. Mommy Margie would be home any minute.

It felt good to have his face and hands bathed in the warm, soapy water; to be clothed in soft, flannel; to be loved as only a mother can! In that, young Kenny was twice blessed.

As Mommy J.J. tucked him in, he planted a kiss on her cheek. "I love you, J.J.," he said.

"I adore you," she said, going him one better.

J.J. backed slowly out of the room. The night-light illuminated the serene face of the boy hugging his monkey. She left the door partly open.

She sat in the adjoining room, watching the TV news with the sound down low. Outside, the night had fallen.

It wasn't long before she heard a key in the door, the rattle of the knob.

She rose unhurriedly, making her way to the top of the stairs.

It was Margie.

"How was your game?" J.J. asked, wanting to make small talk.

Friday nights Margie played darts; J.J. got to babysit. She looked forward to it all week.

"It wasn't a game, just a practice," she called up. "But it went well, thank you for asking."

Margie put away her umbrella. She tossed off her coat onto a chair.

"The big game's next Friday," she said. "We're going to trounce Tally's."

J.J. didn't really give a damn about darts, but she was trying.

The phone rang.

"Could you get that?" Margie hopped on one leg, then the other—like an Irish jig. "I got to go real bad. I've been holding it the whole way over here. I should've gone before I left the pub."

"Are you sure you want me to get it?" J.J. said. She was still thinking about the visit from the broad-shouldered policeman. She could see where some woman might find him attractive.

"Don't be silly. Just get the phone, okay?"

The downstairs bathroom door closed with a slam.

J.J. shrugged. She walked over and picked up the phone: "Hello."

"Is this Margaret Danser?"

It was a man's voice. Her heart automatically shifted into overdrive. With a dry mouth she asked, "Who is this?"

"My name is Lance," said the voice. "And it's very important I speak with Margaret Danser, the mother of the three year old.... It's about the child."

Warning lights flashed in J.J.'s head. The maternal instinct is not bound to biology. Without giving it a second thought, J.J. answered, "Yes, what is it? This is the child's mother." By now her heart was pumping pure adrenaline. Her hackles were up and her head was down. She lowered her voice letting the R in *mother* trailed off in a low growl.

The caller couldn't see the fury building behind those eyes. But it wouldn't have mattered. He was that crazy.

"Four years ago, when you went to the Women's Health Center, you received sperm to conceive the child."

She listened; her face went hard, her lips curled back, she exhaled venom.

"That was my sperm," he said self-righteously. "I am the father."

He said he needed to see her as soon as possible. Right away. He said it had to do with the wellbeing of *their* child.

From where she stood, J.J. could see K.J.'s little head poking out from under the covers. Sleeping peacefully in this little bed, he was such a good boy.

What should she do? What must she do?

She wondered, *Did he know where Margie lived? How could he? But then how did he get the phone number? He wasn't supposed to have any information!* She had to think fast. Okay, she would agree. If he asked about the address, she could tell him they had moved and kept the old phone number.

"Okay, I'll see you!" she told him. "You can come over to my apartment." For effect she stipulated, "But it's getting late, you can't stay very long."

He agreed; he'd stay only a few minutes. He thanked her repeatedly. He took down the address she gave him, which was of course *her* apartment, and *not* Margie's.

"In one hour then..." she instructed, emphasizing that she needed at least an hour to get ready. She added that she was looking forward to meeting him. And she hung up.

It was so unthinkable! He actually believed her. Like any mother would expose her child to a total stranger! In the middle of the night!—he had to be crazy!

"So who was it?" Margie was coming up the stairs. "On the phone?"

"Oh, no one. One of those surveys... wanted to know which radio station I listen to."

"At this time of night!"

J.J. gathered up her things and got ready to go.

"Thanks a million for coming by and staying with Kenneth." Margie was forever thanking J.J. for helping out.

J.J. had asked her not to do that—he was *her* boy too!

A shadow loomed in J.J.'s eyes. She was looking to Margie for validation. Her world lay in the balance.

Margie answered the question without J.J. having to ask. "I'm sorry. I don't know why I do that. Of course, you're right. He's your child too. I would never have had him if not for you. We planned him together. We had him together. Nothing could ever change that! Kenneth J. is our child."

That was what J.J. needed to hear. She smiled as she took a last look around—at the sleeping boy; the warm, safe home; the face of her lover.

She turned and bounded down the stairs, to the door.

"Were there any other calls, or messages?" Margie called after her.

She stopped at the open door, crossing the threshold. Her right hand was in her pocket, touching the handle of her knife. She looked back over her shoulder.

"No, no messages."

Chapter 34

Turner was having a rough time of it. He was tired and frustrated. But there was something else...

Something had been bothering Willy Turner ever since he got involved in this case. The whole business of sperm banks and artificial insemination, for some reason it upset him. It was a gut level reaction, and at first he told himself that it didn't make a whole lot of sense. If some woman wanted to inject herself with semen purchased from a stranger... Why should he care?

William "the Tomcat" Turner, was a thirty-eight year old veteran of the sexual revolution. He was never married, had no children. Now suddenly he found himself trying to come to terms with his own values. He was even feeling a little guilty, which didn't make any sense! There were a lot of men like Willy, men who were commitment-phobic, men who avoided the responsibilities of family life. If these women chose to resort to radical measures to have a family... that wasn't his fault.

He was giving himself a headache. He rubbed his hand across his face and stared blankly. He put on his coat and closed the locker door.

Then he just sat there—like he was waiting for something.

Taber had gone home to his wife and kids. The station house was quiet; it was between shifts. Turner just couldn't get himself in gear. He spent the past hour sitting at his desk staring out the window. What was he waiting for? He pulled on the ends of his moustache and thought... *Kids!—that's what it's really about.*

Turner could not believe himself. What had gotten into him!—and all on account of some psycho sperm donor. He always considered himself relatively content. So why was he all of a sudden thinking about having a child? Wasn't that something exclusive to women?

He stroked the ends of his moustache and he thought of the child he'd met earlier that day, at Margaret Danser's house. What was it the boy called him?—Whiskers. *Whiskers!*

That was it! He thought back to last spring, to a sun-drenched field at a Father's Day picnic and a small boy reaching up to touch his moustache. That was it! That was where he knew the child! And Margaret Danser!—that must be Margie, the pretty redhead he'd met, the one who worked with his brother-in-law. He'd forgotten all about her and her little boy. He hadn't made the connection. Margaret. Margie. Of course, it had to be.

He stood up and walked into the station. He stopped in the hall, between the watch commander's office and the report writing room. It was slow, but there was some activity. Cops were working on reports, talking on the phone, bringing in suspects.

One of the front desk officers looked up from his terminal. "Detective, you still here?" He waved Turner over, handed him a sheet from the station fax. "Something came in for you."

It was from Sheriff Boomer. They'd found Mandy Greenleaf. Turner should call him as soon as possible.

Turner needed to speak to him anyway. The lab report had come in comparing the evidence from the Greenleaf house with that gathered at the clinic. It was a match. The same man had been in both places.

Turner had no doubt that it was the same man who visited Sigreid Calhoun earlier that day.

"I need to speak to Sheriff Boomer right away.... Tell him it's Detective Turner."

Willy couldn't sit down; he paced in front of his desk.

Then the sheriff got on the line, and he had to sit down.

Mandy Greenleaf was still alive, but just barely. She had indeed been kidnapped.

She was found by accident—seven hundred feet under the ground, below the hills of South Central Kentucky.... Some cave explorer.... If it wasn't for him, nobody would've found her in a thousand years.... The man's name? Jink Ray Cooney.

Boomer had him checked out; Cooney wasn't a suspect. Apparently he was a local legend in those parts. "He's an albino who roams around under the earth like some kind of mole man. Anyway, it was a lucky thing for Mandy Greenleaf. She was abandoned down there without any food. No blankets. No light."

Turner shuddered to think of it.

"Sheriff, you said 'It was a lucky thing for Mandy Greenleaf.'" Turner asked, "What about the boy? You haven't said anything about her little boy?"

"He didn't make it. Hypothermia."

Chapter 35

J.J. stopped in her tracks and listened to the rain. The wind blew in gusts, slapping sheets of rain against the windshield. She was feeling very philosophical. Life was full of bittersweet ironies.

Water sustains and water drowns,

Ride the wave or get knocked around.

"Hey that wasn't half-bad," she thought aloud. "I got to remember that."

The weather was just one more thing she couldn't control.

She had told the creep that she needed time to get ready. Which was true. She had to prepare a proper welcome. She drove straightaway to her new apartment, which was only a few blocks from Margie's. She parked behind the building and started gathering up the things she would need. She loaded them into a cardboard box.

There was the stun gun—intended to deliver sixty- to eighty thousand volts. She tested the device; pressing the button sent a ripple of electricity buzzing between the terminals. It was supposed to be enough to bring a two hundred pound man to his knees. In the locksmith business she often had to go into neighborhoods that weren't the best. She usually kept "the cattle prod" in the truck. Tonight, it would stay with her.

There was a set of handcuffs. She had them left over from a

196

service call. This couple, a man and woman, they were experimenting with light bondage, and they lost the key. When J.J. got the cuffs off, they told her to keep them. They didn't want to have anything to do with it anymore. J.J. couldn't bring herself to throw them away. "That was classic." She held them up. "Not likely to forget that call." She dropped them into the box. "What else?"

There was a length of motorcycle chain. She took that. And a lock, the U-shaped kind with the crossbar—"Should make an effective shackle."

With the box in hand, she ran through the rain to her apartment.

And she waited.

She didn't know what to expect.

There was a knock at the door. Her heart jumped inside her chest.

"Who's there?" she called out. She moved cautiously toward the door. In her left hand she held the stun gun; in her right hand, her knife. "Who's there?" she said again.

"It's me, Lance."

He sounded younger, more vulnerable than the voice on the phone. Maybe because he was out in the rain, while she was in her warm house. Or maybe it was because she had had time to think, to re-consider. This man was a part of K.J. He might even be like a larger, grown-up version. And if there was a part of him in Kenneth, how could she not feel a connection to him?

She put down the weapons and opened the door.

In an instant, she was face-to-face with a ghoul—so pungent was the odor; so foul the figure. A fish smells like the sea, an ape sounds like the jungle, a camel conjures visions of desert dunes— the creature in J.J.'s doorway was a peek into a primeval cave. Small of stature, his prickly beard dripped rainwater. His face was lined with festering sores and crusted lesions.

She stumbled backwards, groping for the knife or the gun.

He lunged forward in the wake of her retreat, filling the room with revulsion and terror.

Her hand locked around the grip of the stun gun. She turned quickly.

The piton hammer was poised above her head.

Click-buzz. The stun gun rattled in her hand. The rainwater made an excellent conductor. It sprayed from his body as he shook with the charge. *Click-buzz.*

He crumpled down onto the floor, convulsing into a fetal position. J.J. bent over him and continued to administer jolt upon jolt. She didn't want to stop. She wanted nothing left of him but smoldering ash on her living room floor.

But after a while, she stopped.

He continued to twitch and whimper at her feet.

She was satisfied.

Now to secure the wretch. Grabbing his right arm, she dragged him across the floor. His wet clothing made a squeegee sound and left a wet streak. She wasted no time, handcuffing his right arm to the leg of a heavy couch in the center of her living room. She used the motorcycle lock to shackle his legs. Then, keeping his left arm pressed close to his side, she wrapped the length of chain around his torso, ran it up between his legs, none too gently, and padlocked it behind his back. She was not taking any chances.

She stood up and stepped back, looking over her handiwork, and scrutinizing the monster that just tried to bludgeon her.

"Okay, so what was it you had to talk to me about?" She nudged him with her foot. "Something about a child?" She pulled a chair alongside and sat down.

He rolled over and looked up at her. "The child... the mother..."

This was not at all what J.J. imagined. She thought he might be a slick flimflam man running a con, wanting a payoff to have him stay out of their lives. This was a whole other animal.

"What do you want?" she screamed.

His eyes were swimming in his head, two flames in a sea of madness. She couldn't hold his gaze—it made her sick. She looked away, her eyes falling on the piton hammer that lay several feet away, on the floor.

"Why did you want to hurt me?" she asked, not that she expected an answer from such an abomination. It was like something that crawled out of a hole.

"You are the mother...?" he cried. "I need to find the child of my seed. We must go inside the Mother Earth. That's how it's supposed to be!"

"Jesus! You are sick, man! What the fuck are you talking about?"

His head was turned awkwardly up, and his eyes were ogling the picture of Margie and Kenneth J. that J.J. kept on the end table next to the lamp.

"What are you looking at?" She jumped up and turned over the picture frame so that he couldn't foul it with his eyes. "You ain't going inside anyone, creep."

That was when J.J. felt it: the odd sensation, the unpleasant taste in her mouth.

Did she remember to take her meds? She thought she had. Maybe it was the exertion, the emotional upheaval. Whatever it was, it was too late now. She could feel the epileptic seizure being triggered.

If there was any doubt, it vanished as images of her childhood floated in front of her; she saw her father's face.

J.J. Twomey fell headlong into an altered state. She lay thrashing on the floor alongside Lance. Almost on top of him.

Lance was already crazy; this made him frenzied. He let out choppy, disconnected screams: "Eh, eh, eh, eh..." He began to kick at the couch with his shackled feet, jangling his chains.

But J.J. was lost to her surroundings. She didn't hear the cracking sound of the wooden leg being torn loose from the couch. She wasn't aware of the demented laughter or the shrill cry of pain issuing from Lance as he dislocated his shoulder in order to free his arm.

Her pupils were fixed and dilated, and she didn't see him drag himself over to the piton hammer.

And even if she had, there wasn't a thing she could do about it.

Chapter 36

As his unmarked car splashed through the rain-slicked streets, Turner's mind flashed on the scene from that sunny Father's Day afternoon in the park six months earlier. That day had somehow converged into this. He did not know it then, but Margaret Danser had made an impression. He spent a few hours in her company at a barbecue, and six months later, she's vivid in your thoughts. She had a quality; she stayed with him. She had the most irrepressible laugh, and just a trace of mystery.

Now he was caught up in that mystery. He needed to see her. He needed to see her because her life was in danger. And because he wanted to see her.

It was as if all this time, she was in his subconscious, the redheaded mom with the curly-haired boy, only he didn't know it.

Fishtailing around the corner at Queen City Ave and Ferguson Road, he was mighty grateful that the intersection was clear.

The water running in rivulets down the oil-slicked asphalt reflected the street lights, throwing stars at his windshield, to get batted away by the wipers. Turner leaned forward behind the wheel. He had the odd feeling of being outside himself, watching events unfold. He knew that any detail could be significant. Every step could have consequence.

It was like he was writing the police report in his head and trying to figure out which details he'd need to include.

Margie Danser was in her bathrobe, in her living room. She was watching the evening news, scenes of calamity from around the globe. Police cars, ambulances, shattered lives, a parade of victims—on the small screen.

The doorbell rang. It rang again.

Someone is impatient, she thought, and went to see who it was.

When the voice on the other side said "Police", she felt like she hadn't fully dissociated herself from the TV. She looked through the peephole.

"Good evening... Ms. Danser? I'm Detective William Turner. You may recall we met once before. I'm Rhonda Duberry's brother, Paul's wife."

She opened the door. "Funny, you don't look like Paul's wife."

She was too quick. Besides, he wasn't there to be clever. He couldn't help but smile, although weakly. "No, you know what I mean. Rhonda is Paul's wife, and I'm Paul's brother-in-law."

She chuckled. "Yeah, I know what you mean. I remember you, Detective."

"I'm here on police business. Can I come in?"

She invited him in. She offered him a cup of tea? He declined.

"Well, I gotta say, you're scaring me a little, Detective. Tell me, what brings you out here on a rainy night?"

"I'm sorry to scare you, but that's kind of why I'm here. You've got good reason to be scared." Talking fast he began to explain.

He started by telling her about the break-in at the Women's Health Center.

Margie listened intently. It wasn't until he got to the part about Mandy Greenleaf that she began to tremble.

This was too much! This couldn't be happening!

He assured her *it was happening,* and she needed to take the threat very seriously, or she and Kenneth could become Lance's next victims.

Kenneth! She ran up the stairs, three at a time.

A few seconds later she came back out of the boy's room. She stopped, put her hand on the banister, and sighed. Turner stood at the foot of the stairs looking up. He saw her nod—
Thank God! He was alright!

She came down the stairs slowly, still shaking.

"He's in his bed, right where I left him, sleeping peacefully."

Turner felt an urge to fold her in his arms.

But she looked at him only as an official presence, an officer of the law, the brother-in-law of a friend. She didn't need comforting from him.

Her mind was racing. There was a lot to take in. She wrapped her arms around herself, as if it had suddenly gotten cold. She thought of J.J. *Her* J.J.

"When I was here earlier this afternoon, I spoke with a—"

She interrupted him: "Did you say that you were *here* earlier this afternoon?"

"Yes, why? I assumed you knew.... I left a message with—"

"I never got any message."

Panic kicked in again. She replayed the last minute, right before J.J left. There was a phone call, someone taking a telephone survey. Something wasn't right...

Ugly images sprang up inside Margie's head; she couldn't keep them out. She was being overrun by terrible thoughts.

She ran to the phone. The detective followed close behind, into the kitchen. She talked as she dialed: "Something's not right. It isn't like J.J. to not tell me about a message, especially something like this, involving the police, involving Kenney. Oh God! I hope I'm wrong! Let me be wrong!"

No answer! The phone just kept ringing...

She hung up and began pacing. This wasn't happening.

"We've gotta do something. I know it!—J.J. did something foolish." Then she started saying, "No time... there's no time!" She must have said that a dozen times.

Turner said he was going to call in for a patrol car. "They can look in on her."

"J.J. lives five minutes away. We have to go. There's no time!"

"What about Kenny? I'll get a couple uniform cops out here to watch him."

"No time. Besides, he's staying with me. I'm not letting him out of my sight," as she hurried upstairs.

"Give me a minute to call for backup. They can meet us

there."

"Do it from your car?" she shouted down at him.

A moment later she was carrying K.J. out to the car. All bundled-up and half-asleep. She spoke to the child using soothing tones. It helped to keep them both calm.

Turner held the door.

They got in the car. She sat in back with the boy and fired off directions at Turner as he pulled away from the curb. The night was sucking them in like an undertow.

Turner didn't say anything as he navigated the wet streets leading to J.J.'s. Or if he did, nothing registered in Margie's mind. It was awash in dread. She stared out the window into the shiny darkness. It was like the night was made of glass, waiting to be shattered.

She remembered a female officer coaxing Kenny out of her arms.

There was a scream, a mournful wail ringing in her ears.

She was on her knees when she realized it was her; she had screamed.

That was right before she passed out.

Light-bars flashed up and down the street as more and more officers arrived. Crime scene tape went up. Detectives arrived. Photos and Prints were called out. The preliminary investigation would stretch long into the night, and the next morning.

It would be a while before the coroner would remove the

body.

Cause of death: repeated blunt force trauma.

J.J. Twomey was bashed beyond recognition.

Chapter 37

They say there are five stages of grief. Five, seven, however many there are—Margie Danser didn't have time for that. She was afraid for Kenny. Fear takes precedence over grief.

They also say there are five stages of dying. J.J. didn't get time for stages—dying takes precedence over everything.

"We're going to do everything possible to protect you and your boy." Detective Turner said *We*... What he meant was *I*... *I am going to do everything possible*...

Margie was doing all she could to hold it together. She probably would have liked to hear him say *I*. But he said *We*.

She had police all around her. But that didn't keep her from feeling terribly alone. It was a nightmare. She kept flashing on the image of J.J.'s apartment. The stun gun on the floor next to the body. The broken couch, balancing on three legs. And the end table where the picture frame lay shattered, the photo of Margie and K.J. ripped from its frame. When she closed her eyes she could see that photo: she and Kenny were sitting on the stoop outside their house, squinting at the sunshine, grinning at J.J.

The thought of that animal feasting his eyes on that photo... her knowing that this man might be the father of her child, holding their picture in his bloody hands... it was enough to make her sick.

"This guy won't get away!" It was the lead detective

speaking, the one assigned to J.J.'s case. "Not the way he looks. Sigreid Calhoun was able to provide us with a very good composite; we know what he looks like. One of J.J's neighbors came forward. She states she saw 'a monster' running out of the building moments before we got here. It's the same man. He's injured; his face is badly scratched. He won't be able to go anywhere without arousing suspicion. What's more... it sounds like he could actually be hobbled, dragging chains. We should be picking him up any moment now."

Margie looked at him like he was speaking another language. Then she looked past him to Detective Turner.

"None of this is real—a monster with a torn face, dragging chains, hammering people to death."

First her head shook. Then her whole body shook. Then she broke down crying.

Detective Turner held her as the pain overflowed—a part of the job not in any of the training manuals. It's not unprofessional to be human. And you just can't ignore someone in that much pain.

"That's it. Let it out." He patted her on the back.

The agony threatened to shatter her.

His arms held tightly.

~~~

The days that followed were slow and unsteady, coming back from the edge. Just getting out of bed in the morning took all she had.

J.J. and Margie had been separated, but they were never

really apart.

Now a part of Margie was gone.

She would have to learn to live with a hole in her soul. What other choice did she have? She was a fighter. She had K.J. to think of.

She didn't explain to him what had happened, not really. How could she!

She said that J.J. wouldn't be able to visit with him anymore. J.J. had gone to heaven. She didn't want to leave him. She loved him very much.... She was in a wonderful place, and she was watching over him.

She could see that he didn't understand. But they weren't going to talk about it anymore. His mommy wasn't feeling well.

Chapter 38

The monster stole away to lick his wounds.

Parking the Plymouth under a nameless bridge, he sought refuge along the riverfront, just another mentally ill homeless person picking through the garbage. An urban eyesore; and at the same time, invisible. Such people went unnoticed because they didn't count.

Lance was hurting, and more confused than ever. That woman—she was so rough, so... mannish. Why had she tried to electrocute him? to imprison him?

Now he had to shuffle about with tiny steps, very quickly; his feet were still shackled. His mind felt like it was convulsing. Padlocks and electric shocks!—What was that *she-he* trying to do?

No matter. He decided not to hate her. But he was glad he knocked her in the head. He nodded to himself, shivering in the raw dark hours.

His car had become his home, stocked with supplies left over from spelunking. He pocketed several cans of food and a bag of trail mix. Using a can of motor oil that he kept in the trunk, he set out to free himself from his chains.

Why are they trying to punish me?

He laid down in an empty lot. His night-vision picked up movement—rats in the weeds. Taking off his shoes and his socks, he poured the motor oil over both feet. Painfully twisting

211

his feet and pounding at the lock with his hammer—after an hour of rolling around in the weeds—he finally managed to free one foot.

He fell asleep in the mud and the tall grass.

The first light of day was cold and blue like smoke. It crept up over the junkyards and fell upon the fiend in the weeds, a pile of rags bathed in shimmer and haze.

The glare was harsh against his mind. The sunlight was repellent to the landscape of his soul. He was homesick for the caves.

He got to his feet and he stumbled off, to wander the urban blight. The banks of the polluted river, where bag ladies and shopping cart men roamed freely, was a place where he wouldn't cause too much attention.

Under a highway overpass, far back from the factory streets and the torn fence, amid the rubble and rubbish, he found a cave of sorts, a sanctum where he could wait out the day amid shadow and stone. Giant underpinnings supported the highway above. Cold to the touch, stained with graffiti and mold, and caked with pigeon droppings, the walls reminded him of gnarled calcite columns he'd seen in underground caverns.

He sat down in a heap.

From his coat pocket, he fished out a can of chili.

"Now how am I going to open this?" he said out loud. "I could hit it with my hammer, but that would make a mess."

Then he remembered the knife he'd taken from that bitch.

"That butch bitch!" He tried not to think about her. It was making him upset all over again.

He got out the knife and began to jab at the can till it was open. The smell of the food reminded him that he hadn't eaten in twenty-four hours. Using his fingers he spooned the cold gooey beef into his mouth. Chunks of goo stuck to his face and beard.

And when he finished devouring the contents, he felt much better.

He placed the empty can on the ground next to him. The handcuff that dangled from his right wrist clattered against the stone floor, echoing softly, causing him to smile as he dropped off into the chasm of his subconscious, where he dreamed of tunnels and passages. No out-world sounds were allowed into his inner-vision. If they penetrated the depths of his stupor, through the filter of his fantasy the sounds of pigeons became bats; the breeze was the mouth of the cave inhaling; the traffic above was the *whirr* of his descent.

Further and further... Down. Down. Down...

The lead dog made a pass like a shark bumping its prey. Then he jumped back. Not clamping down and tearing, just testing, getting the sharp scent of blood in the air, sending a spill of saliva down glistening fangs.

Half-starved animals with ribs protruding at their sides, moving as a unit—the pack wound tightly and cautiously around the sleeping man. Each dog was linked to the others by an invisible band. When one got too close, the band snapped and growled, and jumped back. In that manner they closed in, hackles raised.

The quarry didn't react. He stirred slightly, but he didn't seem capable of mustering a counterattack.

From the rear of the pack, two dogs moved in. Their muzzles were bowed low. It was a posture signaling the attack was about to begin.

The lead dog hung back. He was a smart old mongrel.

The man made a noise, stirring from the maze of his mind, coming up slowly from his dream like a diver from the cool and the tranquil. He blinked back the pale gray light. His eyes opened.

The snapping jaws ripped him from ear to cheek, pulling him into a spiral of pain. Blood sprayed everywhere.

One of the animals had his hand in its mouth. Tugging and shaking with incredible ferocity, it was trying to tear the arm loose. He went sprawling onto his face, thrashing about like a man caught in a shredder. Five shredders. All fighting for the flesh. Mad to get beneath the fabric, frustrated by the clothes. Every animal knows:

The feast is in the flesh; the banquet, in the blood.

The feast is in the flesh; the banquet, in the blood.

The feast is in the flesh; the banquet, in the...

Lance desperately needed a weapon. He couldn't get to his hammer; he tried. It was tucked down his pant leg, held securely on his right side under his waistband and belt.

The lesbian's knife! He'd laid the knife alongside the can of chili before drifting off. And now he couldn't see it—he couldn't see anything out of his left eye—but he could feel the shape of it under his left hand. He closed his fist around the handle: a life preserver to a drowning man. He rolled over and thrust upward as hard as he could, slicing through the underbelly of one beast. Intestines came spilling out. Yelps and growls and snarls—all tangled in the blood and the guts. And suddenly, he was one of them, tearing wildly. Savage and terrible, he staggered to his feet.

One animal lay dead. Another lay dying. Its body twitched in the throes of death, its tongue falling slackly from its mouth, trying to lick at its own innards.

The others backed off, still holding in a tight circle, a life-and-death circle. A circle of bloodlust.

At the center of the circle, standing on two legs, was Lance Manly.

Directly in front of him, the lead dog held its ground, watching his every move. Manly turned the animal in his arms belly-up, bringing the gore inches from his face. With one eye he glared at the beast before him. Then he plunged his mouth into the sanguineous soup still warm with life.

The lead dog retreated, taking his remaining brothers with him. They looked back briefly, then scampered out of sight.

A hundred little black dots, fleas from the belly of the dying dog, jumped onto the mange of the man. It takes life to support life. He licked his lips. He was the victor, not the victim. A rush shot through his spine.

Chapter 39

Margie was sinking into a quicksand of depression. The harder she fought to lift herself out, the deeper she sank. Recriminations resounded inside her head.

Had she been mean to J.J.? That last time she saw her—the last time she would ever see her—had she been needlessly cruel? Did J.J. die thinking that Margie didn't love her? Oh God, please, don't let that be so!

It was becoming apparent that she was losing it; grief was winning. At stake, her much-loved spirit.

Friends from work came by. They tried not to look worried: They wanted to be helpful. But nobody knew what to do. It was a difficult situation.

You should take some time off from work. Take however long you need, she was told.

The police said the same thing. For them, it made it easier to keep an eye on her and Kenny. They had reason to believe that Lance would come after them, so uniformed officers were assigned to protect them around the clock.

Margie had a list of things she planned to do around the house, if she ever got the opportunity. Now here she was, a stay-at-home mom, and she wasn't getting anything done.

William Turner was hanging around a lot—in an unofficial capacity. His being Paul's brother-in-law made him an instant friend of the family. He seemed to take a genuine interest. She found she welcomed his concern. He quickly became Margie's trusted liaison with the police investigation.

So it was a little surprising when he suggested that it might be better for her to go back to work. He'd been watching her, seeing how she was getting more and more depressed. Willy (she'd started calling him *Willy*) thought it might help if she was busy.

So arrangements were made to have special security at K.J.'s daycare; she had to be sure that he was safe. But she was going to take Willy's advice. She wasn't going to let some sick creep run their lives. J.J. wouldn't have been okay with that. Neither was Margaret.

She was going back to work.

The Airport Police were notified; they would provide additional security.

She would go about her business as usual. She wasn't going to let herself get bogged down in fear and self-pity. She was tougher than that.

Willy couldn't help but admire that about her.

~~~

A little girl came up to Detective Louis Taber. She handed him a container of milk and a napkin with four cookies.

Lou made a big deal out of thanking her. He chewed the cookie with gusto, making all kinds of yummy noises.

Kindergarten milk and cookies!—it was amazing how it brought back memories of being unequivocally safe and protected... and of nap time.

The children each got three cookies. Mister Taber got four, probably because he was a lot bigger. He smiled over at the preschool teacher, Miss Beasley, Prisilla Beasley. What a nice lady!

She was a little older than Lou, but not by much. Not especially pretty, but beautiful. Lou recognized that right off. From their brief conversation, he learned that she was never married and had no children. She was flat-chested and had a face like an otter—full of mischief and playfulness. But what stood out most were her eyes. She had hazel eyes that seemed to smile from behind laugh lines, and just a trace of makeup. The more the detective saw her, the prettier she became.

She was also a very good teacher. That too was very attractive.

Hearing what Kenny was going through, she made a special effort to be patient and caring with him. It wasn't easy for him adjusting to new surroundings. But the boy was doing a fine job. He was a fine boy. The past couple weeks must have been very confusing. He wasn't even supposed to be in preschool yet... but he was almost four, and now that J.J. was gone... No, it wasn't easy.

This was his third day at the Wildwood Day-Care Center. He'd made some friends, and he seemed to be getting along.

His mother, on the other hand, was a nervous wreck, constantly checking on him. She'd phone and want to know, *Was Kenneth alright? Was he crying? Did he want to go home?* Then she'd ask if Mr. Taber was there. No, she'd say, she didn't want to talk to him; she just wanted to make sure he was there. This happened several times a day.

The police hadn't been completely upfront with the school. They explained that there were some "special" circumstances involving the new enrollee. They said it was a custody dispute within the family, which was basically true. The world being what it is, teachers and administrators alike were all too aware of the consequences of bitter divorce. In such cases, there was a very real threat that a child could be abducted by a parent. The days of being able to release a child to an adult without authorization and positive ID were gone forever. And so, Wildwood Day-Care was quite sympathetic to the request that a police officer be permitted to remain in the classroom. They did, however, ask that the officer not be in uniform. They didn't want to cause any unnecessary concern among the parents. If anyone were to ask, Mr. Taber was just an overly protective parent there to monitor his child's adjustment during the first few days. Had it been the start of the semester there would have been other parents hanging around. The first day of pre-school brings out the video cameras; it ranks right up there with *first step* and *first haircut*.

A shrill cry went up, disrupting the relative peace of milk 'n' cookies. At the far corner of the room, a little girl had had an accident. Her dilemma was sufficiently stressful to set a second child to crying.

Miss Beasley and her teacher's aide, Mrs. Kasdan, responded like firefighters to a two-alarm blaze. And judging from the looks on some of the other children's faces, the fire could spread at any moment.

Detective Lou Taber suddenly felt the urge to go.

He managed to catch Miss Beasley's attention; he gestured; he literally raised his hand and mouthed the words "I'll be right back. I gotta go to the bathroom."

He walked quickly down the hall to the rest room marked TEACHERS.

The door closed behind him, shutting out the tumult, replacing it with solitude and the catharsis of the commode. He did some of his best thinking on the can. He thought about Miss Beasley. Here was someone who had never married, she lived alone, and yet she seemed so complete, so fulfilled. Lou wondered if he could say the same for himself. It was hard to believe that he'd been married sixteen years. If he thought about it, he'd have to say it was a good marriage, as good as any. The problem was, he didn't think about it very often. It's not a good sign—taking things for granted. He thought some more about Miss Beasley.

The bathroom door slammed open.

Mrs. Kasdan shouted hysterically, "Mr. Taber! Mr. Taber!"

He didn't need to hear more; the flush drowned out what she was saying.

Rushing from the stall, he had his gun in his hand. His other hand was trying to buckle his pants. He saw that Mrs. Kasdan was too panic-stricken to provide any information; it would take too long. He dashed from the bathroom.

The classroom was in pandemonium. The children were all

screaming and crying. Miss Beasley was sitting in the middle of the floor. Blood was pooling all around her. Playtime was over.

Taber knelt by Prisilla. She'd been slashed. Her arms were dripping blood.

Mrs. Kasdan came out of the bathroom; she was standing in the corridor looking dazed. He barked at her: "Call 911. Tell them you need an ambulance. Tell them what happened. Then I want you to come over here and apply pressure to these cuts."

As he spoke, his eyes made contact with those of the wounded teacher. "You're going to be alright," he said. It was what they always say.

She nodded, and tried to point with her bloody hand.

"You must chase after them," she said. "A street person, dressed in rags, covered with filth—he had one eye and horrible wounds all over his face. He has Kenny."

Lou shot an urgent look at Mrs. Kasdan. She jumped; a second later, she was on the phone.

Detective Taber took off like a shot, out of the building and across the schoolyard. The cold air against his skin, the shimmer of daylight—everything was amplified in the rush of the pursuit. The leather badge holder was now out of his breast pocket; the gold shield clearly visible. As he reached the sidewalk, he looked right, then left. That's when he saw him—nearing the corner. At a distance, he didn't appear human.

In his arms—little K. J.

Pedestrians on the street had their backs turned, eyes following the progress of the ogre with the young boy—letting him get away.

"Out of the way! Police! Out of the way!" Taber shouted as he raced up the street, desperate to not let them get away.

The creature heard. He stopped. Standing next to the Plymouth parked on the other side of the street, he turned to look at his pursuer.

Detective Taber stopped in the middle of the street. His gun hand was extended; he brought his other hand up to steady his aim. His pulse was pounding in his ears.

And then, as he caught sight of Lance Manly, he felt worms begin to crawl under his skin. The left side of Lance's face was chewed up, the cheek laid open to the bone, the eyeball caved in—just flesh rotting in the socket. Crusted in blood, the half-face cracked a twisted smile.

The cop took it all in: the child, held under the creature's left arm; in *its* right hand, a knife ready to tear the throat of an innocent three year old. J.J.'s knife. And her handcuff still hung from its wrist. Chains dragged the ground behind it.

Taber shuddered. This was a ghoul!

The door to the Plymouth was pulled slightly ajar.

This maggot had already killed. Howard Greenleaf was dead, his little boy Brad; this was the monster who murdered J.J., and he just got through slashing Miss Beasley. There was no way in hell Lou Taber was going to let him take that boy into that car.

"Don't move! Drop the knife! Do it! NOW!"

Taber took aim at the creature's right eye. If he had to, that was where he would put the shot. In the head, yet as far from

222

K.J. as possible.

But what if I miss? What if he doesn't die right away? What if he slashes the boy's throat? Even worse, what if my bullet hits the kid?

Taber didn't want to think about it. It was the stuff of nightmares.

Lance's jaw moved, but no words came out, not at first. Then, pained and garbled: "This is the way it's supposed—"

"I'm not going to say it again. Drop the knife or I blow your *fucking* head off!"

There in the street, Detective Lou Taber, poised on the brink of deadly force, did not see the car turn the corner. What's worse, the driver of the car did not see him. Not in time. There was the screech of brakes. A shot rang out a split second before the impact. There was the sickening thud as the body hit the pavement.

And as consciousness was leaving him, Detective Taber could hear the monster cackle, and the Plymouth start up.

Chapter 40

You don't *Go to Hell!* It comes to you.

At that moment, it came to Margaret Danser. Up from below, out of the muck and depravity, it was to be her new dwelling, to go with her wherever she went, relentless to torment, until Kenneth J. was back with her.

News of the abduction reached Turner in his car. Compounded by news of the traffic accident—Lou Taber was in critical condition. He'd gotten off a shot. But it wasn't known if anyone was hit.

Detective Turner made a few quick turns. Activating his emergency lights, he rode the carpool lane down. It didn't take him long, he was out of the downtown and approaching the airport. *What do you say to the mother of a three year old kidnapped by a deranged killer?*

He turned onto an empty stretch of road that paralleled a runway. It was a little-used shortcut into the terminal; emergency vehicles only.

There were no tall buildings in his field of vision, just the control tower and the sky. And the sky was like one long ceiling of clouds, gray and black, mottled convolutions like folds on a giant brain. It loomed sinister. Turner shook his head and tried to clear the doom from his thoughts.

A jumbo jet roared out of the cold brain-sky overhead. He

watched as it came in for the landing.

Turner parked in the loading zone. A recorded voice threatened to tow any vehicle left unattended. Stepping from his car, he moved with urgency through the noise and the poor air quality, then into the terminal, up the escalator, and across the glass-enclosed concourse.

Whatever he was going to do, he had to do it now. The FBI would be taking over the case soon, if they hadn't already. There was a bulletin out on the missing child, and the suspect's vehicle. A suspect description would be going out to all law enforcement agencies across the country: Be on the lookout for a male white, thin-build, approximately 5' 9", 150 pounds, missing his left eye; when last seen, he was covered in blood and dirt, and dragging chains.

Good God, the boy was taken by a ghoul!

Turner flashed his badge as he past the NO ENTRY/RESTRICTED AREA. He kept going, down ramps and through tunnels. AUTHORIZED PERSONS ONLY—he kept going.

He wondered about Taber, *Was he conscious?*

The thought hurt—not being able to go to the hospital to see his partner. But he knew Lou would have plenty of visitors at his bedside. He also knew that the one thing Lou would want more than anything else would be to have that boy back home. That would go a long way to speeding his recovery.

Turner arrived at the heliport. As he stepped out onto the tarmac, there was Margie. He thought he'd find her there. He was beginning to realize that they often thought alike. She was standing alongside the Channel 9 News Chopper.

News travels fast, which was precisely what Margie needed—to travel fast.

The pilot was trying to dissuade her.

Everyone at the airport had already heard about the kidnapping. Margie's co-workers were family people, and they pulled together like a family. They all had children of their own and their hearts went out to her, even those who didn't really know her. They'd all seen her around. You couldn't miss her, the spunky redhead who worked on the ground crew.

The chopper pilot hadn't requested clearance, yet he was receiving the *okay for take-off.*

"This isn't *my* helicopter," he was trying to explain. "I can't just take off whenever I want, no assignment, no cameraman. What am I supposed to do? Go on a wild-goose chase? Search every highway in the state for a brown Plymouth? There are a lot of cars out there."

Margie turned away. She looked in every direction, looking for help. Anger, panic, helplessness—all registering on her face.

Then she saw Willy. *Her* policeman. He came right up to her, meeting her desperate, sad eyes head-on. There was no room for blame in those eyes, just pleading: *Help me save my baby!*

Turner knew he was about to overstep his authority. He went ahead anyway. He showed the chopper pilot his badge: "This is a police emergency. I'm going to commandeer your helicopter."

The pilot took a moment to consider. Then he nodded; he was satisfied. He was off the hook. "Okay, since you put it that way... It's your call, Officer. Let's get this bird in the air."

Workers nearby put their hands together in applause; and then, the hands remained clasped together in silent prayer: *Good God, let her find her little boy safe and sound.*

The chopper blades began to whirl. The sky, so solemn and gray.

It soon became too noisy to hear anything.

Turner shouted to the pilot. They would leave the interstate to the troopers, following instead the old highway down toward the Flint-Ridge Mountains, toward South Central Kentucky.

Turner was thinking about the cave where Mandy Greenleaf had been found.

He kept his thoughts to himself. Margie had enough on her mind. She was determined to spot a needle in the haystack—*an old brown Plymouth, Kentucky license plate AJE 570.* It was a long shot, but it was better than sitting around doing nothing, and waiting for the worst. As long as there was light in the sky, she wasn't going to take her eyes off that road. No breaks, no distractions.

They flew parallel to the horizon, desperately tracing the highway.

As the light began to fail, the temperature fell. An orange-red color filled the sky, and Turner's hope began to fade. Sitting next to Margie, watching the sunset, he held her hand.

She squeezed his hand.

227

Chapter 41

It wasn't until mid-morning of the following day that the brown Plymouth was found.

It had been abandoned along a private road several feet from a massive sinkhole. When they searched inside the sinkhole, they discovered an entrance that led into the underground cave system.

In a matter of a few short hours the mouth of the cave began in take on the appearance of a Hollywood movie set. The F.B.I. cordoned off the area, but it was impossible to stem the tide of curiosity. There were reporters from all over, as far away as England. They crowded into the pastoral setting of hills and valleys. The story of an anonymous sperm donor who returns as a depraved monster to steal back his son—this was a story that captured the imagination. The news media was having a field day. It didn't take long for them to dig up Lance's bizarre history. His grisly past provided a jumping off point for the drama that was unfolding, all against the incredible backdrop of endless labyrinths and impenetrable darkness. Members of the psychological community were called to offer commentary and insight. The caves themselves became a metaphor for the landscape of the human soul.

The mother's relationship with another woman, allegedly murdered by the monster—that was another angle that raised eyebrows.

Meanwhile, a lonely young woman drew upon her dwindling reserves of endurance, and courage that she didn't even know was there. Love for K.J. spurred her on.

She was in constant fear for K.J.

Turner had to walk fast to keep up with her. The detective had become Margie's constant companion. He was definitely afraid for her, but he was working overtime to not let it show.

They strode past a small pack of hungry journalists, snapping questions and cameras. The earth beneath their feet was soggy with dead leaves and twigs. The air was cold and damp. It was late afternoon. The sun shone hazy on the surrounding hillsides. An eerie vapor clung to the ground. It seemed to seep up from out of the earth.

Local authorities, working together with the F.B.I., had set up a base of operations. Up ahead, the brown Plymouth was in the process of being loaded onto a flatbed. It was being taken into evidence. A team of experts would go over every bit of mud and metal.

Front and center, a bear of a man was speaking with a pair of federal agents. He was bearded, wearing coveralls and holding a miner's helmet. He wiped a bead of sweat from his forehead. He was doing most of the talking. Otto Gothard, President of Otto's Speleological Tours, stopped his prattling when he saw the cute redhead and her tough-looking companion.

The agent nudged his partner to get his attention, which was brought to rest on the approaching couple.

"You must be Turner."

It didn't sound like a question. Turner didn't bother to answer.

He had plenty of respect for the Feds. They had the resources, they had the capabilities. But they were usually condescending pricks, which made it impossible to work with them. *For them*, maybe, but *with* them.... Not likely.

Straightaway, an agent said, "Your Commanding Officer has been calling all day."

The other agent put himself between Turner and Margie.

The agent with Turner sounded very official: "He says you are to get in touch with him the moment you get here."

Margie's agent had ushered her off to the side. "Ms. Danser, the F.B.I. wants you to know that we are doing all we can..."

Reluctant to take his eyes off Margie, Turner continued to glance over his shoulder as *his* agent led him toward a newly installed bank of phones.

"Detective, why don't you use one of our field phones? See what your C.O. wants, and then, afterwards, we'll talk."

Meanwhile, Otto was left standing there looking confused. He was in somewhat of a predicament. The F.B.I. wanted him to guide them to find Lance. But if they found Lance, they would probably find out about the ill-fated raid on the quarry. But suddenly, the F.B.I. men were leaving. He had gotten his wish? They were walking away with *Red* and the big city detective.

The agent with Turner spun around: "Gothard, don't go anywhere. We're not through yet."

The big man's shoulders slumped. *It had been too good to be true.*

Meanwhile, Turner listened with half an ear as his C.O. chewed him a new one.

But the captain was behind a desk, and Turner was in the field—literally, in a field. Turner was losing his patience. "This is bull–! ...I don't care that the helicopter company submitted a bill for eighteen hundred dollars. ...You're right! I can't concern myself with that right now. ...No, I don't care about jurisdiction either. Now tell me about my partner."

Willy listened as the captain repeated what the doctors had told him.

"So what you're saying is *There's no change*. It's still touch and go." Willy's fingers drummed on the wall of the kiosk. "Okay, that's all I needed to know."

But he wasn't getting off that easy. He listened some more as the captain went on about how he was jeopardizing his career. Except Willy wasn't thinking of his career. He had a job to do— to keep Margie from harm. He had to find her child. It didn't matter what some captain back in Cincinnati had to say.

Then suddenly a commotion broke out at the entrance to the cave. Several men in coveralls were coming up out of the hole. The agent with Turner broke away and hurried to the hubbub. Moving like a sprinter, he covered the thirty yards to the edge of the sinkhole in no time.

Off to his right, Turner heard somebody say something—he wasn't sure if he'd heard correctly—something about *a body. A*

231

child's body!

He slammed the phone down and ran to the hole in the ground.

The hole had become a grave. He could see the men carrying out a child-sized body bag. They laid it on the ground.

He had to stop Margie from seeing this...

But Margie was already standing at the edge of the pit. Her face was like chalk. Her lips were trembling. Her mouth was open. Her throat was tight.

Turner stepped in front of her, trying to shield her, to move her away.

Something strange was happening. It wasn't a conscious gesture, but all those standing around the sorry little body bag lowered their heads in a moment of silence.

Then, speaking softly, one of the men stated, "It's a little girl. She looks to be around five years old. I'd estimate she's been dead a week, maybe two. It's hard to tell."

A scream rose, puncturing the stagnant air.

It had come from Margie. She dropped to her knees and ripped at the shroud. Before anyone could stop her she had opened the body bag and lifted out the doll-like cadaver of *Princess Lulu.*

A puff of wind stirred slightly, carrying the sickening-sweet smell of rot into the nostrils of those downwind. Part of Lulu's face had been eaten away by cave rats or crickets. Upon her head, a coronet of beetle larvae was crawling, wriggling through the baby-fine tresses.

With a dozen law enforcement officers present—local, state, and F.B.I.—all just stood and watched the mother of the kidnapped boy cry her eyes out.

They knew better than to intervene or try to comfort her. Hers were tears of relief.

Margie Danser cradled the dead child in her arms, racked by wave upon wave of sobbing.

It was a painful spectacle that should have been private.

Turner walked down into the sinkhole, to the entrance to the cave. With the sound of Margie's wailing behind him, he stood staring down into the narrow hole. Chills ran up his spine.

Chapter 42

It took a while, and an injection of tranquilizer, but Margie finally went with Turner back to the motel.

The F.B.I. told her repeatedly: "There's nothing you can do here, ma'am. Go back to your motel. Try to get some rest. We'll call you the moment anything happens."

Their motel was a half hour's ride from the site of the cave mouth. There wasn't much choice; the only accommodations were in Cave City, which was more a town than a city. With tourist season months away, the hotels and guest houses had plenty of vacancies; some were closed. Everything looked so bleak. Or maybe that was just Margie's perspective. And Turner's.

Last night, when they put down on the tarmac at Cave City Airport, the helicopter pilot called it. "Welcome to the boondocks," he said. Then he wished Margie good luck and took off—like a leaf from a "Polly nose" tree. Maggie missed Kenny so much. Her face began to scrunch up, about to start wringing out tears.

Turner saw the pain. He went to her to offer a shoulder, but she steeled herself and pushed him away.

They would make their own luck, she said. "There's no time for tears."

That was 24 hours ago. Now Turner occupied the straight-backed chair next to the bed where Margie fitfully slept.

His mind was elsewhere. He stared out of focus. He was only now beginning to understand how vast the cave system was. You could hide an army down there. How did he hope to find one lunatic in a place like that? They didn't even know how deep it went. Portions of it that were mapped were as big as the Grand Canyon—only underground and in total darkness. He was glad Margie was sleeping; he didn't want her to see the frustration that was building inside him. This trip was turning into an exercise in futility. They had tracked the monster to his den, and now they were helpless to do anything.

And that wasn't the whole of it. He hadn't said anything to Margie, but the F.B.I. agent had confided in him; they found blood at the scene of the abduction, outside on the street near where Lance Manly's car had been parked. There was no point worrying her unnecessarily. It could be that Taber wounded Manly. That was certainly a possibility. The lab couldn't rule it out. The initial tests weren't conclusive. It seems Lance Manly and Kenny had the same blood type.

Turner wrung his hands. He felt like banging his head against the wall, but he didn't want to wake Margie.

The window was closed and the curtains were drawn, but he knew that outside, the sun was going down. He was also becoming aware that he was hungry. They hadn't eaten anything all afternoon. He decided to let Margie rest. He'd go out and get some food, bring back a nice warm dinner for her to have when she woke up.

235

He got up to go, but then, as he reached for the door, he stopped and turned. He stood there transfixed, watching Margaret as she slept.

She was going through so much—the loss of her lover, her son stolen by a psychotic killer. No one should go through that kind of nightmare.

She was so strong, yet so fragile.

And so incredibly beautiful.

A knock at the door broke the spell.

He started to say *Who's there?* but he didn't want to risk waking Margie.

He opened the door a crack.

On the other side—a pair of pink eyes set in a gaunt, white face.

The apparition didn't speak, not right away. He just stood there and let Turner give him the once over. He was a thin man with narrow shoulders. Even so, Turner got the impression of strength—the kind of strength that's in the bone. The Cincinnati cop looked him up and down, from the hobnailed boots to the two half-fingers on his left hand, and back to the hollow cheeks and the disconcerting eyes. This was a hard man—the kind of hard that comes from a hard life, not from a gym.

The sun was down. The gray tide of twilight was fading over the hills. And this sallow stone of a man stood on the doorstep like something left behind in its wake.

"Mister Turner, my name is Jink Ray, Jink Ray Cooney."

It took Turner a moment to recall where he'd heard the name. "You're the man who found Mrs. Greenleaf in the caves?"

He nodded that he did. "It's my understanding you've come to fetch the boy back to his mama…?"

Turner stepped into the darkness, closing the door part way. "Go on... I'm listening."

Jink Ray spoke without averting his eyes. "I can take you into the caves." He paused, waiting on the policeman's response.

There was none.

"I can find the boy." There was a glint of gold off his front tooth. "And I can bring you out again." The albino didn't mince words.

Neither did Turner. "Now why would you want to do that, Mister Cooney? Why come to me?"

"Because… you're not with the federal government. I seen you out at the cave today. I give some thought to what I seen. I believe you are here to deliver that boy to his mama. This isn't just work for you. This is personal." He held up his three-fingered hand to still any objection, at least 'til he finished his say. "I heard about your partner. I'm sorry. I pray he mends real soon. Mister Turner, I know you're a cop, but you're also a man.

"Detective, did you happen to hear about an accident out at the Elkhorn mine?" Jink said, changing the subject. "It happened about a month ago. A man died."

Turner shook his head. He couldn't quite get a read on this hillbilly.

Jink Ray proceeded to tell him about the ill-fated raid, in which Lance Manly played a regrettable and deadly role. It was obvious that Jink felt somewhat responsible. He had involved the others. He made sure not to name any names.

Turner flashed on the nervous cave guide he'd seen talking to the F.B.I. earlier in the day.

It was beginning to become clear. Jink Ray wanted to find Lance before the F.B.I. did. He was afraid that if Lance was captured, the Grotto's involvement in the kaolin mine incident would come out. He and his friends would be accessories to murder.

"So how's it going to be any different if you and I go down after that maniac?"

Turner pretty much knew what the answer was going to be. He just needed to hear it for himself.

Jink's words were solemn as a pledge: "Because, Mister Turner, if we go after him, I'm going to make sure he doesn't come out of the caves."

"Least not alive!"—It was Margie who had spoken. She was awake and standing by the door.

Both men were taken back by the sound of her voice. The words were hissed. They were pure venom.

The two men exchanged looks, pained by the paradox—to hear such hate coming from such a sweet lady.

Chapter 43

Crossing onto campus gave Professor Albert Bunnell the feeling of passing into a separate reality. It was as if there was a bubble, an invisible sphere around the university buildings and grounds, even portions of the neighboring community. A kind of preserve set aside to protect academia, and academics, such as himself, from the outside world.

He was in trouble, and it didn't take a university professor to figure that out. He was in contact with Otto Gothard, who in turn, was in contact with Jink Ray.

Albert wasn't fooling himself; he knew that the campus didn't really provide any sanctuary. Nevertheless, he welcomed the illusion. It had been a while since he'd been on campus. Emeritus faculty has its advantage. On that morning, he was going to speak in front of his wife's class. He got to bask in the esteem of young, eager minds and not have to deal with curriculums and tests, and grades. If only his other problem was that simple.

Outwardly he seemed unperturbed as he walked along the footpath. Beneath the surface, his thoughts were acutely troubled. He couldn't stop thinking about the drama unfolding miles away in a Kentucky cave.

He walked faster, and faster.

When he got to the lecture hall, he was in a sweat.

239

The room was a modern mini-amphitheater. It was beginning to fill. There was a good turnout, despite the early hour. Dr. Bunnell was a sought-after lecturer, besides being the husband of the professor.

Several latecomers scooted down the aisles; seats were saved by friends. Amid the low murmur of students getting settled in, and notebooks being opened, Dr. Bunnell set up his slide presentation. He retrieved his lecture notes from his briefcase and laid them out on the podium.

Jill Minter approached her husband. Placing one hand over the microphone, she made sure the switch was off before she spoke. Her back was to the assembly.

"Have you heard anything else?"

"Nothing new," he whispered. "No news is good news." He didn't sound very convincing. "Now Jill, there's no point making yourself crazy. There's nothing we can do. I spoke to Otto. He's working with the F.B.I."

From the startled expression on her face, Albey realized his wife had misunderstood. He hastened to clarify. "No, it's not what you think! Otto tried to get out of it. He explained to them that Lance was an acquaintance. They didn't care. They insisted that he guide them. From what he told me, he didn't have much of a choice. Anyway it may work out. At least there's someone in the caves looking out for our interest. A mutual interest I might add. Otto told me he's going to do whatever he can. Lead them on a merry chase if he has to. They'll never find Lance."

"He's going to do *WHAT!*" Her voice rose up

spontaneously, but then quickly lowered again. "What about that poor child? He can't..."

Albey silenced her with a look. "Perhaps you would prefer we turn ourselves in?"

She started to say something then decided against it. She didn't know what to do. Dealing with moral questions is so much easier when you're not in the middle of it.

"We'll talk later. Right now I have a lecture to give." He gestured to the rows of students gathered before them. "It's too early to panic. A lot can happen."

She bit her tongue and nodded, *Okay for now.*

Facing Archeology 201, Dr. Minter cleared her throat, rendering the lecture hall sufficiently quiet.

"It is a special honor for me to present to you an internationally recognized anthropologist and renowned spelunker, a man who has explored caves on five continents, a pioneer in the field of speleoanthropology, my husband, Dr. Albert Bunnell."

Excerpts from Dr. Bunnell's lecture:

...Someone once said, "If it wasn't for women, men would still live in caves." Perhaps. I wouldn't underestimate the role of Woman as a civilizing factor. There were a lot of reasons man traded in the cave for the split-level with the two-car garage. Anthropologically speaking, man's — and woman's — social nature is inextricably linked to the caves. The cave was the incubator for our subconscious... for at least two hundred thousand years...

As Dr. Bunnell spoke, the slide projector flashed images on the screen behind him. They went from cartoon cavemen to contemporary Stone Age Aborigines, to the slides of Dr. Bunnell's spelunking expeditions—unreal photographs of colossal caverns and monumental stalagmites.

Psychologists may look to early childhood for clues to behavior. I suggest that for some of the reasons we do the things we do, you might want to go a little deeper.

Ever notice how children love caves. They love to play in caves made from blankets draped across chairs, or empty cardboard boxes. Long before we learn of the real dangers in the world, we instinctually regard caves as places of safety. Could that be a vestige from our great- great- great… grandparents?

The shapes and colors of the rock, and the sheer dimension of it all—was absolutely stunning. Slides showing the members of the team provided prospective. There was Otto Gothard checking equipment, standing next to an enormous sinkhole. There were several breathtaking shots of Jill Minter rappelling down a 200-foot chasm wall. But it was the picture of Jink Ray sitting along the shore of an underground river that caused the audience to burst out in wonder and disbelief. *That couldn't be real!*

I know you're all curious about that photo. I'm going to ask that you hold your questions till the end.

And yes, that was real. He is real.

The slide changed.

Moving right along…

With each click of the projector they were transported deeper into a world straight out of Jules Verne's Journey to the Center of the Earth. Gardens of crystals and ceilings where stone hung like moss. Petrified waterfalls of cascading limestone. Mirror images of giant cave columns. Flowstone towers like statues. Skylights that let in shafts of light where humidity rises into the cool air and forms clouds inside the cave.

There is something undeniably spiritual about caves—magnificent vaulted cathedrals of stone. We see it in the architecture of the basilica. The same way prehistoric man used the caves as a sanctum for his faith. The part of the cave near the entrance was his dwelling, but the deeper realms were reserved for cave paintings, sacred crystals, and burials. In the oldest buildings of Christianity, under the central part of the church, there are sacred tombs for saints and martyrs. Our myths and fables are filled with images of the cave: the subterranean river of Styx; the blessed water of the grotto at Lourdes. 'Open Sesame' divides the rock and stores of treasures are waiting. As unexplored as the subconscious. On the surface, we like to think of ourselves as creatures of reason. Below the surface, parts of our brains were developed in the caves. Geologists trace the formation of the earth; archeologists, such as my wife, search for fossils of skull and bone; but for anthropologists, the caves can hold a flood of primordial memory. Through spelunking and spending time in the caves we tap into our nascent brain. It is not so much what the caver discovers in the cave, as what the caver discovers in himself.

There was an appreciative round of applause. The lecture portion of the presentation was over. Dr. Bunnell opened the floor to questions.

A young man in the front row wanted to know: "So who was that ghost in the picture sitting by the river?"

The professor took a moment to ponder his response.

"That 'ghost' is, in all probability, the greatest cave explorer that ever lived."

He thought back over his long career. He had made a name for himself predicated on a single find. He'd written many noteworthy papers, published in scientific journals, but his principal contribution would always be the discovery of the Smilodon, more commonly known as the saber-toothed tiger.

He, himself, didn't know why, but he decided it was time; he was going to tell the true story of the man who really found the famous bones.

After a thoughtful pause and in a careful, measured cadence, he began: It was twenty years ago, a young anthropologist moved to Kentucky to take a position as an associate professor. He had lofty aspirations of publishing a ground-breaking thesis and making a name for himself in the field of Paleoanthropology. On weekends he would go off by himself into the surrounding hills where he would explore old abandoned mine shafts. He dreamed of uncovering an anthropological find of astounding proportions and setting the scientific community on its ear.

Around the same time, a young man from the impoverished hills of Appalachia made his way along the banks of the Green River to the Central Kentucky Karst. He was in search of treasure of a different sort. Long before the Parks Service enacted laws to protect mineral deposits from souvenir hunters, folks thought the highly polished pieces of calcite and aragonite made nice ashtrays and paperweights. Cave onyx was bringing a handsome price in the curio shops along big city avenues. The young man's name was Jink Ray—a peculiar name for a most peculiar individual. As a boy, Jink Ray worked in the mines. The coal company straw boss found use for him, squeezing through the crawlways and crevices too narrow for a grown man. Child labor laws hadn't yet reached into the backwoods of the Smoky Mountains. So the boy just about grew up underground. Now, as remarkable, in and of itself, as that might seem, there was something else even more remarkable. Jink Ray was an albino. Deficient of pigment, his hair was completely white; his skin, paler than pale; his eyes were small and pink. The lack of retinal pigment was accompanied by degeneration of certain eye muscles and focusing apparatus. From a Darwinian perspective, Jink was heir to deadly disadvantage: his lack of color made him conspicuous; his poor eyesight made him vulnerable. Were these manifestations a genetic mutation, or a hereditary throwback? Cave-dwellers are not handicapped by defective eyes. In darkness, even good eyes cannot see. By the same token, a pale individual suffers no disadvantage where all are blind.

The anthropologist met the albino in a cave, a hundred feet

below the surface. Stone shelves shaped like birdbaths were suspended off walls and columns marking the waterline of a pool that had long since receded. It was there, by the light of a carbide lamp, that Dr. Albert Bunnell first laid eyes on Jink Ray Cooney. He stepped out from behind a cluster of stalagmites huddled like gnomes at the base of enormous, elongated shadows.

The ghostly figure padded noiselessly through the chamber. Overhead, a bat darted and veered after some unseen insect. The mirage was drawing closer. The anthropologist was speechless, the sound of his own heart booming in his ears.

There could be only one explanation: He was losing his mind. The long hours hemmed in by velvety blackness had finally altered his logic.

Then the apparition said, "Ain't much of a house, but it's got a hell of a basement."

It was a saying that Albey had heard before. A traditional spelunker greeting. The phantom standing before him was a man—white hair and pink eyes, but a man all the same... The fear took a few moments to fade.

"One hell of a basement!" Albey laughed, responding with the customary reply.

The two men shook hands, introducing themselves. Albey was laughing at himself, an anthropologist, a man of science. *It is amazing how quickly we revert to superstition!* Jink laughed too. Albey could only guess what he was laughing at, but it felt good, and it echoed roundly in the pit of the earth.

The professor paused in his recounting.

He'd never told anyone before about Jink Ray's role in the discovery. But now, for some reason, it seemed important to set the record straight. It wasn't that he felt guilty. Jink Ray had been clear on that account; he wanted no part of the notoriety. He was conspicuous enough, thank you. Albey was the one who identified the bones. He was the one who told Jink Ray what to look for. But it had been Jink Ray Cooney who led the young associate professor to the Smilodon.

The professor spoke with reverence of his friend who could traverse the substrata with the ease of a mole.

Did Albert Bunnell really believe that Jink Ray had evolved differently? Was it even possible that such a man walked among us?

Chapter 44

There were several things about Jink Ray Cooney that bothered Turner. First off, it was still unclear how exactly he proposed to find Lance in that monstrous cave system. One freak to find another. It could work. Some kind of strange radar where they could sense each other. But there was something else: *Why would Jink Ray want them along?* Turner didn't have an answer, not yet he didn't. The thought had occurred to him that since Cooney was the one who found the Greenleaf woman, maybe, just maybe, he was in cahoots with Manly. He decided he was going to have to keep an eye on the albino.

They stood in a holler some twenty-five miles from where Lance had entered his lair. Their headlamps made three waning glimmers in the gathering dawn—William Turner, Margaret Danser, Jink Ray Cooney—a grim hunting party. They stood alongside the ruins of a small stone house, the roof and one wall completely gone. In front of them, an abandoned well stood open. Several boards had been pulled aside uncovering a black half-moon. They peered in; their lights revealing a pair of hickory logs laid across the hole and wedged into the sides of the funnel to provide a fulcrum for the wire rope-ladder, for the 180 foot drop.

"Well, what are we waiting for?" Margie bit down on her words; her jaw muscles set with determination. Her voice was layered with emotion and hung defiantly in the open air, in the open field. About to enter the earth to retrieve her child from the den of a madman, it's only normal that she should feel anxious and scared.

Their guide went first.

The time for last-minute instruction was past. They'd each been outfitted with rope, lifelines, wall-hooks, provisions, and emergency rations. Turner was about to complain that his haversack was too heavy when he noticed that Jink carried twice the load, shouldering it without any apparent burden.

He decided not to say anything.

Jink Ray raised his arms, resting his bone-white hands on the shoulders of his two new friends. A beacon of sunlight began to crest the horizon.

"Take a good look at that sky! It'll likely be a while 'fore we see it again."

And with those encouraging words from their guide and tracker they began the descent.

After the first fifty feet or so the hole opened up, widening as if they had dropped into a bottle. No deposit, no return. Turner hung from the rope ladder, revolving slightly. He peered into space with the light from his carbide lamp falling away into the darkness, barely able to discern the outline of the cavern walls. A rush of momentary vertigo forced him to close his eyes. He opened them a split-second later, looking up and breathing heavily. The half-moon above had become small—a thin band of sunlight swimming with specks of dust, becoming more and more distant. All around, nothing but cold, forbidding blackness.

This was beginning to feel like a bad idea.

Margaret didn't allow herself to think of the dangers. The sky itself could be forever eclipsed if that's what it took to find her boy. She descended the ladder on the heels of a strange albino hillbilly. Down and down, and she didn't think of anything except K.J.

A three-fingered hand steadied the ladder, helping her as she stepped down into the rubber dinghy. She instantly sat down and held on, the light from her helmet rocking over the sides onto the veneer of shiny black upon which they were floated.

The surface rippled as Detective Turner joined them.

It was a small inflatable. If Jink and Margie weren't such lightweights, it would be doubtful that they'd all fit. As it was it was crowded.

They drifted into the throat of the mountain. Such were the mental images that played on the fringes of their minds. Margie felt like a mouse on a floating cork. Turner felt like Jonah being drawn into the whale. Jink Ray felt like he was going home.

Some two hundred feet above, a few sparse raindrops fell.

The National Weather Service estimated three to four inches of rainfall over the next twenty-four hours. A second storm front was said to be moving into the region sometime tomorrow, which could very well drop an additional four to five inches of rain on the Central Kentucky Karst.

This was one instance when the weatherman was in

complete agreement with the Old Farmer's Almanac.

Local radio stations were alerting spelunking expeditions to the possibility of subterranean floods.

The F.B.I.'s search for young Kenneth Danser was going to have to be put off. At least until the threat had past. It was only prudent. To venture into an active water-filled cave with a storm brewing would be to risk inordinate peril. Rainwater seeps into clefts and fissures, the flow builds, a torrent roars down what used to be a dry passageway, a basin fills, and the way out gets blocked! It can happen very suddenly. It has been known to happen that an entire expedition of speleologists was trapped and drowned.

Caves can become death traps from which there is no escape.

Chapter 45

Within the earth, between the strata of debris, rubble, and sinter, man's history is preserved. A calendar of evolution. A chronology of steps leading to the rise of civilization. Clues and traces left behind for scientists to read. The deeper they go, the further back...

Charred stone walls tell of the conquest of fire. The vestige of a rudimentary lamp may be nothing more than a depression in a slab of stone bearing minute traces of grease. Bone needles tell of skins for clothing. Split skulls and hollow bones tell of a means for tanning the skins using substance from the brain and the marrow. Traces of the preparation on the bone confirm the method of preparing skins. Snares, weapons, pottery and weaving, and most striking of all, the origins of art—all protected in the earth, preserved within the constant humidity and temperature of the cave.

Lance Manly descended the long tube-like passageway keeping his head bent forward and low. The chains of the lesbian still rattled from his skinny frame. It was she who had tried to trap his soul, to rob his seed. He growled, grumbling and snapping at the air as he went. A lantern swung from his outstretched hand and he followed it like a dumb beast of burden chasing a carrot-on-a-stick, trundling down tunnels. His back was bent by the weight of the sack he carried. Its rough burlap, sticky with blood, glistened darkly, licked by the light that filtered back. The shadows danced on the walls in patterns that felt cool and calm in his brain. And it was all so familiar, somewhere down deep.

Deep down keep down, low down slow down...

A wall appeared in the path directly ahead.

Lance stopped, still as stone. Only his face continued to move, the nose and cheeks twitching forward; his right eye, the good eye, remained closed as his whiskers scratched at the air. His nose separated out the mix of smells: There was his own characteristic scent. There was the reek of urine and terror that clung to the sack he carried. And then, there was the musty odor of the cave itself, a smell that came from the walls which were covered with beads of condensation collected around tiny molds that Dr. Bunnell had called *Actinomycetes*.

Yes, Lance had learned a great deal from his friends in the Grotto. From Albey and Otto, and from Jink Ray. Especially Jink Ray—white like a real cave dweller, like the blind beetle and the white spider, like the eyeless millipede and the ghostly flatworm.

Lance thought about Jink Ray and he listened to the cave.

The raw patches of flesh and exposed nerve within his ravaged cheek functioned as a supersensitive organ of touch, picking up on the most infinitesimal vibrations in the still, damp air. And in turn, the skin over his whole body prickled with the new sensitivity, feeling the cave breathe.

He put down his sack.

Then he turned and merged with the blackness, running his

hand along the sinter ridges, up between the tunnel wall and ceiling, till he found what he was looking for, what he knew he'd find. Reaching in as far as he could, he pulled out a most treasured bounty. A handful of darkness. The parameter by which all is defined, out of which all is born. A yawning crevice, a black slit into which he could crawl.

It is thought that the caveman only ventured into the coldhearted, unwelcoming inner recesses to make offerings, hunt magic, and petition the blessing of some Higher Being.

Lance returned for the lamp and the sack. For the light and the son—in the twisted black corridors of his brain, they were one and the same. A means by which he could see beyond the span of his time to what lies ahead. The sack shivered; the light fluttered, as a droplet of water fell from above and sputtered onto the lamp. The caveman let out a small sound of animal distress. He snatched up his light, his emissary through the darkness, and merged into the long-forgotten, ever-present past.

The crevice was nasty with mud, made sticky and slimy by by-products given off by bacteria. He crawled in, pushing the lamp ahead. Tied to his waist by a rope like an umbilical, the sac was being pulled along behind.

Entering further and further into the hole he felt a pressure building inside himself.

~ ~ ~

Detective Turner hadn't yet admitted it to himself, but he was having a difficult time keeping up. He was becoming increasingly vexed.

Their foray into "inner space" had taken hours, down the vein of velvety blackness that their guide referred to as "Purgatory Crick." Then they got out and walked for miles, through vast resounding chambers with vaulted ceilings. When you're underground, hours and miles are misleading, and the amount of effort expended does not translate into the distance covered or the time spent. They climbed over massive blocks of limestone where sections of the roof had fallen.

"How's it going back here? You want we should stop and take a rest?" The albino dropped back to check on Turner, to see how the big city detective was holding up.

Willy tried to catch his breath. "No. I'm alright. Just a little hay fever is all.... Happens sometimes when I leave the city. My allergies act up."

"Ain't no allergies in a cave." Jink said matter-of-factly; then added, "We're coming up on Firefall Hall shortly. We'll stop there, eat, and rest a spell." Then he turned and hurried to rejoin Margie up ahead in the lead.

"Damn!" Willy cussed himself. *Maybe Margie didn't hear that!*—but then sound did carry farther down here. *Of course there are no allergies in caves. There's no pollen!* Not only was he out-of-shape, he was stupid too. That was one thing he didn't want—to seem foolish in front of Margie.

She was so spectacular! Determined. Tireless. Up ahead her light shone into the great hall.

Without warning a shriek reverberated into huge hollow echoes.

255

Willy suddenly found the strength to bound up the slabs of broken limestone, through the narrow opening, and into the room beyond.

There, all three stood on a glistening terrace of flowstone. Below, waterfalls of rock, all yellows and reds, all streaked from the iron in the limestone. Waves of red like blood.

"Welcome to Firefall Hall." Jink flashed a rare glint of gold-toothed smile. He knew that his guests weren't looking at him. Hell, they couldn't take their eyes off the cascade of fiery brimstone.

On the earth's surface a heavy downpour had already dropped four inches in the past two hours. And still more angry storm clouds were rolling in. Rivulets of rainwater raced down muddy hillsides filling sinkholes with swirling brown water, seeping into the underground, leaving the terrain dotted with white foaming bubbles.

Chapter 46

"He passed this way."

Turner sat, practically falling onto the ground next to where the guide squatted.

"You sound pretty sure of yourself." He was glad for any excuse to stop, even if only for a minute.

They were no longer amid the grandeur of spacious caverns. It was over an hour since they'd entered into this twisting funnel of cramped, ever-enclosing walls.

Jink lifted off his haunches. They'd rested long enough. He was ready to continue down the tube-like passage. The ceiling pressed low and Jink was no longer walking upright. Instead he was using a method called "scrambling." Resembling an ape, he bent forward, using his hands for balance and to help propel him along.

Still on his ass, Turner grabbed at the albino's pant leg: "So how do you know he passed this way?"

"What? You want me to explain how I know...? We don't have time for this..."

Jink Ray had been pushing hard right from the start, but for the past three or four hours he had become relentless.

Turner wasn't letting go.

"Okay... I can smell his urine. On the floor of the cave... he's been marking his path, leaving his scent like a pack rat. The damp, motionless air holds the odor close to the ground and I can smell his piss, even at a distance. Can we go now?"

The cop let go.

A strange image popped into Turner's mind. He imagined their guide as a scrawny white lab rat running through a maze, penis hanging down, stopping every now and then to squirt a few drops on the walls.

Turner laughed. His mind was getting away from him.

No time to fantasize!—his cohorts were getting too far ahead. *Light in sight! Keep the light in sight!* If there was one thing he didn't want, that was to be left behind. Not down here.

He'd been trying to ignore it, but he was beginning to feel a little... claustrophobic.

He stumbled after Jink and Margaret. It was the fear making him clumsy. An urgency was building inside of him. He told himself: "Suppress it! Maintain control! You have to maintain..."

The walls were folding in. The passage was no more than four feet high and so narrow that he would not be able to turn around without difficulty.

Then something started happening. His senses were playing tricks. His equilibrium began to waiver. The beams of light on the helmets ahead were floating. It was as if the blackness that surrounded them had turned to liquid. He was being suffocated, drowned in a tube of oozing black paste.

And the lights... they were floating away.

He had to get out of there: "Let me out! Let me out!"

Then William Turner was gone. And in his place, desire

beyond identity, fierce and struggling. Pulling the gloves from his hands, he began to tear at the rough, stone walls. Solid walls, cold and drenched in piss; wet from fear; raspy, like a file. Electricity shot up his arms. He could feel the flesh being scraped from the palms of his hands.

Then something big hit him on top of his helmet. It was the ceiling. He kept trying to stand up. And again, it came down on him like a club. A giant black club.

And then he was looking up.

Yellow-white lights hit him square in the eyes.

He could hear a voice saying "It's 'cave-frenzy.' I've seen it before, many times."

Turner began to emerge; he began to return. Everything around him began to solidify again. The black ooze receded.

"The frenzy can end as quickly as it began. Or not."

"Is he going to be alright?"

It was Margie. And the albino.

"Yeah, but right now we've got to get through this passage. Here, help me to get him up."

"He might have a concussion. Maybe we shouldn't move him yet?"

"If we don't keep moving..." The pink bunny rabbit eyes cut into Margie with the seriousness of a lathe, "we're all going to die right here."

"What are you talking about?" She didn't mean to sound scared, but she did. It was the way Jink Ray was looking at her.

"I didn't say anything sooner. I was hoping we'd make better time. Thought it best not to worry you. Figured you had enough to worry about."

She held his gaze; she didn't flinch.

"An hour from now, this passageway, this entire section of cave, is going to be underwater."

It seemed like forever before anyone said anything. It couldn't have been more than a second or two. Turner sat there with his mouth open, gasping, his brain still stinging from the snap. He felt confused and ashamed, somehow less a man. He looked to Margie for reassurance. Any at all.

The albino was saying something but it wasn't registering.

The next thing he knew, they were up and moving.

Was this the plan from the start?

Jink was using his knowledge to corner the monster—his knowledge of the caves, his knowledge of the floodwaters; his knowledge of the places of refuge. It was an incredibly dangerous scheme. Having tracked Lance to this section of cave, he knew there was only one small gallery which would remain dry during the downpour. Lance would be sensitive to changes in the atmospheric pressure within the caves. He would know. He would retreat there, to wait for the danger to pass, for the waters to recede.

Now it was a race to the high ground.

If everything went as planned, they'd soon be trapped between a river and a rock, and a deranged killer.

Chapter 47

Since his early days as a beat cop, William "Tomcat" Turner walked the mean streets and felt no fear. Whispers of "the Man" preceded him; crooks and villains scattered before him.

Now here he was—limp and spent, and being led through a dank, dark tunnel by a plucky, little redheaded mother.

"Okay, this is it," the albino was saying. "This is the stricture I told you about."

Willy didn't remember being told about any *stricture*.

"Take off your packs, we're leaving them here. If there's anything you got to have, get it out and give it here."

Willy couldn't believe his eyes. Jink Ray was standing there in his underwear, boots, gloves, and knee pads. "I know it's cold, but you better shed any extra clothing." Jink had opened the canister: a large tin shell, three feet long, marked with reflective tape and tied to several feet of string. He removed several items from his own pack, putting them with the emergency provisions.

That was when Turner saw the crevice. At the top of the wall, behind the slug-white physique of Jink Ray, a narrow slit ran horizontally through the rock.

He couldn't be serious. It was way too tight. There was no way he was going to be able to fit through there.

Margie had begun to shimmy out of her coveralls. Yellow-white lights played on the swell of her small, full breasts; and on the curve of her hips. With a helmet lamp, wherever you look, that's where the beam falls. They hadn't meant to be so obvious. Just being men.

Margie piped up: "No time for modesty."

A light was falling on William. She was talking to him. Looking at him.

"I can't fit through that crack! I can't!"

"Here! Rub this over your body." The albino tossed something.

Turner caught it—good reflexes.

"Do it! Do it fast!" the albino cautioned.

Turner stared at the gunk in the jar, horrified. It looked like animal fat, had the consistency of motor oil, and smelled of putrefaction.

"You can't be serious!"

Margie had a jar of her own. He watched her as she wiped gobs of the gel on her panties. She'd removed her bra and was rubbing the stuff on top of her T-shirt. It glistened, soaking through to the skin.

Suddenly he became aware of the sound of rushing water coming from somewhere behind them.

"Oh, God!"

They weren't listening to him anymore. Nobody was listening, least of all God. And if He was, He was having a good laugh.

The water rushed in, covering the floor where they stood.

Jink Ray balled up his clothes into a tight bundle, along with his helmet, which he pushed out in front as he bellied up the crack. He moved fast like a lizard, pulling the canister through after him, vanishing quickly out of sight.

Margie was about to follow. She'd put her clothes, along with her helmet, on the ledge, just as Jink had done.

She hopped up. But then she stopped and jumped back down with a splash. She crossed to where Willy stood shivering in the dark.

He could feel her warmth lean in close to him. Her lips pressed warm against his mouth—making him realize he'd been mumbling to himself.

Behind them, the caverns were gurgling louder, water was spurting from every crevice in the ceiling. He looked down. The water was past his ankles and rising fast.

"C'mon, Willy, let's get out of here."

He looked up and she was gone, boots disappearing into a crevice. And then her light was gone too, leaving only his one light to hold back the pitch-black.

It was a long few seconds later 'til Margie heard him climb into the cleft after them. She looked back and saw the beam of his lamp, and she let out a sigh of relief.

The inside of the crawlway was relatively dry. Directly above, far, far above, the makeup of the soil differed from that of the surrounding karst; a canopy of trees and a steep grade on a hillside all combined to provide a kind of geological umbrella.

"You okay, Willy?"

"Yeah, I'm okay."

He didn't sound so sure. But at least he was there, crawling up the ant hole. That's what it felt like to him, an outsized ant hole.

Margie shifted her weight to wedge around a tight corner. She wondered how Willy was going to make it; he was so much bigger. As she pulled herself through, her hips scraped on the rock. Something struck her as funny and she started to laugh: *It was painful reliving the birth trauma.*

But that made her think of K.J.—and that made her start to cry.

"You okay back there?" the albino asked.

She bit down hard on her lip, trembling uncontrollably from the ache in her heart. It racked her violently. She wanted to tear at the walls around her, to rip the mountain apart—to find her baby.

"Your mama loves you, K.J. Your mama would move mountains for you," she called to her child as she pushed through.

"You okay back there?" Jink repeated. "I can't hardly hear you."

"Yeah, I'm okay. I'm okay." She twisted her body like a corkscrew, pushing her way out the stricture. Her gloved hands pressed hard against the rock like frog fingers, the tendons in her arms popping through the skin like taut little cables.

"What is that? On the rock." She was looking at the ceiling where long brown and white hairs seemed to sprout from the stone like a mold. A mold that was moving. It was a moving carpet of daddy longlegs, *harvestmen*. Their small rounded bodies and slender long legs wove into a fuzzy thick fabric: a living wall-covering.

She stifled a shriek and jerked her hand back, knocking a wave of the creatures off the wall. They fell on top of her and scampered across her body. She brushed frantically at herself, her hands shaking like they were about to fly off.

Breathing in gasps, she struggled to steady her nerves.

"They can't hurt you. They're not *true* spiders, they don't bite." It was Willy. He'd made his way up to the bend in the shaft. Like a talking head, he peered through the opening: "I guess we're not the only ones trying to keep dry."

He smiled.

It had taken all his effort, but there he was. And he managed a smile, feeble as it was.

She smiled back.

Both terrified and half-naked, neither one suspected that at that moment they shared the same thought:

If we ever get out of here alive, we really should become lovers.

Chapter 48

It is the water that shapes the caves. It is water that erodes the rock and carves a place for the tears of women, the thirst of men, the domicile of emotions and hostages.

Lance had shed all his clothes which were, by this time, little more than rags. He sat on the edge of a vortex and pondered.

A raging river flowed along a previously dry passage. A deep pit in the riverbed had created a churn-hole in the center of the current, swirling swift and deadly. Lance eyed the phenomenon with his one good eye.

He rocked back and forth, aware of the shadows and the growl emerging from behind the veil of the mystic past.

From within the cave.

From within himself.

He was also aware of the dim lights and distant voices emerging from the shaft at the far end of the gallery.

The way back was blocked. There was the present to contend with.

Out went the light, as he pulled back the cover of darkness. A profound animal alertness within his brain fanned out to meet the utmost night.

~~~

The albino lifted Turner out of the hole.

"Sssh!" He pressed the stub of his index finger to his lips.

Listening.

The policeman tried to listen, but he couldn't hear a thing above the hammering of his own heart. He felt like he'd been in a fight. Only his opponent suffered no pain. The stone didn't bleed, it didn't groan, it would never cry *uncle*.

Margie whispered: "The light! It went out!" She pointed across the chamber.

Willy looked in the direction. There was nothing there.

He looked to the guide.

Jink Ray acknowledged with a slow nod of his head. The pink eyes stabbed into space; the lizard-lips mouthed the words: "He's here alright."

All three looked out upon the chamber, the far reaches of which were lost in monstrous gloom, making it impossible to tell the size of the hall. Contained within its walls: the deepest dark forest of stone, ancient and grotesque, curling and twisting like a kingdom of worms lost and frozen in the carcass of the earth. Preserved in perpetuity in the murky recesses of the psyche.

Jink Ray and Margaret were already dressed. Willy hurried to don his woolen shirt, his coveralls, and webbed belt.

Meanwhile, Jink Ray kindled a small fire.

A confused Detective Turner stared from the fire out into the lurking eyes of the blackness beyond. "He'll know we're here."

Jink Ray didn't look up: "No matter. He already knows." Then he added, "If he's hungry enough, he might just come join us."

Was he serious?—Turner didn't take his eyes off the perimeter, where the light got swallowed up.

It didn't take long for Jink Ray to prepare a clear soup. The cap from the canister served as both pot and bowl. They passed it among themselves, feeling the heat through the dampness of their gloves. It was just a simple herbal broth, but to Turner the warm liquid felt like a transfusion.

Lowering the oversized bowl, he suddenly realized that Margie was walking away. Faster and faster—a few more steps and she would dissolve into the shadows. Her voice came drifting back, tearfully pleading: "My baby. My baby is out there."

Jink Ray was already running after her.

Willy started to react when—

A cry filled the chamber. A shrill, dreadful wail. Shrill, like scraping marrow from bone. Dreadful, like a heart being slowly torn out.

It was not coming from Margie.

It seemed to be coming from everywhere.

She fell to her knees as the sound washed over her. The color drained from her face.

Turner remembered hearing a sound like that once, a long time ago, when he was a boy. He'd run away from home, and he ended up sleeping in a field. A city boy listening to crickets, gazing at a sky full of stars. It was the shank of the evening when it started—an ungodly bawling from across the field. Loud. Oddly compelling, though not quite human. And long. It went on and on, for hours. In the morning, he awoke from his dew-covered sleep. The sound had stopped. Later, when he was walking up the road, he came upon a farmer and asked about the sound.

"Oh, that," said the farmer, "That was the sound of a cow calling for her calf." He explained that the calf was taken from its mother shortly after it was born. "It's a dairy cow, son."

Willy made a mental note: So that was the sound of sorrow.

Margie was down on her knees. She began to scream, tearing at her clothing, ripping the breast pockets from her blouse. The cries in a cave blended with one another in agonizing discord. This was *a funeral*. A funeral *inside* a grave.

The albino was on guard, his head turning from side to side trying to pinpoint where the sound was coming from.

But it was impossible.

It was rebounding from every wall.

It seemed to Turner to be drilling into his head and bouncing off the inside of his skull. He desperately wanted to cover his ears.

Instead he ran to Margie, fell down to his knees beside her, and held her in his arms.

It is as it was—before the invention of words. Language never adequately conveyed grief.

The same was true for all life's more powerful sentiments. The fundamentals are the realm of the scent, not the sentence; the muscle, not the mind. Matters of blood get communicated in carriage and bearing, in howls and snarls, and telepathic waves.

The rescue party no longer had anyone to rescue.

Kenneth J. Danser was dead.

As surely as the chill that ran up the spine of each person within earshot.

Chapter 49

The headlamps huddled like fireflies. Jink Ray unsheathed the vicious gleam of a hunting knife. Detective Turner unholstered his service revolver. Man's work needed to be done.

Jink Ray explained: They were to fan out across the cavern, which was no more than fifty meters at its widest. Each man was to keep his back to the wall. He would move up on the left, Turner on the right. Margie would stay near the center. She was in no shape to move. Turner and Margie would use their lights to scan ahead and to the side, maintaining visual contact at all times. Lance must not get past them.

As for Jink Ray, he would move blind.

He glided away smoothly, like a fish in water. When he got to the far side they could still see his ghost-like visage. He signaled the *go-ahead*. Then his carbide lamp dimmed and vanished. He was lost in the ink that was all around them.

It was now clear why the hillbilly needed them along. It was their job to drive the quarry onto his blade.

Turner wiped the clammy perspiration from his forehead. The rim of his helmet cast an odd shadow that exaggerated the ridge of his brow, making his shadow look like that of a brutish caveman.

Proceeding along the shale covered floor, he began to hallucinate that the walls of the cave were decorated with cave paintings, like he'd seen in pictures. Only these weren't from any books or magazines. They seemed to be projected onto the wall from *inside* his head. Vividly. If he had a brush and ochre, he would be able to step up to the surface and trace the outlines accurately. A bison, borrowing the shape of its hump from the curve of the rock. A dotted horse ensnared in a trap, arrows and spears protruding from its flank. There were geometrical designs, which he intuitively understood to be sexual—triangles for the female, ovals and bell-shapes; the male symbols were barbed, short strokes and dots. Turner felt like he was entering a dream, a sanctuary. A place of ceremonial magic and secret ritual. He could no longer trust his senses. With adrenaline pumping, still reeling from the attack of cave-frenzy, how much of this was real? How much, a product of his imagination?

He trod slowly and cautiously, like a man who, with each step, turns a corner.

He looked over at Margie. Sitting in a heap on the cave floor, she had her helmet in her hand, methodically sweeping side-to-front, as Jink had instructed. Once again he found himself regarding her with awe and admiration. She was struggling in a nightmare, bearing-up bravely. While his light was lingered on her. He brought his light into play, scanning slowly along the opposing wall.

With his gun raised, he was in his element. *She* was under *his* protection. In this place from before memory, his was the role of the hunter.

They were now closing in, throwing a net of light over the

heart of darkness. They were turning over a rock and cornering the slimy thing that lived beneath.

Turner could feel sweat trickle down his back. He could feel his clothes sticking to him. In the cool of the cave, the heat of his body practically dried the clothes on his back.

The floor began to slope, as though drawing him in.

Was he the hunter? Or was he the prey?

There was a sound coming from up ahead. A rushing, sucking noise.

Getting nearer.

An ugly pig-nosed rat with wings hung just inches away from Lance's face. Perched ten feet above the floor of the grotto, the two creatures commiserated in the dark.

Lance first spotted the tiny ball of yellow fur when he was sitting by the swirling river. He saw the solitary pipistrelle as a cave spirit. There had been an incursion upon *their* world. Lance needed an ally. Forsaking the light, he went to join 'the archangel' in the domain of dripping crystals. Climbing into a snug crevice, he worked his way up to its roost. In the absolute darkness he could no longer see it, but he knew it was there. Just as it knew he was there. Even in its current state of hibernation.

Lance envied the pipistrelle its long sleep. Its breathing and heartbeat were nearly stopped. Its body temperature had sunk to that of the rock to which it clung.

Perhaps that's what happened to Lulu. Perhaps that's where K.J. is.

Beaded with moisture, its sharp-nailed toes kept it fastened to the smooth stone wall.

But the awakening process had begun. Its temperature was rising—a couple degrees per minute. It was going to take several minutes to rouse from its dormant state.

Lance stayed perfectly still.

Odd though it may seem—given the place and time—he had become aroused. Inexplicably and uncontrollably. He held fast to the wall, without moving a muscle. He could hear the floodwaters below. He could feel a stillness in the air all around. And within himself, a mysterious tide. He was becoming immersed in the flow of recollection. There he was, under the porch. He could see his mother and his father. He could see within himself, something less than a man.

He reached down.

He felt his tumescence.

At that moment the light hit him squarely.

He squinted past the glare, to the man. To the woman. He smiled. Infinitely sad. Thoroughly depraved.

The bat took flight.

He leaped down.

Margie Danser thought she was seeing things. Some kind of weird, fertility statue. Primitive and foul. A wretched, erotic icon in bas-relief, high on the cavern wall.

It was smiling.

It was smiling for her.

Then suddenly something flew out.

Chains rattled.

The gargoyle came alive—bounding through eons to break free at this point in time.

A shot rang out. A deafening roar.

A thud.

A grunt.

The dust was flying. Light, flickering.

Margie could make out the detective—a tangle of arms and legs, fending off the thing. The undergroundling. Subhuman and hideous, and naked. She started to run toward them. That was when the detective's light went out, and the darkness swooped in. In the blink of an eye, she stumbled and she fell.

Margie had no idea how long she'd been out. It couldn't have been long. *Seconds? A minute? Two, at most.*

She lay there, a small island in hell. Her helmet lay next to her on the floor of the cave. The beam from its carbide flame, directed down in the ground. There were no sounds. Only the wash of running water. Ringing. Incessant. Hypnotic.

She stood up and began to turn slowly in the dark whispering void.

She wanted to call out, to let the others know.

Something was stopping her.

She was being watched.

She could *feel* it.

Her skin grew clammy, crawly; her mouth, dry.

She stepped back, away from the gleam on the cavern floor.

Away from the lamplight.

Instantly she was enveloped by the dark.

It was scary in the dark. But to be in the light was to be exposed, so she pressed herself further into the blackness.

Chapter 50

In the pocket of Margie's woolen cardigan was a small but powerful flashlight. Jink Ray made sure they all had three sources of light with them.

So where was Jink Ray? Why hadn't he turned on his light?

She moved her finger off the penlight switch.

There was something else in her pocket: darts. She must've left them there the last time she played. She forgot all about them. Those days seemed a million years ago.

What was that!—She thought she heard footsteps. The clink of chains.

What was going on? What had happened to William?

Her breath came in paroxysms.

How had the world suddenly become so filled with terror?

Early on we know the truth, when we first come into the world: In the dark there are only children and bogeymen.

Lance Manly was a bogeyman, connected to the cosmos and powered by intrinsic brutality. He was free from rationality. By all accounts he should have been dead. Perhaps ten thousand years ago.

He moved unthinkingly—like spermatazoa, shimmying and gyrating through the moist, dark tunnel. He moved toward the female.

She waited in a place of vulnerability, held fast in the dark.

By nature a woman's defenses are not impregnable.

As soon as she heard the tinkling, piddling sound, she knew exactly what it was.

She didn't mean to, but she let out a shriek.

The bastard was peeing on the lamplight!

The sparkling yellow stream found its mark. Sprinkling the ground, arcing high and wide, he squirted the helmet. The reflector plate resounded *pitter-patter* and *hiss*.

They were plunged into a world where sight did not exist. Her reaction—to bring her hands up to her eyes. It felt like a blindfold had been placed on her, literally. Such was the weight of the dark.

Then she caught a whiff of the odor, pungent and sharp. Repulsive. She thought she was going to gag.

A noise rattled to the ground. It seemed to be coming from right in front of her, from where the light had been. It was hard to tell.

A gun discharged and thunder echoed painfully round the room.

For just an instant, there was illumination. It was as if the flash of the gun barrel ignited the air, revealing an underworld swimming in sparkles and glimmer.

The light was actually coming from a powerful torch beam in the hands of Jink Ray. The albino was on the other side of the cavern, standing partially behind a stalagmite, not wanting to become an unwitting target.

Against a backdrop of shadow and stone, William Turner

and Lance Manly appeared to be dancing.

Man versus monster—the combatants did not look remotely akin.

Yet as Margie watched them grapple she got a strange and vague impression—not something that could translate into words without sounding insane—but it was as if she were witnessing an *internal* struggle, a conflict within the species that had followed them down the corridors of time.

Somehow Lance had managed to wrestle the gun from Willy's grasp.

Shots rang out.

The light went dead.

Another shot. A grunt. Then silence.

Horrible silence.

Margie fidgeted in the dark.

She held the small but powerful penlight in one hand. She waited, listening. Smelling. Feeling—even the faintest movement in the still, rank air. A wisp of cordite smudged across her olfactory palate, mingling with the stink of Lance.

She thought: *How have I come to this godforsaken pit?*

She began to shiver, thinking about all she'd lost. About J.J. and K.J. And now... about William.

Anger was building inside like a small volcano ready to erupt. She was going to get that bastard! Make him burn in hell!

She switched on the flash, sweeping the chamber with its long, narrow beam.

Nothing—she could see nothing in front of her.

Then she noticed the body. Face down on the floor in the corner. It was Willy.

A noise. Behind her. She turned.

There he was, no more than eight feet away. Standing there, grinning.

She didn't hesitate. She let the dart fly. Just as she had a thousand times before. Holding the shaft gently between thumb and index finger she drew back her wrist, eye-level. With a snap she straightened the arm, directly in front of her, never taking her eyes off the target. The fingertips uncurled, pointing along the line of flight, releasing the projectile at the precise moment of full extension and sending the tungsten steel tip slicing through the beam of light.

It struck with a sickening thud.

For an interminable second Margie stood there transfixed by what she'd done. The brightly colored plastic flight protruded from the eye socket at an upward angle. The right eye. Now he was completely blind. A small geyser spurted a thin pulse of blood down the front of his face. He didn't scream. He didn't jump. He merely stopped grinning. His tongue slobbered out of his mouth to lap at the sticky stuff of life.

He began reeling about, pointing the gun and laughing.

He squeezed off a shot. It smacked into the dirt just inches from where Margie stood. She sprang back and to the side as a second shot whizzed by her head.

Then something hit the ground, like a handful of pebbles. They scattered along the floor. Lance Manly turned, tracking the sound. And as he did, a phantom came lunging out of the shadows. The blade in Jink Ray's hand streaked fire across its path as a glimmer of light was captured and refracted off the savage steel.

Margie couldn't be sure what she saw. The light source was weak and shaky—no match for the cave. She was beyond exhaustion, her nerves stretched thin; her imagination was quite possibly playing tricks on her. The two men appeared to hover above the floor. A cloud of dust billowed at their feet. Surrounded by a cluster of man-size stalagmites. Behind them, a surface of glittering white gypsum. Crystals loosened by the heat of their bodies snowed gently down upon spectacle of the life and death.

It was beyond fantastic. The way the two men continued to fight—the albino slashing unmercifully, the depraved killer firing until there were no more bullets left. Bloody pieces of skin and fragments of bone went flying everywhere. It was unreal in its brutality.

Margie watched in horror, expecting at any minute that one of them would drop. Her flashlight went on the fritz. Suddenly the whole grotesque manifestation started to blink, fading into a hazy afterimage. And they continued to fight.

They simply would not die. Not their pace, nor their fury. They thrashed about the grotto locked in supernatural combat.

Lance was tearing at Jink Ray's throat with his teeth. Jink was slicing with his blade. Then, with a howl and the cry of a banshee, they lifted off and went sailing, through the air, out over the surging waters, where they were sucked down under the swirling turbulence.

Still fighting as they disappeared into the shiny black hole.

Chapter 51

Hey little girl... What are you doing sitting in the dark by yourself?
Did those mean boys hurt your feelings? Poor dear! Pay no attention. You
didn't want to play with those boys anyway. They don't play nice.

Margie had not moved for hours.

Time itself had ceased to exist.

She had switched off her flashlight. In the subterranean
night she felt disembodied. It was as if nothing existed but her
mind, her thoughts.

Deprived of a reference point, a new vision imposed itself
upon her mind's eye. She saw herself inextricably woven onto a
tapestry, the fabric of which was suspended in a void. Coarse and
warm, smeared with blood and feces. And breathing ever so
imperceptibly. Inhaling. And exhaling.

Her hands trailed the contours.

Oh my God!—It was Kenneth. He was alive!

She did not know how she came to be beside the sack. But
there she was, connected once again to her offspring.

She clicked on her flashlight.

Manly had taken the dying child—or perhaps he believed
young K.J. was already dead—and he suspended the body from
what appeared to be a natural belay, a protruding spine of stone.
Twisted and tangled in the worn, dirty pouch, the boy was
interred like some kind of cocoon or Indian mummy.

Margie became frantic. She tried pulling down the sack, but it wouldn't give. It wouldn't tear. She pressed her face against it, alternating between kissing and tearing at the fabric with her teeth. Finally, she managed to make a small tear in the burlap. She could widen it with her fingers. Several heartbeats later she had him. She laid him out gently on the cave floor.

It wasn't until then that she became aware of the structure from which K.J. had been suspended. She'd never seen anything like it. This was no haphazard collection of stones. It was more like a burial place. A dolmen: a prehistoric monument of two upright boulders supporting a horizontal stone slab. At the foot of the sepulchre someone had laid out a pattern of stones and bones and crystals, like liquid sapphire.

"Mommy...? Mommy? Is that you?"

"Yes, baby, it's me. It's your mommy." She held him and she cried. "You're going to be alright now, baby. Your mommy loves you. Your mommy's here for you."

Little Kenny opened his eyes as though waking from a bad dream. He was safe and secure now. His mommy had moved mountains for him. That's what mommies do!

She peeled off the green cardigan and blanketed him against the dampness. Her undershirt was soaking wet and clung to her breasts, points straining against the cold ravenous night.

Food! It suddenly occurred to her that he must be starving. *What about water? Had that madman even thought to give him water?*

She had to find the supply canister. Where did Jink Ray leave it?

284

Then she remembered it was near the entrance to the grotto, left as a buoy at the spout of the stricture. Once the flood water recedes, that would mark their way out.

She stood up slowly, shining her flashlight into the murky soup. She had no bearings. The beam went only so far then cut out like a spill on a blotter.

She didn't dare leave her baby. Not ever again.

But she had to get to that canister.

She couldn't risk moving K.J. Not yet. He'd been shot in the shoulder. She could see where the bullet had passed through—both entry and exit wounds marred his tiny shoulder. He'd lost a lot of blood. As soon as she laid his head back down, his eyes closed and he drifted off—somewhere between dream and coma.

She looked at him. Her heart felt like it would bust.

She made up her mind they were going to get out of this grave! Whatever it took, she was going to get him back to the sunlight.

What choice did she have? Reluctantly she moved away from K.J., and began her search.

"*Aaah!*" She jumped and stumbled.

There was something there, on the floor—a hand reached up and grabbed hold of her ankle.

Almost immediately, as she pulled free, she realized it was Willy. He had crawled along on his belly, crawled toward the light. He was badly wounded, shot in the chest. He floundered at her feet.

Working quickly she fashioned a pressure bandage from his

shirt, managing—at least temporarily—to plug the sucking chest wound. She had to find that supply canister. There would be first aid materials, food, and additional sources of light. She removed hard hat and carbide lamp from Willy's head. Now if she could only get it to work. She scrutinized the damaged lamp. She was terrified that she'd leave in search of supplies and not be able to find her way back. But with this light she had a fighting chance.

It took several tries and too many precious matches from her supply belt, but she got it up and glowing. Light flooded the grotto, illuminating a much wider angle than the spot from the flash. She took the headlamp and left the flashlight with Turner.

There was a story Margie remembered hearing, or perhaps she'd read it in a magazine. It was a lamentable tale of three college students. They decided, on the spur of the moment, that they were going to explore a cave which they'd come across when hiking in the woods. Poorly equipped, they entered the cave with only a flashlight and a book of matches. When rescuers finally found the boys it was too late. There was an aspect to the tragedy that made it all the more tragic. It soon became apparent that the young explorers had fallen prey to curiosity. They'd entered farther into the cave than they'd planned. A common failing among new cavers. There's a name for it: "borehole lust" or "virgin passage fever." It becomes hard to turn back. You become obsessed with what's around the next corner—to discover a new cavern. You are Lewis and Clark, Sir Edmund Hillary, Neil Armstrong. But alas, in the case of our fledgling spelunkers, there would be no more frontiers. The batteries in their flashlight died. Lost and disoriented underground, they began using their matches. They followed along the wall of the cave. When their matches were all used up, they continued to follow the wall. If only they had paid more attention to the incline of the floor. They went deeper and deeper. *Is it still considered a discovery when you find a new cavern but you're not being able to see it?*

Margie's headlamp flickered. She knew she was getting low on carbide. She tried not to think about it. But she couldn't help it. Even without having recalled the story of the ill-fated students, she knew that without light, the cases where men successfully emerged from deep caves without help from outside were rare or nonexistent.

Chapter 52

It was three days since the rains let up.

There was talk of going back down.

"Professor, you really think there's a chance of anyone being alive down there?"

Professor Bunnell got the feeling that the head of the FBI's Anti-Kidnapping Unit couldn't care less. He was going through the motions, making conversation.

It had been two days since Professor Bunnell and his wife Jill arrived to join the contingent of lawmen and newsmen, the curious and the morbid. All camped by the mouth of the cave. All waiting.

"I can assure you, sir, I would not be here if I did not think there was a chance of rescuing them."

Bunnell's wife stood behind him.

The FBI man narrowed his eyes, allowing a smirk to settle on his mouth. He didn't need to say what he was thinking.

"Jink Ray Cooney was well aware of the impending storm before he ventured down. He knows these caves like you know your own house. I have to believe he had a plan. He was not a foolhardy man."

"No...? So how come you're using the past tense?"

The Professor ignored that remark. "There are a limited number of areas in the caves likely to provide a dry haven. Since

288

we know that they entered at an abandoned well on the old Collin's place, it stands to reason—"

"Yeah, I know, you want me to send the rescue party down the well. I just got through talking to your buddy, Otto.... Okay, let's say I do it your way. I pack up and move the whole operation twenty-five miles down the road. You know, Turner and Ms. Danser were told to stay out of the caves. I already had my hands full looking for her kid. Am I supposed to drop that and go off looking for her? What am I supposed to do about a murderer named Lance Manly? Am I supposed to just forget about him?"

"Do you want to rescue a murderer or three innocent people? Besides, you don't think anyone is alive down there anyway." Now the Professor was getting irritated. "I don't seem to be getting through to you. Underneath this limestone plateau that we call Flint Ridge, there are literally hundreds of miles of caves... *interconnecting* caves. Just because Lance entered a cave at this particular site, doesn't mean *we* have to. If you really want to find Lance Manly, follow Jink Ray. You find him, you find Lance."

The FBI Man didn't take his eyes off Bunnell. He was a law enforcement officer with thirty years of experience. He was wary. He was resolute. But one thing he wasn't... he wasn't a dumb man. He knew *what's the point of consulting experts if you're not going to take their advice?*

~~~

Medicines, bandages, cans of carbide (precious lumps of

acetylene-producing fuel), even a sleeping bag—all neatly packed in Jink Ray's canister. A veritable life preserver. Margie hung on to it with renewed strength and hope.

She found her way back to Willy and K.J.

Willy's mud-coated, stubble-bearded face looked up at her. "Forget about me, I'm dying anyway. Try to save your son. Save yourself."

She managed to spoon a little soup into K. J.'s trembling mouth before he dropped again into a deep sleep.

Then she tended to Willy's wound. It did not look good.

She considered the task of transporting an injured man out of the caves. She bundled the three of them under the sleeping bag. In her mind she retraced the different obstacles they'd have to overcome. She began to grow sleepy. There seemed to be no choice; she was going to have to leave them! At some point she would have to go for help. It was a terrifying prospect. She was thankful that for the time being there was nothing to be done. She would have to wait for the floodwaters to recede. Till then— conserve light, conserve energy, try to heal.

They lay on their sides. She curled in Turner's arms with K.J. spooned against her. They shared body heat. They could feel each other's heart beat. They could cling to life.

In an instant they had drifted off into a profound, seamless sleep... and beyond.

Margie's eyelids began to flutter.

~~~

Screaming swirls of fog and fume tear deep grooves in the surface of the world, ripping handfuls of grainy soil from the parched desert floor, flinging them out across the darkened plain. The wind is angry at the moon and is throwing clouds of dust at the eye of the night. Huge and silver... and watchful.

The young female is angry as well. She has begun to bang her bottom against the ground. To spread her scent.

The dominant male moves as the elements move, a ripple of power. A swirling mound of fur, teeth, and claws. His eyes flare in the night.

The young female sniffs the air.

Fear and anger hold the world together.

And hunger in the nethermouth.

She begins pulling on her breasts, crying and singing—a most unearthly noise—and running her bottom in the soil.

Margie finds herself standing face-to-face and mind-to-mind—as if the thoughts of the young female are filtering through to her own. One moment she's looking into those eyes, familiar and compelling; the next, she is looking out.

Looking out at the prehistoric pit-dwelling that rises vertically around her some sixty-five feet to the surface. Walls of clay and gypsum eroded by nature, excavated by hand. A hole, a hundred feet in diameter. Fires burn in the mouths of the many caves burrowed into the sides of the pit, their smoke adding to the veiled texture of a distant place, a forgotten past.

The center of the floor of the pit lies empty except for a cistern and, of course, the young female. The edges of the cistern are shaped like giant tongues to lick the sky, to collect as much rain as possible.

The courtyard is accessible by a long sloping ramp that begins a third of the way up. In places there are ladders and stone steps dug into the walls.

She can vaguely make out several ropes, dark and vine-like against the wall. Her people are not that far removed from the trees. Pit-dwellers living in state of the art shelter—warm in winter and cool in summer. Safe from the fierce desert winds.

The dominant male stands on two legs, on a bulge of rock that overhangs the young female. He palms a large gnarled stick like a cudgel, like a scepter.

It is then that the young female notices the others. The other women. They giggle softly, watch unabashedly from inside their burrows.

The young female realizes it is her time. Time for "the stab." The dominant male is there. She has, after all, come of age.

She strains to see, pressing her face against the night. But he turns and disappears inside a cave. The sight of his bare back causes strange tingling between her legs.

She starts in again, banging bottom more wildly now. She feels anticipation within, fear and excitement. She nervously toys with the downy red fur that covers her belly.

The dominant male emerges. Devoid of self-consciousness, he strides the earthen ramp.

Still unable to see his face, she can see his mighty stick, waving in the air as he stretches toward the surface-world and the heavens beyond.

The young female recoils at his show of dominance. She resents. She is confused by the pull and the purpose. She struggles to slow her heart, to stem the flow. But it is too late, she has responded. Posturing submissively, she bends over to expose her pink and glistening labia.

A knife suddenly appears in her hand—the same knife J.J. used to own. And as the dominant male begins to mount, the young female slashes.

Looking down at her hand, the knife is no longer a knife. It is a lipstick. Now it is a qp doll. But it doesn't matter, it is still able to cut, to wound. It is his turn to bleed. The barren earth runs red with blood. And the knife continues to shape-shift. Now it is a tampon. Now it is a corsage.

She attacks the phallus, slashing and cutting. Whacking and hacking—try as she may, she cannot cut it off. It is inseparable. And soon it begins to grow. Long and thick, and longer still. It grows to enormous proportions until the man himself becomes the penis. Angry and lovely. And aching.

The young female's mouth hangs open. Faced with the power of creation she begins to cry out, "Oh God! Oh my God!"

She looks away. And at that moment she notices the stick on the ground. The staff of the dominant male. The symbol of his power.

Snatching it up, she begins to run.

The night opens before her onto a vast and changing scenario.

Early morning fog has lifted. The tall reed-grass of the veld is pushed back to reveal a makeshift encampment.

The young female enters.

She is at once confronted by a mangy tribe of ape-men. Diminutive hunters with baboon faces and red testicles that dangle to their knees.

She is wearing a crinoline party dress. She becomes aware of this as she fends off the pawing and tugging of a dozen grimy hands. She combatively raises the large, gnarled stick. The ape-men fall back, duly impressed by her authority. They cower and they cringe. The staff has procured for her a level of deference.

But then, in a sudden onslaught, they all rush her. She is knocked off her feet and the staff falls easily away, out of her hands; it is not part of her.

293

They tear at her ruffles and her bows. Her breasts fall free and they pull at her nipples. Her panties are pulled down around her ankles.

How can she endure these monkeys in her womb? She begins to cry—tears of rage, tears of panic.

One of the little buggers is inches from her face. His eyes lock onto hers. It is Lance Manly. And the others—they too are Lance Manly. Climbing all over her. Sniffing and poking.

She manages to break free.

Now she is running through tunnels, pursed by the tribe of monkey-men. All of whom are Lance Manly.

She tries to outrun them but she cannot; she has been transformed, turned into the most helpless, vulnerable of creatures. She is a pregnant woman. A newborn clings to her breast. She waddles as fast as she can but it is not fast enough. They are almost upon her.

Suddenly J.J. is there.

The men are no longer men. They are sperm. They are pulsing through the tunnel. They are swimming ever nearer.

J.J. Twomey is on ice skates as she uses the staff to bat away oncoming sperm, knocking them out of the air like a hockey goalie. The young female, trying to cover her nakedness with shreds of her tattered party dress, dabs a tear from her cheek. J.J. skates past and stops briefly to smile and wink.

All at once two ape-men have broken through. They are trying to mount her. Out of nowhere the dominant male is there. Furious with jealousy, he begins to lash out. Each time his fist collides with one of the 'Manly' creatures, the monkey vanishes in a puff, until all other males are gone.

And the dominant male comes to her. He does not take her, not right away. Instead he licks her. First under the arms. Then her breasts. And finally, between her legs. His breath is hot and whispers to her thighs. He licks her knowingly, and her thighs answer.

And when he stops, she continues to do it herself. Her head between her legs, she contorts like a four-legged animal. She is comfortable with her nature. And she is comfortable with his.

She is ready to take him in, to accept him for the man. More the woman for it.

She sees between her legs: his stiffness presses against her spreading her petals and pushing up inside her cave, he stirs the fragrance. She licks his balls, the saliva splashes from her mouth as she runs her tongue along his fullness.

She feels his hand upon her head, grabbing her hair, pulling her face up to his. Her eyes close. A shiver courses through her slender frame and her mouth finds his mouth.

Her eyes open.

It is Willy Turner's face she sees.

~ ~ ~

Otto "the Cave Bear" Gothard was the first to reach the sleepers.

Professor Albert Bunnell said he'd never seen anything like it. All three of them were suspended in a dormant state, very near death. Their pulses and metabolic rates were practically nonexistent.

"So what do we do now?" he asked the Professor.

Albey didn't answer. He was too busy tearing through the boxes of medical supplies. They had a paramedic along with them; the two men worked in tandem, rigging an IV. Kenneth was the first to be hooked up: an infusion of plasma, a glucose drip. It didn't take long—the color began to come back to his cheeks.

Chapter 53

It was 8:37 A.M. when the rescue party brought the survivors to the surface. Heavily anesthetized, they would not recall the slow and painful journey up through tortuous passageways. Just as the dreamer rarely recalls the dream. Yet it's there, somewhere, locked in the basement of his brain.

The stretchers were hoisted one by one out of the hole and into the warmth and clarity of a new day.

There wasn't a cloud in the sky.

And the sun shined mindlessly.

Made in the USA
Las Vegas, NV
26 January 2022